FAMILY
THE ROAD
A POST-APOCALYPTIC
NEXT-WORLD
BOOK SERIES
VOLUME 2

LANCE K. EWING

Families First ~ The Road
A Post-Apocalyptic
Next-World Book Series

Volume 2

Copyright © 2019 by Lance K. Ewing

ISBNs: 978-0-9996765-1-6 (Kindle)
978-0-9996765-2-3 (trade paperback)

First Kindle edition: September 2019
First paperback edition: October 2019

Printed in the United States of America

Dedication

To my wife, Hannah, our three awesome crazy boys, Hudson, Jax and Hendrix, and to my mom, Shareen, for her tireless editing.

To the readers who took a chance on a new author without knowing if there would be a second volume.

Thank you to all readers who left honest reviews on Amazon, Goodreads and Audible, making this continued series possible.

Foreword

FAMILIES FIRST

Recap of Volume 1

In *Families First ~ Post-Apocalyptic Next-World Series, Volume 1*, we are introduced to a cast of characters spanning multiple locations across the United States, with each group having diverse points of view and hardships to overcome.

We learn that North Korea dropped an EMP in the center of the United States, knocking out power to all states except Hawaii, as well as parts of Canada and Mexico. With no electricity, food or running water, and few working vehicles, the country is instantly reduced to the hardships of days long gone. It's every family for themselves in this new and hostile world.

The story begins with a Chiropractor, husband, father and starting prepper, Lance, with his wife Joy and their young boys: twins Hudson and Jax (age 4), and Hendrix (age 3), from McKinney, Texas. They band with friends and neighbors as they prepare to leave their homes and head nearly 800 miles to Saddle Ranch, in the Rocky Mountains near Loveland, Colorado.

With help from new friends, including two McKinney police officers and a former military couple, they gather a formidable group of prayerful and like-minded men, women and children.

McKinney police officer Lonnie is always cool-headed and is a great leader of people.

Lonnie convinces his old friend Vlad to join the group and bring the entire inventory from his nearly looted gun store in Plano, Texas, in return for full membership in the group and the hopeful promise of long-term safety in the Colorado mountains.

The other McKinney police officer, Mike, has a soft spot for kids, females, and anyone close to him that needs his help. This behaviour is closely pared with his propensity towards violent acts with seemingly little remorse. His conduct in Volume 2, and beyond, is sure to escalate and provide the groundwork for a wild ride.

With the good Lord always watching over them, the group sets out on the journey of a lifetime in Volume Two.

The cast of Saddle Ranch in Loveland, Colorado, is diverse, with more than 100 people living in the community.

John is the leader of Saddle Ranch. With the help of Bill, Sharon, and their head of security, Mac, they need to secure their territory quickly. However, they realize that nothing stays locked down tight for long.

Close by is the Church of the West, just up the road in Green Valley, with Samuel as their leader.

Working together, but still maintaining their separate groups, they do their best to secure the four miles across the valley where they all live, surrounded by foothills and mountains.

In Raton Pass, New Mexico, almost halfway between McKinney, Texas, and Loveland, Colorado, live the Jenkins family; older son David with his mother Beatrice and father Dean, and David's son, Mark.

Banding with neighbors and an old friend, who is a moderate prepper at least, they have staked out their territory and formed the Raton Pass Militia.

James and Janice VanFleet also live close by Raton Pass, in Weston, Colorado. As a saved former gang member, James and his wife have longed for a family of their own for years. They now have their home filled with new friends, children, and a loyal dog they will stop at nothing to protect.

* * * *

Dear Reader,

If this is your first look at my *Families First* series, please consider reading Volume One first. *Families First* is a planned series of 5-7 volumes, depending of course on you, the reader.

Thank you for purchasing and, most of all, for reading this first book in the series. In this day of Internet publishing, I realize you have many other choices in this genre. I am honored you would spend your money and time with me. As writers, we now, more than ever, are judged by our reviews online. If you enjoyed this book, please leave an honest review on Amazon. I am working hard on Volume Three.

For those of you interested in this series, please consider keeping in touch at FamiliesFirstNovel@gmail.com. I will not distribute your e-mail anywhere else. I will only contact you as a reply to a question you may have or to let you know of an upcoming volume or series I am about to release.

In return for your e-mail, I will forward you my Quick Guide e-book (free of charge and not yet available for sale). This short e-book introduces the main characters of *Families First*, including their backstory, much of which you will not find in either Volume One or Two.

Lance K. Ewing

Reviews from Amazon

"A most interesting story about life after an EMP and how it affects the families involved. The reader will follow families in Texas, Colorado, and New Mexico as they determine their next moves.

"I read a lot of EMP fiction, and this one is different for me in several ways. First, I appreciate the fact that these groups put their faith in God first and foremost. Loved that concept. And, secondly, they all banded together either before the EMP or after it.

"For a first novel, this is excellent. Hope that the author is writing the second one now! Definitely will read on.

"Highly recommended."

* * * * * * *

"Awesome book. I can't wait for the next one. The characters were all real; the story was great. I loved this book. Would highly recommend it."

* * * * * * *

"This was an enjoyable storyline. I liked it because the author was able to keep your attention throughout without gratuitous violence and sex. Yes, there is violence, but it was in context of the story. Very good book! Give this story a chance."

* * * * * * *

"I loved this book and the story line. The characters were all people you could see out in the real world, even the bad apples. Thank you for the GREAT read and please hurry with Book 2."

* * * * * * *

Chapter One ~ McKinney, Texas

Lonnie had the laminated Rand McNally map of Texas on the dash.

A few of us had marked the trip yesterday and highlighted alternate routes in case we didn't have a choice.

The first big goal was Amarillo, Texas, by way of Wichita Falls.

Jake was humming to himself, and I recognized the tune—an old George Strait song called "Amarillo by Morning."

"Well, we won't be there by morning," I told him.

"It's about 350 miles. Used to only be about 5½ hours, but in this next world it's at least 18," he replied. "I'm sure the kids are only good for about 8, maybe 10, and I damn sure don't want to be driving in the dark," he added.

"That's what I figured," I replied. "It's why I told David we would be about four days out from Raton Pass."

Our caravan headed straight up Ridge Road to Highway 380, then turned west.

"It's a good thing this bomb thing hit about 10 a.m., instead of the rush hour," said Vlad.

"That's true," added Jake. "At rush hour we would be stuck behind a gridlock of cars, instead of just weaving around them like this," as he pointed ahead.

We had 55 miles to go on Highway 380, heading to Decatur, Texas.

"Let's stay sharp!" came the voice on the radios.

"We've got running vehicles," said Lonnie, "and it will draw attention; we can count on that."

Highway 380 West cut straight across the countryside. Abandoned stores and gas stations flanked both sides. Some burned out, others just deserted, but nearly all were looted.

"It looks like they spared that McDonald's over there," pointed out Vlad.

"Not much to loot after a day or two, except maybe the Happy Meal™ prizes," I replied. The liquor store next door was picked clean, from our view.

I looked towards the Bronco at my kids and saw Hendrix giving me "the look." It's one-hand in a circle over one eye, like a monocular. I gave it right back and could see him laughing. At that moment, I would have given everything to have one more day with my wife and boys before this all happened.

At nearly 15 miles per hour, we were making great time. Nearing a long stretch of road nearly void of broken-down vehicles, we picked up speed, with nothing but trees on either side.

"We must be doing at least 35, if not 40!" I yelled over at Jake.

"Yeah," he replied. "At this pace we might just be in Amarillo by mor…."

There was a loud thud, followed by a crunching sound I couldn't identify. I looked up at a large brown object coming over the cab of the truck and onto the trailer. Jake and I both jumped to the sides, but Vlad was not so lucky.

The large deer landed on his left leg, and there was the audible sound of breaking bones as he screamed in pain.

Lonnie's truck rolled to a stop, with smoke coming from under the hood.

"Well, crap," said Lonnie, as he got out to see what happened on the trailer.

Vlad was lying on his back, with the deer still on his leg. Jake and I were working on getting the nearly 200-pound animal off him as he cried out in pain.

"How did the deer come over the top of the truck?" asked Jake.

"I don't know," I replied, "but Vlad is in bad shape. Let's get Nancy over here to help."

Nancy examined Vlad. "It's broken," she said—"the left femur."

"Am I going to be okay?" asked Vlad through his pain.

"Just lie down, and don't move," she said. "We'll get this fixed."

With the caravan immobilized, all eyes were on Vlad. She gave him a shot that quickly calmed him down.

"What did you give him?" asked Lonnie. "Morphine," she answered.

"How did she get that?" I asked Jake.

He just smiled and shook his head, saying, "You have no idea, my brother… Let's check the deer out. It's a lot of meat, and we have more than a few mouths to feed."

Jake and I conferred with Lonnie and Mike.

"We have been on the road for only a couple of hours, and we're already derailed," said Lonnie.

"I don't know much about getting the truck fixed, but I can get this venison processed so it will keep for a while," I said.

"What do we do about the truck?" asked Lonnie.

"We can take a look at it," offered Jim and Steve. "I've done some tinkering over the years on my old truck," said Steve, "and Jim has helped me with a few projects as well."

"Far as I know," said Jake, "Vlad is the only one with any extensive mechanical experience, so we may be out for now."

Lonnie, Steve, and Jim quickly agreed that they could not fix the truck after an hour of trying.

Jake and I processed the deer over the next two hours, with the ladies, led by Lucy, cutting the meat into long thin strips that could be smoked and preserved for up to a year.

Lonnie provided support for Nancy as she worked on Vlad. She was able to set his femur with a crude but effective splint made of two-by-fours cut to fit his leg, and electrical tape.

When Vlad was stable and comfortable, Lonnie went again to look at the damage to the lead truck. He approached the front from the passenger's side and saw two work boots sticking out from under the front bumper. "Any luck?" he asked, not knowing who was looking at it.

"I can fix it!" came the voice of a female from under the truck.

"Who's under there?" asked Lonnie, confused.

"Sheila," came a response from a man out of sight by the tree line.

"Who are you?" asked Lonnie, with his hand now on his still-holstered pistol.

"Dan's the name, and my girl under there is the best mechanic in these parts."

"We don't need any help," said Lonnie flatly.

"We saw what happened and the truck's been down for near three hours," she said as she poked her head out from the front bumper.

"We just figured," said Dan, "that y'all could use a little help."

"Come on out," said Lonnie in his officer voice. He was surprised to see a tall fit woman in her mid-twenties, he guessed, with a beautiful face and long curly blonde hair to match.

"What are you doing to my truck?" he asked, as they were both standing in front of him.

"We're headed west and thought we could tag along," said Dan. "It's pretty clear you need us," he added.

"Can you fix it?" asked Lonnie, speaking to Sheila while he ignored the comment from Dan.

"I think so," she replied. "If I do, can I hitch a ride?"

"We're a package deal," said Dan quickly. "She goes, I go."

"We'll see," replied Lonnie, "if you can fix it."

Jake and I finished with the deer, and he made the call to circle the wagons.

"We're here for the night," he told our group. "Let's organize the vehicles and set up the tents."

The children were excited to exit the vehicles and run around, even if only inside the newly formed circle of safety.

"No kids outside the circle!" called Lonnie, "except to go to the bathroom we will set up in a few. Mike, let's have you and Steve scout out our position about a quarter-mile in each direction."

"Sure thing," Mike replied. "We're on it!"

Jake and I dug a two-foot-deep pit, four feet long and three feet wide.

Finding dead wood for the fire was easy now, although I knew that would change over the next few months. We needed a good bed of coals to have any chance of smoking all the meat.

With the fire blazing, the ladies cut the meat into thin strips. Jake and I cut green branches off nearby trees and made hanging racks.

"It will take all night to smoke but should be ready in the morning. There's probably 80 to 100 pounds of edible meat, including organs," said Jake.

Mike and Steve returned from their perimeter check with exciting news, according to Lonnie. He made an official announcement to the group:

"Thanks to Mike and Steve, we are now proud owners of one more trailer and our very own porta-potty! It seems the porta-potty was left over from a now-abandoned construction site and is nearly brand new. They will be bringing it back with the trailer in just a few.

"Anyone needing to use the bathroom will use this one only, as it will be inside our circle of safety. We have already had some of our group wandering about, and it's important we stay close together while on the road.

"The last thing I have for now is we have someone outside our group trying to fix our lead truck, and Nancy is getting Vlad fit with a temporary cast on his leg until the swelling goes down. Oh, and we have venison steaks for dinner tonight. Keep close inside our circle and stay on high alert."

When Mike and Steve returned with the nearly new bathroom on a trailer, both adults and children applauded their efforts. "There's a bonus," said Steve. "Approximately 20 rolls of toilet paper inside! Please use sparingly!"

Lonnie headed back to his truck and met Sheila and Dan. "Well," asked Lonnie, "what's the verdict, Sheila?"

"She fixed it," said Dan, before she could answer. Lonnie was getting annoyed with Dan, and his cop instinct kicked in, telling him something wasn't right about him.

"So, what's the verdict, Sheila?" he asked again, looking in her eyes. She didn't answer and looked at Dan. "Do you mind if she answers, Dan?" he asked.

"Okay," he replied. "Go ahead, Sheila."

"Well, sir," she finally spoke. "It's fixed, I'm pretty sure. Can you start it up and see?"

"Lonnie," said Mike, overhearing the entire exchange. "Can I have a word?"

"Sure, Mike. What's up," he asked, as they met out of earshot of the two strangers.

"What's the deal with the girl?" Mike said with a grin. "She looks like she's going to wash the grease off her hands and head straight over to take first prize in a beauty contest." Then, in a serious tone, he added. "You want me to take care of this guy?"

"Take care of him how, Mike?" asked Lonnie.

"With Vlad down, we need a good mechanic," Mike continued. "And if your truck does start, we may need to add to our group, but we don't need him. I can take this asshole for a little walk, and it's done. It sounds like he doesn't know the first thing about trucks anyway."

"Hold on, Mike," said Lonnie. He got in the truck and turned the key. It started right up and sounded good, better than good, he thought. He put it in gear and drove forward about 30 yards before returning to the circle.

"You fixed it!" he told Sheila. "I'll talk to the group tonight. Come back first thing in the morning if you want to hear my answer."

"We were looking to stay here tonight and get some food too," said Dan. "We fixed your truck," he continued. "Looks like you owe us now."

Lonnie laughed at this as Mike's face was turning red with anger.

"No, Dan. Sheila fixed my truck, and without being asked to do so. We're done here for today," as he put his hand on Mike's shoulder.

The night was a feast of fresh venison, canned corn, and pantyhose sprouts with Italian dressing.

"Who wants to say the prayer tonight?" asked Vlad, now comfortably sitting up on the trailer.

"Me, me," said many of the kids, all raising their hands. "Okay," he laughed. "Jax, you're up."

Jax stood and asked everyone to close their eyes and bow their heads.

Dear Lord, thank you for this special day. I just love the way you made us, and I love you. Amen.

"Amen," we all said in unison.

"Oh, and I forgot," announced Jax:

Thank you for making Mr. Vlad better, and for the deer to feed us and for the new potty, as he giggled.

We all had a good laugh and relaxed just a bit.

"I know it's the first day of our trip," I said, loud enough for all to hear, "and it's not what I or any of you expected, I'm sure. We had some bad things happen, and some good as well. That's how it goes."

"Kelly...have you seen her?" asked Mike loudly to the group. There was some quiet talking between the other women when Joy spoke up.

"Mike, we last saw her about an hour before dinner. We thought she was with you," she added.

"Kelly!" he called out. "Can you hear me?"

Everyone was silent, even the children. There was only the sound of the crackling fire and the wind in the trees.

"We have to find her!" said Mike. "She must have wandered off and gotten lost."

"Okay," said Lonnie. "Here's the plan. Lance and Jake, you take the north side of the highway. Mike and I will take the south side. There are a lot of open areas, so I don't think she got lost. She may be hurt, so let's be thorough.

"You guys go out about a half-mile," he said, looking at me, "and go around east to south in a circle. Mike and I will do the opposite. Let's get night-vision binoculars for each group. Jim and Vlad will each have a pair, as well, to keep an eye out over the group. If we come up on trouble, be sure you know which way our group is. There can be no friendly fire here.

"All six men going and staying will have a radio. Everyone else stays inside the perimeter, with no exceptions."

Jake and I headed out without our flashlights on. It was one of those clear nights with a nearly full moon that lit up the landscape enough to see clearly. It reminded me of my childhood days, roaming the Ranch as a boy after dark on a clear summer night.

I didn't want to draw any attention by using a light or calling out. We walked slowly about 30 feet apart, side-to-side. Jake and I carried an AR-15 and our pistol of choice. Lonnie and Mike opted for the same.

We all met up in a clearing.

"I've got something up ahead, about 200 yards out," said Mike.

"I see it," replied Lonnie. "Looks like a small campfire." There was a man's voice raised and sounding agitated.

"We have the advantage, unless they have night vision as well," said Lonnie. They crouched down and, using the binoculars, saw two people sitting just beyond the campfire.

"Any sign of Kelly?" asked Lonnie.

"No. It's Sheila from the truck and that asshole what's-his-name," said Mike.

"Let's approach but real slow," said Lonnie. "I don't think they're armed, but who knows."

They slowly reached the makeshift camp and were undetected until the last ten feet, when Lonnie yelled out, "Don't move," shining his flashlight into Dan's eyes.

"Hey, what the hell?" yelled Dan, standing up.

"Where's my girl, Danny?" said Mike, in an accusing tone.

"What the hell are you talking about?" replied Dan.

"Kelly. She's missing. Have you two seen her?" he asked, unzipping the gray tent just beyond the fire.

"Hey, man. That's our property!" yelled Dan.

Mike, ignoring Dan, shined his light into the near-empty tent. Two sleeping bags, a small cooler, and a toolbox were all there was to see.

"Listen," said Lonnie. "One of our group, Kelly, went missing a couple of hours ago. Have you seen anything out here?"

"No," said Sheila. "I'm so sorry, but no, we haven't heard or seen anything here."

Lonnie noticed a small trickle of blood coming out from the right corner of her mouth.

"What happened," Lonnie asked her.

"She tripped over a rock and had a little fall," Dan said quickly.

"Sheila," he said again. "What happened?"

"I just told..."

"I'm not asking you, Dan," said Lonnie. "I'm asking her."

Dan stood up again, clearly unarmed, and Lonnie met him chest-to-chest, only feet apart. Dan had a good five inches in height on Lonnie, but both knew the score if it went bad.

"Have a seat, Danny boy," said Mike, feeling flushed again, like earlier in the day. Dan slowly sat down.

Sheila replied, "It's just like he said. I'm good at fixing things but get a little clumsy from time to time."

"You hear or see anything, you let us know," said Lonnie, clearly as a statement.

"Hey man, I've got something over here on the road," Jake said to me in a low voice.

As I reached him, he was looking at a neatly folded stack of items on the side of the road but visible to anyone walking or driving by.

On the top was a hair clip inlaid with turquoise, a ring, and what appeared to be a note held down by a small rock.

"I recognize the clip," I said. "I'm pretty sure it's Kelly's. I don't know what that note says, but I think Mike should be the one to read it," I added.

Jake was way ahead of me as he radioed Lonnie. "Hey, guys," he said. "We've got something over here about 150 yards up on the road.

"Is it her?" asked Lonnie?

"No," replied Jake, "but we think it's some of her belongings."

Ten minutes later, Lonnie and Mike walked up. Mike had wanted to run the whole way, but Lonnie convinced him to take it slow and observe their surroundings.

Mike saw the pile and reached for the note. Lonnie pulled out a small BIC lighter so Mike could read it.

"Dearest Michael," it read. "Do you remember this hair tie? You gave it to me four years ago, along with this promise ring.

"For nearly three years, I kept waiting for you to ask me those four words every woman wants to hear, but they never came. I gave up somewhere along the way and had been waiting for something big to happen that would point me in the right direction. Well, it doesn't get much bigger than this.

"The group, this group, is one of families, and I don't belong. I thought I could stick it out, but I can't. I do love you, Michael, and I wish you the very best. Please don't try to find me.

"Love, Kelly."

Mike handed the note to Lonnie and walked towards the camp.

Lonnie quickly read it, setting the lighter to it, and watched it burn on the pavement.

"Let's go," he told Jake and me. "We've got a big day tomorrow," and started walking.

He caught up to Mike, leaving Jake and me behind.

"Guess we leave the stuff?" asked Jake.

"Yeah. I think it's done," I replied.

We headed back, lagging behind, so Lonnie could talk to his old friend and partner.

Lonnie made a point of addressing the group before bedtime, including the kids.

"Kelly," he said, when he got their attention, "has decided to go her own way and leave our group. Any adult here is welcome to do so at any time along the way if they so choose. We will not be discussing this anymore, so if there are any questions, ask me now."

There were no hands raised.

"Mr. Lonnie?" asked Jax, standing up. "Do you think God will watch over Ms. Kelly?"

"I think He will. Yes, I'm sure of it.

"We have a big day tomorrow," Lonnie continued. "As most of you know, we had damage to our lead truck today. A woman outside of our group was able to fix it and get us back on the road. With our good man and most excellent mechanic, Vlad, down right now..."

"But not out!" yelled Vlad from inside his tent.

"Well, we could use a hand. She comes with a companion, and if all here agree, maybe they could tag along for a little while before we make a firm decision about them. All agreed say 'aye.'"

Most every adult replied "Aye."

"Any opposed?" asked Lonnie.

All were quiet.

"Okay, we will get a schedule together for tonight, with each man spending one hour tending to the fire smoker and one hour on perimeter patrol. This plan will give everyone enough time to get rested."

Our first night outside was quiet by new-world standards. Occasional gunshots were heard far off in the distance. Each family had a tent, and there were a few single tents mixed in.

My shift was from 11 p.m. to 1 a.m. Jake lent his pocket watch, having the only one that still worked, and it was passed down with each shift change.

Daylight came about 6:30, and Ringo was barking for the first time since yesterday.

Dan and Sheila approached slowly, and Lonnie met them just outside the camp.

"You're up early," said Lonnie.

"We still have a little packing to do if you're taking us on," said Dan.

"Did you find the girl?" asked Sheila.

"We got everything worked out," replied Lonnie.

"Lance, Jake. You guys got a minute?" Lonnie called out.

"Sure," we each replied, and headed over to where they were talking.

He had filled us in last night on the duo and wanted us to help keep an eye on Dan.

Lonnie addressed Dan and Sheila: "The group has decided to bring you guys along as our mechanic is down for a while. It's a temporary thing for now, and we will see how it goes.

"You will be under our roof, and we have a particular way of doing things. Any questions?" asked Lonnie.

"Maybe Mike can help us with our belongings?" asked Sheila. Both Lonnie and Dan glanced at her with a questioning look.

"No. He's busy, but maybe Jake and Lance have a few minutes."

"Sure," I said. "We need about 15 minutes to finish with the meat."

Joy, Lucy and Tina were inspecting the venison strips.

"If they snap when you bend them, they will keep for a long time," said Joy.

"Just like the Indians probably did," replied Tina. "Veronica and Suzie have been a great help, right girls?"

"Yes, Ma'am," they both said. It was clear to me that Tina was now the adopted mom of these two beautiful girls. She loved them, and they loved her.

"Thank you so much," Tina whispered to Jake and me, "for bringing my girls home with you. We talk about their mom and dad every day, so they don't forget."

"I knew from the first day you met them that you would be their new mom," I told Tina.

After breakfast and our first camp pack-up, we were ready for day two. Nancy gathered a few of us together to talk about Vlad.

"He's doing okay, considering everything, but he's going to need a proper cast. He had a rough night."

Lonnie went over the day's instructions, including keeping an eye out for a hospital or a medical center. They would most likely be picked clean of meds but should have supplies for casting left.

Lonnie pulled Joy and Nancy aside.

"I want Sheila to ride inside with you. Maybe she will open up to you about Dan. I'm pretty sure he's abusing her, but she won't talk about it."

"Sure, Lonnie," said Joy. "We will see what we can find out."

We took up the same positions as yesterday. Lonnie introduced Dan and Sheila to the group.

"Dan, you're in the trailer with Lance and Jake, and Sheila you will be inside with Joy and Nancy."

"Now wait a minute," said Dan. "We ride together or we don't go."

"Okay," replied Lonnie. "Grab your things and go." It was a bluff, and Lonnie knew it could go either way, but the ground rules had to be set.

Sheila spoke up and said, "Dan, I'm going with them."

"All right. All right," replied Dan. "We'll go."

We pulled out of camp at 9:30 a.m., according to Jake.

"Slow and steady today," said Lonnie over the radios. "We have some miles to make up, but let's be safe about it."

Jake and I were talking with Vlad. "Are you nervous about riding back here in the trailer?" I asked.

"Nah, that's was some crazy shit, but lightning never strikes the same place twice, so I'm good. Plus, now I've got deer jerky," he said, laughing and holding up his Ziplock bag filled with six-inch-long strips.

"What do you think about the new mechanic?" I asked.

"She's good, far as I know. I didn't get to see the damage firsthand, but I know it was bad. Not sure about her guy pal, though," he added, nodding towards Dan, who was out of earshot at the end of the trailer.

Joy was expecting her to be reserved about discussing what Lonnie believed to be accurate.

"He hits me," she said, without being questioned. "I'm sure Lonnie told you about the blood he saw last night. I just heard that he was a cop, so I'm pretty sure we didn't fool him with our story."

"Where did you two meet?" asked Joy, hoping to bring down the tension just a bit.

"We met at a mechanic shop," replied Sheila. "I used to work for his dad, who owned half a dozen garages across North Texas. Dan was the trust-fund kid who was always around but didn't do a lot. I liked him at first, but that faded quickly over a few months, when he started hitting me. The first time I was shocked that it happened, you know. I was packing my things as he apologized over and over, saying it would never happen again."

"I believed him and gave him another chance. It was just two weeks later when it happened again, but this time it was different."

"Different how?" asked Janet.

"Well," Sheila continued, "this time he beat me bad…real bad… I went to the hospital after collapsing at work the next day. But I covered for him, telling the doctors and his dad that I fell down some stairs, giving them pretty much the same type of story I gave Lonnie last night."

"Do you love him?" asked Joy.

"Not anymore," she replied, as tears rolled down her face, dropping onto her jeans.

"I'm sorry," she said, regaining her composure quickly. "I want out, but he won't…I mean, he won't ever let me leave."

Sheila glanced over towards the trailer and saw Dan staring at her, slowly shaking his head back and forth. She started to shake.

"It's okay, sweetie," said Janet. "You're safe here with us. I can assure you our men won't tolerate this behavior from anyone in or around this group. And don't quote me on it, but I'm pretty sure Lonnie, and even Vlad, were impressed with your mechanical abilities."

"Where did you learn that?" Joy asked.

"My dad," Sheila replied. "I was the boy he never had, but he was so good to me. Never hit me, not even once."

* * * * * * *

Chapter Two ~
Outside Decatur, Texas

Two hours later we were just outside Decatur, Texas. We stopped to group up.

"Let's take 30 and strategize before we hit Decatur," said Lonnie after circling the vehicles.

Jake and I met with Lonnie, Mike and Steve to go over the maps and have alternate routes around the town. Jake pointed out a few roads leading around the main part of town.

"What's going on?" asked Lonnie, as we heard loud arguing coming from the front of the caravan. We jumped down off the trailer to investigate.

As we neared the front truck, we heard Dan screaming at Sheila. He was yelling about her talking behind his back and trying to leave him behind at the last camp spot.

Coming around the side of the truck, I yelled, "Hey" at Dan, but it was too late. His clenched fists connected first left, then right, with Sheila's chin and nose. She fell backward, with blood pouring out of her broken nose, deviated grossly to the right side of her face. Jake was able to catch her as she fell, keeping her head from slamming on the ground.

Mike immediately grabbed Dan in a headlock, saying, "Let's go, big guy," and walking off the road and into the trees, out of sight. We could hear Dan yelling to let him go.

"What do you think?" I asked Lonnie.

"Well, it's a new world, and I don't think Dan's coming back," he replied.

Mike let Dan out of his headlock. "You've got a tight combination," he said. "Right-left, or was it left-right? You should be proud of yourself; it looks like you broke her nose. She must have had it coming, isn't that what you think?"

Mike swiftly swung his right arm, connecting his fist with Dan's face, knocking out his front tooth.

"This is none of your business," Dan spat, as blood poured from his mouth.

"That's where you're wrong," replied Mike. "You've made it all our business now, and that's where it ends." Mike drew his Ruger SR 40 pistol from his right hip, pointing it at Dan's forehead.

Without emotion or another word, Mike fired his weapon, catching Dan between the eyes. Mike turned without watching Dan fall.

He emerged from the trees to a quiet, wide-eyed group, who all heard the gunfire. All were stunned, apart from us present outside the gun store when he shot the family man in the back.

Nancy was treating Sheila, who was unaware thus far of Dan's fate.

"This is going to hurt," said Nancy, as she grabbed Sheila's nose, straightening it with a swift pull and a crunch. Sheila screamed out and immediately fell silent, breathing heavily through her mouth… With the bleeding all but stopped, they got her back in the truck.

Mike poked his head in, asking Sheila if she was okay. "She will be," said Nancy, with no one asking about Dan.

"Mike?" asked Lonnie. "Do you have something to tell me?"

"Only that Danny boy won't be joining us for the trip, after all," replied Mike.

He turned and walked back to his vehicle at the back of the caravan. Lonnie looked up at Jake, Vlad and me, shaking his head.

"All right, guys. About three miles up the road we're going to head north on County Road 4003. It connects to a few more that wind through the Lyndon B. Johnson National Grasslands. We'll then cut west to Highway 287 North, staying clear of the city of Decatur by about 15 miles all the way around.

"I'm guessing we'll run into a fair number of folks that headed out to the grasslands looking for food to hunt. They will probably not be grouped up, but we can't be sure.

"Let's go," said Lonnie to a few people walking about. Five minutes later, we moved out.

We found the county road a few miles up and headed north.

I was taking in the scenery of the grasslands, knowing it wouldn't be long before the area went up in smoke.

Small makeshift camps with two to ten people lay scattered across the land. Tents of red, green, blue and orange stretched as far as I could see. In the old world, it could have easily been mistaken for a music festival, like the one made famous by the band originally from Palo Alto, California, called the Grateful Dead. In this next-world it was just another death trap, as they slowly ran out of food and water.

Most just stared at our caravan, and a few stood up, pointing in our direction.

"Eyes peeled," said Lonnie over the radio. "Let's take it nice and slow."

"Beautiful country," said Vlad to Jake and me. "Reminds me of Mother Russia in the countryside, kind people living off the land."

"We've got something up ahead, 150 yards," yelled Lonnie over the radio.

"It looks like a blockade: Let's lock and load, boys, and everyone in the vehicles down on the floor."

The road appeared blocked all the way across with a combination of large logs, rocks and old tractor tires.

As we slowed to a stop, a shantytown of tents and tarps spanned the horizon.

"It looks like they grouped up," said Jake.

"That's not good," replied Vlad. "Hand me my AK," he added. "I may be down, but I'm still a threat."

Lonnie slowed the lead truck a hundred yards out and stopped, with the rest of the caravan following suit.

"Here they come," said Lonnie over the walkie-talkies. "Women and children down on the floor. Shooters at the ready but stand down for now."

A growing crowd of refugees flanked the caravan on both sides. Men, women and children slowly enclosed the vehicles.

"Why do they have their children here?" asked Vlad.

"Do not engage," said Lonnie over the radio. "There are women and children. Hold all positions."

As the growing crowd closed in on the caravan, everything moved in slow motion.

"Please, Lord," I prayed. "Let us resolve this situation without harm on either side."

With our group surrounded by everyday fathers, mothers and school children, it was clear we were all getting nervous.

"Having firepower does no good if you're aiming at women and children," said Jake to Vlad and me.

"What do we do?" asked Vlad. The surrounding crowd was eerily quiet. Even the children didn't speak.

"Nothing," said Jake.

"I never expected this," I added.

Lonnie, Mike and Steve all joined us on the trailer to come up with a plan.

"Guys," said Lonnie, "this isn't good; we can't just shoot our way out of this. We all have families to protect, but I'm not shooting at women and kids."

"We're with you," I said, with Jake and Vlad nodding in agreement. Mike was stone cold and didn't respond.

"Lance and Jake," said Lonnie. "We need to find out who's in charge and figure this out.

"Who's in charge here?" yelled Lonnie, in a toned-down voice. The crowd was silent.

"Who's in charge?" he repeated loudly. Several of the adults pointed towards a military-style tent, 100 yards off the road.

"Okay, Lance and Jake. We've got to do this," said Lonnie. "Mike, Jim and Steve, you help Vlad cover.

"Mike," he added, "promise me you won't shoot anyone."

"I'll do my best, buddy," he responded, "but don't be too long."

Jake and I glanced at our wives and kids. Hendrix gave me the monocular look. I gave it right back, hoping it wasn't my last.

"Danny," said Hudson, "look at the kids," pointing around the caravan. "They look like zombies, just standing there."

We approached the tent, weapons pointing towards the ground. Two guards stepped aside, opening the tent and motioning us to go inside.

I was nervous about it, but I didn't see any other way.

"Sit, please?" asked a man at the back of the enclosure, seated on a colorful blanket.

He was easily over 60 years of age, with long gray hair pulled back in a ponytail and a leathery face, signifying he may have lived out here for years.

"Welcome. We have been expecting you," he said confidently.

"I'm not sure what you're talking about," said Lonnie, "but we just ran into your barricade a few minutes ago."

"I'm guessing you think we are unorganized, not capable of having scouts out 10 or 20 miles to alert us of incoming dangers. Is that right?" asked the man on the blanket.

"Why do you think my people surrounded your caravan without saying a word?"

"We're not sure about that," I said. "What do you want?"

He smiled. "My name is Ronna, and I'm the leader of our growing group out there.

"We want the same thing you do. Peace for our families, women and children. Food, protection and prosperity in this new and exciting world."

"How did you come to be the leader so quickly?" I asked, genuinely interested.

"I was a barista at a coffee house you may have heard of, started in Seattle," he said in a low voice, "and my real name is Harry.

"I headed out here after the power went down and found a large population of unorganized families looking for direction. What may have taken many years in the old world took just days in this next world for me to establish myself as the leader and caretaker of our growing family.

"With that being said, I need to provide for them as their new leader.

"We are short on weapons, as I'm sure you have surmised. However, most men I know would not fire on women and children unless it was absolutely necessary; and even then, I'm not sure."

"So, you use them as pawns for your agenda?" asked Jake angrily.

"Whatever it takes," responded Ronna.

"If it were just me and a few of my men manning the barricade, you all would be two miles down the road and we would be dead. Does that sound about right?" he angled. After a long pause, with no one speaking, he added, "We're just like you, trying to survive."

"It sounds like you're nothing like us," I threw in.

"Okay, we understand," said Lonnie. "What do you want for our safe passage?"

"Protection," said Ronna. "It won't be long until we get someone passing through who doesn't care about the children."

"How about an AR-15 and a 9mm pistol for safe passage?" asked Lonnie.

"That won't do," replied Ronna.

Mike opened the tent, overhearing the conversation, entering with his pistol drawn.

"How did you get in here?" asked Ronna.

"Seems your guards don't want to die today," replied Mike.

"I think my buddy Lonnie here has offered a deal that's more than fair, with a little ammo, I'm guessing."

"What if we say no?" said Ronna.

"Well, that's easy," said Mike. "Your little group here gets to pick a new leader, and by the time they do, we'll be down the road. I'm short on patience at the moment, and I assure you I can go either way on this, so what's it going to be?"

"It's a deal," said Ronna, "and we can have you on your way in 15 minutes or so."

He led the way out of the tent and back down to the vehicles. All eyes were on him as he approached, stopping 20 yards out.

Raising one arm, and without a word, he pointed to the east, and his people followed.

One of his guards came to the trailer to collect the trade weapons and ammo.

The blockade was opened enough for the vehicles to proceed, and the caravan moved forward slowly and steadily.

Three miles north, Lonnie stopped the group and called for a circle. "Time for a potty break," he said to the kids. They lined up, nearly all having to go.

He addressed the adults, saying, "I'm sorry about the scare back there, but it could have been much worse. Thanks to our good friend Vlad, we have some things to trade.

"It won't always be that easy, I'm afraid, but no one got hurt today, and that's fine with me."

"Except for Dan," Jake whispered to me.

"That's why I told you to stay away from Mike," I replied. "He's a loose cannon, and I don't want my new best friend getting caught in any trouble."

"Awe, that's nice," replied Jake, "but I can handle myself."

Winding around the town of Decatur was slow going. "Eyes in all directions," called Lonnie over the radio. "It's open country out here and we stick out. We'll hold steady at about 10 miles per hour."

There was a steady migration of families walking with all their belongings. Some had backpacks, and others pulled kids' wagons.

A few had grocery carts, but most just pulled rolling suitcases or had large garbage bags over their shoulders. They all carried themselves slumped and defeated, eyes void of the life they recently enjoyed, now marching with free will from their once-comforting homes towards the unknown and probable death.

"I'm betting only one in five families have any kind of shelter, tents or sleeping bags," I said to Jake and Vlad.

"If even that," replied Vlad. "Where are all the Refugee camps we heard about? These people will never make it on their own out here. It's sad, yes?"

Jake and I nodded our heads in agreement.

"I'm guessing Ronna will be adding some more to his group, now that he has a little firepower," said Jake.

The miles slowly rolled past, with more of the same.

Once clear of Decatur we got back on Highway 287, heading northwest.

Lonnie stopped the lead truck and called to circle the vehicles. "Time for lunch and a look at the map," he called over the radio.

"We've got lunch covered," said Joy, Nancy, Tina and Lonnie's wife.

"We're about 50 miles outside of Wichita Falls, near as I can tell," said Vlad, pointing to the map.

"Lake Arrowhead is here, about 20 miles south of the city," said Lonnie.

"We can hit the south side of the lake for the night and catch the main highway again, 35 miles northwest of the city, tomorrow without losing much time.

"We can get everyone a much-needed lake bath, and we can set up my yo-yo fishing reels."

"Yo-yo what?" asked Vlad.

"They're automatic fishing reels that look like a kid's yo-yo. You just tie them to a log or stake them into the ground, bait the hook and wait. When a fish is on, the reel brings it in and holds it until we check it."

"Sounds like cheating to me," said Vlad.

"Yeah," I responded. "It kind of is. That's why it was illegal in most states, and now it's just a cool food catcher."

"I wouldn't mind some good fish jerky," said Jake. "Most folks coming out of the city will head to the north part of the lake, as the path of least resistance, so we should stay relatively secluded to the south. With any luck, we'll have a nice big fish fry tonight and some left to smoke."

Sheila had been resting quietly since the incident, not talking at all.

Only now she asked about Dan. "Is he gone?" she asked Nancy.

"Yes, sweetie, and he won't be bothering you anymore."

Sheila started to cry. "I know it's hard," said Joy, "but he didn't treat you right."

"No, it's not that," she replied. "Lonnie said this was a temporary thing, and if I can't stay I'll be all alone. Even staying with Dan is better than being alone."

"Let me work on that," said Lonnie's wife.

Shredded venison sandwiches were on the menu. The gas generator on the trailer was powering two freezers, now filled to capacity.

"About time for a gasoline run," I said out loud.

Crossing back over Highway 287, we unhooked Lonnie's truck from the trailer.

"Lance and Jake, can you help me out?" asked Lonnie. "Mike, Jim, Steve and Vlad, you're on security."

"Hey, Vlad," I called out. "Can you please…"

"Keep an eye on Mike?" he asked.

"Yes, that's it," I replied.

"No worries, new friend. I'll do just that."

Finding cars full of gas was the easy part. Even out here in the middle of nowhere, there was one every hundred yards. Every car was at least half full of gas, having just passed a larger town.

The siphon hoses made the work easy. Just fill up the gas cans, transfer to the vehicles and generators, and store the rest.

An hour and a half later, we had as much gas as we could carry. It was 2 p.m., and we were still 50 miles out from Lake Arrowhead.

"All right," said Lonnie, addressing the group. "We have about 50 miles to get to the next stop.

"We can make in a couple of hours if all goes well, or stop here just off the road a bit for the night. All in favor of stopping, raise your hands."

Only a few hands went up. "All in favor of heading forward to the lake?" Most hands raised, with a few hollers. "Okay, let's move out."

Off the main road, with open countryside, we were making good time.

"Finally, we're moving," said Jake. "Last time I commented on our speed, Vlad got messed up by that deer."

The road ahead was easily navigated, with open country on both sides as far as we could see.

Vlad was smiling, with the wind in his hair.

"At this speed, we'll be fishing soon, with maybe just a shot or two of vodka to ease the stress," he called over the radio.

"Vlad, you've been the most upbeat patient I've ever had," said Nancy.

"I'll pour you the first shot, but only one for now. You're still healing. Just as soon as we get to camp," she radioed back.

The next two hours went by in a flash. I didn't mind the break of smooth travel, knowing it was a luxury.

Lonnie slowed, and the caravan stopped nearly two hours later.

"According to the map, we have a bridge crossing the lake about five miles up ahead.

"We don't have to cross there, but a detour is another two to three hours out of our way. I'm just not sure if it will be blocked."

We agreed to try it. "We should be able to observe it from a ways out with binoculars," added Jake. I handed him mine.

"Take a look. Is that what I think it is?" asked Jake.

Military trucks were blocking the entrance to the bridge, and there appeared to be 50 or more soldiers milling around on the bridge.

"Let me take a look," said Lonnie.

"What are they guarding? The bridge only covers a small part of the lake... There's a broad line of people headed down from the north, most likely from Wichita Falls, and it looks like they are being interviewed before being allowed to cross the bridge."

"Womp Womp...Womp Womp..."

The adults were all so focused on the bridge that no one saw the Blackhawk helicopters approaching from the east.

I turned around and saw most of the children pointing up to the sky. I looked up to see them both fly overhead fast.

"Keep going, boys. That's it. Just keep going," said Vlad aloud.

Just before reaching the bridge, one flanked left and the other right in a large circle. They met side-by-side, hovering over our caravan at no more than 300 feet.

"This situation is not good," said Jake.

"Get ready for a fight, boys," said Mike, smiling.

"No, no, no!" yelled Lonnie, over the noise of the turning blades. "Everyone stands down. This is a fight we won't win."

"Drop your weapons," came the voice over a loudspeaker from one of the helicopters.

Each of us holding rifles laid them on the trailer next to us. Thankfully, Mike did the same.

"This is the United States Army." With one helicopter still hovering, the other came down slowly, landing no more than 50 yards from our trailer.

I counted eight men exiting in full combat gear, rifles at the ready.

"Cool and calm, boys," said Lonnie. "We haven't done anything wrong that I know of."

"Who's in charge here?" barked the first soldier to reach the trailer.

"I guess we all are," replied Lonnie.

"I'm officer Sanchez, McKinney Police Department," he said, reaching out his hand.

"Let's see some ID from all of you," the soldier replied, without shaking Lonnie's hand.

"Sir," said Jake, "I'm former Army Ranger retired, and we all have IDs, but we'll have to dig for them. I haven't carried my wallet in a while," he said with a smile.

The soldier, not smiling back, replied, "Okay, we can do that. You two first," he said, pointing at Jake and Lonnie.

"That's good," I whispered to Vlad. "I think they're trying to establish credibility."

"We can do that, sir," replied Lonnie. "We have a fair number of women and children with us," he added, "so can we take this nice and slow?"

"IDs," replied the soldier.

Jakes ID was in the vehicle with Nancy and Joy and all our boys. They had the windows up and didn't hear everything that was said.

"What's going on?" asked Nancy, in a worried voice.

"I'm not sure yet, honey," he replied. "Stay down and be as quiet as possible. No sudden moves in here," he added, as he emerged with his wallet.

He and Lonnie made it back to the soldier about the same time, handing over their credentials.

"Any other military or police here?"

Jake motioned to Nancy to come out of the vehicle. "Former National Guard," said Jake, as she exited the vehicle.

"Sir," asked Lonnie, "with all due respect, can I ask why we're being detained?"

"You're not being held. We're having a conversation here," replied the soldier. "You're free to go whenever you choose."

"Okay, sir. I guess we'll be on our way," said Lonnie, as he and Jake were handed their IDs back.

"Do you know what that is?" asked the soldier, pointing to the bridge?

"No, sir," replied Jake.

"That's the relocation camp for the area, just across the bridge," said the soldier.

"They take men, women and children. No pets, though," he added, pointing to an unusually calm Ringo on the trailer.

"Also, no weapons or belongings?" asked Vlad, already knowing the answer.

"None of that is needed. In our relocation camps, everything you need is provided for you—safety, shelter, food, water, and even jobs to keep your mind occupied. There are also hot showers and classes for the kids."

"So, the residents are free to leave the camp whenever they want?" asked Vlad in a semi-sarcastic tone.

"Everyone is happy there. No one wants to leave," was the reply.

Our Commander in Chief is recommending that all citizens report to the closest camp until we get things back under control.

"Thank you, sir," replied Lonnie, "for the invitation, but we will have to pass."

"Where you headed?" the soldier asked.

"Colorado," replied Lonnie.

"Well then, I'm sure you'll be passing through Amarillo, and later northern New Mexico. Let me look," he said, pulling out a map.

"We have camps set up in Raton, New Mexico, as well as Trinidad and Boulder, Colorado, if any of you change your mind.

"We just had a talk with the coffee guy, Harry. We understand you ran into them a couple of hours ago. Our camp will give those families protection that they won't get out there in the grasslands."

"What about Ronna...I mean Harry?" Lonnie asked.

The soldier pointed to the chopper hovering 300 feet above.

The side door opened and out came a screaming man, flailing his arms as he fell. He landed hard on the ground with a thud and was silent.

"It's not wise to use women and children as human shields while you rob good people," the soldier replied.

"So, do we get our guns back?" asked Vlad.

"Don't get into any trouble," said the soldier, as he and his men headed back to the chopper.
As the helicopters moved out, we regrouped on the trailer a few miles down the road.

"I guess crossing the bridge is out," I said.

* * * * * * *

Chapter Three ~ Lake Arrowhead South Wichita Falls, Texas

"We can detour to the southwest a couple of hours and still catch a lakeside view before nightfall," said Lonnie.

Staying clear of Wichita Falls to the south and west sides, we made our way back to Highway 287 toward Amarillo.

The south side of the lake was a sight to see. There were camping spots dotted across the shoreline, all empty.

With no houses near this side of the lake, and very few working cars in the area, we had the place to ourselves.

"Five minutes after five," Jake announced, looking at his pocket watch. With the vehicles circled, the adults made plans to get some things done.

"Jake and I can set up the yo-yo reels quickly, and hopefully we'll have a good dinner tonight," I offered.

"Okay," said Lonnie. "Mike and Steve can provide security if the ladies want to get the kids a bath over there, away from the fishing," as he pointed to a shallow inlet partially surrounded by trees and bushes.

"And I'll get a fire going," said Lonnie. "Vlad, do you mind covering all of us from the trailer before you have the vodka shots I've been hearing about?"

"That can be done, yes; the Beluga can wait."

"Honey," said Joy, pulling me aside. "The boys haven't seen you much lately."

"I know, and I'm sorry. We've just been so busy."

"Maybe you two can take your boys and Danny to help with the fish things," suggested Nancy.

"You guys want to go with us?" asked Jake to the four most excited boys I'd ever seen.

"By the smiles and hollering, I'd say they do," I replied.

"Okay, we have 16 to put out," said Jake. "I'll show you guys how to do the first one, then you can each set some. We're looking for bass and catfish, so we will bait them all a little differently and see what works."

I tied the first one to an overhanging branch and threw the pulled line out to a deep spot with some deer scraps that had been purposely left out in the sun for catfish bait.

"That stinks!" said Danny, as each boy grabbed their nose, making a face.

"Yeah, boys. That's what catfish like—the stinkier, the better," said Jake.

"Okay, guys, pay attention over here," I said, pointing to a reel. "Once the line is out, you set the reel, and it does the rest."

"Easy peasy," said Hudson, just as the reel disengaged and started to twist and shake.

"I wasn't expecting that!" said Hendrix, using a line he heard on one of his old cartoons called *Jonnie Test*.

"Yeah! Me neither!" said Jake, looking at me with his eyebrows raised.

"Lucky strike!" I replied. "Let's see what we've got," pulling the line in, using my fishing towel to keep my hands from becoming Swiss cheese.

The hefty catfish was pulled ashore, to the delight of the boys.

"Let's weigh this guy!" said Jake, hanging it on the scale. "Four pounds, six ounces."

"That's a good-looking fish!" hollered Vlad from the trailer. "A few more of those and we will have a feast tonight."

Over the next 90 minutes we hauled in over 40 fish, ranging in size from a half-pound to a monster catfish at 26.5 pounds.

Jake weighed every one, with the boys' help. All said, we had over 100 pounds of fish to cook.

Most of the adult men and women pitched in to get them filleted. A few of the ladies started on dinner, and Jake and I set up the smoker rack for the rest.

"It going to be another long night," said Jake.

"That's right, buddy," I said, "but every long night comes with a lot of new food so far. If we stayed here for a week, we could feed an army."

Everyone ate their fill, including Ringo.

"You missed your bath, boys; you'll get one in the morning, though," Joy told them.

"You boys too!" said Nancy to Jake and me.

After an adult meeting called by the ladies, we agreed to split the security and fish smoking between more people. The ladies argued that they should be on security as well, and we all agreed to give it a try.

My shift tonight would only be an hour and a half. *Not bad*, I thought. *Maybe I can get a good night's sleep, after all.*

Jax, Hudson and Hendrix all wanted Ringo to sleep in our tent.

"When we get to Colorado, he can sleep with you every night, but out on the road, we need him outside," I told them. "He has a very important role because out here he's a Super Dog."

"He's going to need a cape," said Jax, matter of factly.

"Good night, boys," I said, as I stepped out of the tent. "I love you guys."

"We love you too, Daddy."

"Check that out," said Vlad, pointing across the lake. "Those lights out there must be the FEMA camp."

"Looks like it," I added. "Full electricity and all the comforts of home…if you don't mind being a brainless zombie, that is."

"I've heard that they separate the men from the women and children," said Vlad.

"How crazy would it be to have your wife and kids so close but not be able to see them?" added Jake.

"Don't worry, buddy," I said, petting Ringo on the head. "That's not our fate." He barked once, laying his head down for an after-dinner nap.

The sun rose early the next morning, as always, and it reminded me of one true constant thing: the sun will always rise.

Jake and I set half of the yo-yo reels out to catch some breakfast. At this point, with the smoked fish and what we could fit in the freezers, we had all we could carry.

Jake and I took our boys for a morning bath. They were complaining that it was cold.

"A true fisherman fishes first and bathes later, even if it's cold," I told them.

"That's why I'm a fisher boy," said Hudson, getting a laugh out of us all.

Ten fish made for a hearty breakfast, as we packed up to head out. Even the kids ate their fill without complaints.

"Nine a.m. Not bad!" said Jake, looking at his watch.

Our group headed west, then turned north, back towards the highway.

Steve got the ham radio up and tried to reach David on Raton Pass. Mark was operating the radio today and was quick to get his dad.

"Hey, David," I said, getting on the line.

"How's the trip?" he asked.

"It's been interesting so far, but slow going," I told him. "We're going to be a little longer out, but we're coming. Can you let James know we still intend to honor our deal?"

"Sure, buddy, no worries. We're keeping busy up here and will keep an eye out for you all over the next week or so."

"Thanks, David," I replied. "By the way, we have some information about a FEMA camp set up in Raton."

"I hadn't heard about that," David said. "Is the information credible?"

"I think so. It came from a military platoon at another camp in Texas," I told him.

"All right. Then I'm glad we're up here on the pass," David said.

"How are you holding up over there?" I asked.

"Not bad here, besides being mostly isolated from the outside world—except of course for our radio. We reunited with old friends and made some new ones. We've staked out our territory and have a good group working together up here. I'm sure you've heard about our little group, The Raton Pass Militia, by now."

"It's all we hear about out on the road," I said, playing along. "People won't shut up about you guys!"

It was a crisp morning as we headed out, with full stomachs.

I could have stayed at the lake for a few more days, but knew we had to keep moving.

We headed northwest on Highway 25, towards Interstate 287, clearing the city of Wichita Falls by 20 miles. We had nearly 220 miles to get to Amarillo. After an hour's travel, Lonnie called a quick meeting for the adults and a potty break for the kids.

"We have a couple of hundred miles to get to the outskirts of Amarillo. There are small towns up and down the highway on the way. We can count on most of them being less than friendly towards a caravan of people with trailers full of weapons and ammo," relayed Lonnie to the adults. "We'll keep steady at 20 miles per hour if possible, and that should put us closer to Amarillo by tonight, God willing."

It was just after 10 a.m., according to Jake's watch, and the temperature was climbing. The lake water we had filtered the day before would become crucial during this long desolate stretch of road.

The children were now picking favorite buddies and vehicles to ride in, breaking up the monotony just a bit.

Feeling the hot wind in my hair, I looked for Hendrix to give him the monocular look but only saw Hudson and Jax in the next vehicle. *He must have found a buddy in another car*, I thought. *Maybe Veronica or Suzie*, I imagined. I was happy he was making more friends now.

Vlad's leg needed a proper cast, and according to the map there was a hospital 20 miles up the road, right off the highway. I pointed it out to Jake and Vlad, as we radioed Lonnie to be on the lookout.

The miles passed without seeing many people. Just an occasional couple or family walking down the road, but they didn't have any interest in our group.

Just over an hour later, I pointed towards a hospital that looked brand new. It was a four-story building with glass on all sides. A few people could be seen milling around.

"I'm sure the pharmacy is completely cleaned out," I shouted to Jake.

"You know it is," he replied, smiling, "even in a small town like this."

Lonnie called to circle the vehicles 200 yards out, so we could make a plan.

"I'm going in," said Nancy, "since I know what we need."

"Not without firepower," directed Lonnie. "Mike, you go first, and provide cover."

"I'll go," shouted Jake.

"Listen," said Lonnie. "You've got a boy to think about and I can't have both of you in there, just in case."

"Hendrix!" called Joy in a panicked voice. "Has anyone seen Hendrix?!" she yelled, running down the caravan.

* * * * * * *

Chapter Four ~ Vernon, Texas

I jumped off the trailer, bouncing from vehicle to vehicle. "Please, Lord," I said aloud. "Let him be here."

I met Joy at the last trailer, with no sign of our sweet boy.

Joy collapsed in tears, and I felt a surge like a lightning bolt pierce my stomach. I panicked, running back the way we came, shouting his name.

Had he fallen off along the way, or did we leave him at the last stop?

I ran, screaming his name, for more than half a mile when I realized Lonnie's truck was behind me.

"Get in," said a familiar voice, as the passenger door was thrown open.

I jumped in, expecting to see Lonnie or Jake.

"Mike?!" I said, more as a question than anything else. "I…well, I was expecting someone else" is all I could think to say.

"We'll find your boy," he told me in a straight face, with no emotion.

I clicked on the seatbelt for the first time this trip, as Mike laid on the gas.

"Just make sure he's not in the road, having fallen out," I said.

Two miles passed, without a word from either of us, before he spoke.

"So, what do you think?" asked Mike, not looking over from his driving position.

"About Hendrix?" I asked.

"No. About me?"

I hesitated, not wanting to take my focus off my boy, but realizing that this may be a significant moment in the future of our group.

I looked at the speedometer and realized he was going 60 miles per hour towards our last stop.

"We should be there in about 20 to 30 minutes," I told him.

With nothing else to do, for now, I thought I would get this out of the way.

"Well," I told him, "I'm not sure how to read you. You kind of remind me of the fixer from the movie *Pulp Fiction*." Mike laughed at that, not taking his eyes from the road.

"Take an asshole like Dan," I said, "and he gets what he gets. But a guy like Dane, back at the gun shop—I don't get that. I mean, he was unarmed and walking away when you shot him. And here you are, helping me find my boy… I thought Lonnie wanted you to go into the hospital with Nancy," I added.

"He did, but this is more important, and someone may have Hendrix right now. If so, you're going to need my help.

"Did Lonnie ever tell you why I left the department in Brooklyn to move to Texas?"

"No," I admitted. "I didn't even know that."

"My partner and I had a case we were working, involving the Catholic Church. They're real serious about the Church in Brooklyn, let me tell you… Anyway, we were the first in on a raid of one of the preacher's offices, where the janitor had two young boys locked up.

"Father Corraso called me first, before anyone else. He was a good man and stepped in a few times when I got in trouble as a kid. My partner and I kicked in the door of the locked room to find the janitor doing unspeakable things to two young boys about Hendrix's age.

"Well, without hesitation or a second thought, we both opened fire on him. When the smoke cleared, he had nine bullet wounds and died right there in the church, before God and everyone."

"What about the boys?" I asked.

"They were okay. At least they didn't get shot, I mean. They were messed up, man, after that, though."

I was shocked, as tears rolled down Mike's face.

"The trial was brutal for those boys and their families," he continued. "Somehow that monster's family got hooked up with a top-notch group of attorneys who were trying to say that the boys somehow wanted that to happen, and suggested it was just a big misunderstanding. They came at us hard and it was all over the news. They were calling it a murder trial from the very beginning.

"My partner and I were somehow found not guilty by a jury filled with mothers and fathers. The Church filed a civil suit against us both, which was still pending before the lights went out. Father Corraso put in a good word for me, but it was out of his hands.

"For a long time, I wondered how God could let that happen to those boys. Then I wondered if my partner and I were meant to be there to stop it.

"I moved to McKinney to start over and met Lonnie at a neighborhood barbecue, of all places. He got me a job on the force, even with my past record, and I'll never forget that.

"As for the Dane guy, it probably shouldn't have happened. I felt a little bad about it. My mind went numb, having the kid, Sam, in danger on that trailer next to us.

"God help them if someone has your boy, though.

"All that stays between us," Mike said as a statement.

"Agreed," I told him.

"How are you doing without Kelly?" I asked, immediately regretting it.

"Sad, I guess," he replied. "She was with me through the whole thing and never wavered, not even once. I should have married her when I had a chance."

I was on a roll now and wanted to get everything out.

"What about Jake?" Mike said, before I could ask.

"Yeah, I was wondering about that," I replied.

"Don't worry. We're just posturing up, like rulers of two countries might do when they don't agree. We both have a hell of an ego, and I'm not sure who would come out on top if we got into it.

"We're both committed to the group and have respect for both you and Lonnie, so don't worry about it. Hell, he and I may even have a beer together before it's all said and done."

I was suddenly feeling much better about Mike. *He is still a loose cannon*, I thought, but I understood his behavior much better now.

"About ten minutes to where we stopped last," said Mike, navigating the occasional stalled car with ease, even at his now 70-mile-an-hour speed.

I may have asked him to slow, but I knew every second could count with Hendrix. Those next ten minutes felt like an eternity. My mind raced with all the horrible possibilities of what we might find. *Was my boy alive or hurt? Did he survive the heat without water? Was he even there? Was he kidnapped or worse?*

"That's it!" I yelled, pointing down the road a quarter mile. "That's the spot where we stopped."

Mike hit the brakes hard as we approached, squeaking the tires.

"Oh no," I groaned, not seeing any sign of my boy.

"Let's check the perimeter," suggested Mike, "all way around."

I went left and he right.

"I've got something over here," yelled Mike. I ran over to see him pointing down at little tennis shoe prints, leading west, away from the perimeter.

"It's him!" I said, both excited and terrified. "I recognize the under-armor pattern on the sole."

I felt a lump welling up in my throat, as I pointed to the two sets of adult shoe prints, one on each side of my boy's.

"Let's go!" I shouted, still not thinking clearly.

Mike grabbed my shoulder and in a sober voice said, "Listen, Lance. I know you're panicked and your mind is going 100 miles per hour. You need to let me help you."

"Okay, okay," I said, now breathing like I had just run a 10k race.

"Let's take a look," Mike said, handing me a pair of binoculars, while looking through his own.

I scanned the horizon with no one in sight, the ground cracked and fissured as far as I could see under the heat of the desolate land.

"Where are they?!" I said aloud.

"Look at the terrain," Mike pointed out. "There are a lot of valleys we can't see into from here. We need to take five minutes to prep for tracking," he added.

"All right," I agreed. "What's first?"

"Pop the truck hood and pull the distributor wire," he asked. "I don't want anyone stealing our ride back."

Mike grabbed a pre-loaded backpack from the back of the truck. "We only have one of these," he said, "so we'll take turns carrying. We've got enough food and water for a few days, worst case. Last, and certainly not least, the AR-15s," he said with a slight grin.

"All right, buddy," he said. "Let's find your boy."

We set out quickly, following the three sets of tracks in the dusty plains.

I said a prayer, followed by another and another, for his safe return.

I also asked one for Mike, that he might be healed of his past traumas and forgiven for his past indiscretions.

It was about noon, and the temperature was rising. Dust swirled with the occasional gust of wind. My lips chapped as sweat poured from my adrenaline-filled body.

I hope they have water, I thought. *And who took my son?*

Fifteen minutes had gone by when we hit the edge of the first valley. We approached cautiously on our hands and knees, peering down into the narrow opening, with no sign of them.

"Let's be diligent about following the tracks that are now harder to make out," I told Mike. "I don't want us to end up off course and lose them out here."

"They've got a head start, but your boy will have to be carried at some points along the way. See here," he added, pointing to only two sets of adult tracks.

"This one is sunk down deeper than before," so he must be carrying Hendrix.

"I see that," I said, relieved when I saw his little shoe prints 30 yards down the trail.

"Right now, we have the element of surprise, so no calling out his name. Understood?" asked Mike.

"I got it," I replied, knowing he was right. It took everything I had in me not to scream out his name.

I started having flashbacks, like when you do something stupid and you could die. I had experienced them five times in my life, three of which were near-drownings; and ironically, I was a good swimmer.

Now they were all about Hendrix growing up, like a mental slideshow with pictures I would swear I'd never seen before.

Lance, he was just perfect. My little bo…

"Lance," said Mike, shaking my shoulder.

"What?" I asked, realizing I had zoned out.

"We need to be focused a hundred percent," he told me.

"Sorry, man… I'm just…I don't know…"

"Let's stay calm and talk strategy," suggested Mike.

"One of the adult prints is smaller than the other.

"Scenario 1: a couple of guys have Hendrix and have firepower.

"Scenario 2: a man and woman have him and maybe tried to rescue him.

"Scenario 3: an adult and a teenager or other older kid are walking with him.

"They had a couple of hours head start at the very most, so we're close, and we need to have our plan together when we spot them."

"Agreed," I said, looking at the crest of another valley 200 yards ahead.

We approached the same as last time, on our hands and knees. Peering over the edge revealed a lush green valley, at least ten miles wide, with a river running through the bottom.

"They've got water, thank God," I said aloud.

"Let's take our time," whispered Mike. "They're down there. We just have to spot them.

"I'll start right to left, and you go left to right," he said, as we scanned the valley with our binoculars.

"That's them!" I said, as I spotted three people just across the river in the trees. "There," I pointed to Mike.

"They don't see us, but they will if we head down now," he replied.

To see my boy alive and moving around was more than I could have asked for.

"When they start moving again, we'll head down. Once we're in the valley, we will have the advantage again," Mike pointed out.

What seemed like an eternity later, or ten minutes in this next world, they were on the move.

"This is it," Mike called out in a low voice. "Let's move."

"Want me to carry the pack?" I asked.

"Nah. You'll have a 40-pound boy with tired legs to carry soon enough."

Not running full out was the hardest thing I've ever done. To be so close and not grab the prize was excruciating.

"Lance, if they hurt him in any way, don't be surprised if I..."

"Mike, if that happened, you'll be trying to hold me back, I can assure you."

Nearly skiing on loose dirt and rocks down the steep valley wall, we made great time.

"I bet that just saved us an hour," I told him as we approached the river.

Stepping into the clear water, my clammy skin cooled in seconds.

Resisting the urge for a full dunk, I vowed to take a quick swim with Hendrix on the way back.

Crossing the river was easier than expected, given the knee-deep water. Once on the other side, we stopped to plan.

"We made great time," said Mike, and they are no more than a half mile ahead of us. It's going to be dark in a few hours, so we need this done now, in the next 30 minutes."

In a near run, we followed the trio, now in view.

At 100 yards out, one of the adults turned and pointed at us.

"Careful, Mike," I told him. "We don't know the situation yet, and I want my boy on our side if any shooting starts."

Mike was now the one breathing heavy, like he might hyperventilate.

"We're okay," I told him. "It's going to be okay."

Using my binoculars for a quick scan, I saw an old man and woman with Hendrix. There were no weapons visible, except a walking stick he carried.

"Nice and easy," I told Mike. "I think they are trying to help."

We approached straight ahead, weapons pointed into the air but clearly visible.

Hendrix saw me at about 40 yards out and yelled "Daddy! Daddy!" He made a run for me, and I ran to meet him halfway, as I told Mike to cover me.

I had my eye on the man and woman, who slowly walked towards us.

Hendrix jumped into my arms, both crying and smiling.

"Daddy, why did you leave me?!" he asked, now sobbing harder. "Was I bad?"

"No, son, you weren't bad. I don't know what happened, but I'm so sorry. It will never happen again, I promise.

"The people, did they hurt you?"

"No, Rada," as he would call me sometimes. "They gave me water and snacks."

Mike caught up to us, and I told him I wanted to talk to the adults. We met them minutes later, and I saw what appeared to be a harmless couple. Most likely, they were grandparents only a short time ago.

"How did you end up with my boy?" I asked calmly.

"Well," replied the old man, "we were scouting out our property, which runs up to the highway back where you came from, and spotted this little boy crying on the side of the road. Said he got left behind somehow."

"Just so you know," the woman chimed in, "we didn't just take him. He was all alone and could have quickly died out here. We don't have much besides this land, but we agreed we would always take care of this sweet lost boy."

"I am so grateful for your kindness," I replied. "Thank you for helping him get back to us safely."

I looked at Mike, hoping he wasn't going to draw on them and do something crazy. To my surprise, he was laughing out loud.

"I wasn't expecting this good of an ending. I think they're good people." Reaching into his front jeans pocket, Mike pulled out two Silver Eagle coins. "Thank you both for taking good care of Lance's boy here," he added, handing the man the two coins.

The old woman had tears in her eyes. "You don't know what these coins mean to us. Thank you. And Hendrix, we are so happy that you have found your family."

"Let's go," Mike nodded to me. "I want to be back at the hospital before dark."

Hendrix ran back to hug the old man and woman. "Thank you for helping me—and for the good snacks!" he said.

We walked back towards the truck without another word.

I was half expecting Mike to shoot them both in the back, but he was too busy talking with Hendrix about what happened.

"He's going to be fine," Mike told me, after asking Hendrix a series of cop-type questions.

We allowed ten minutes for a swim in the river for Hendrix and me.

"Yay, Daddy! It's just like the river we swam in at Yellowstone," referring to the RV trip we had taken as a family last summer to Yellowstone National Park, driving through Wyoming and Montana. Randomly pulling off the side of a picturesque Montana road, Joy, me and the kids with some grandparents, cousins, aunts and uncles spent an entire afternoon playing in the river. It was honestly one of the best days of my life.

Mike opted to wait on the other side and scout the area.

The walk back to the truck was quick, even with the extra weight of Hendrix on my back. I only wished I could radio Joy and put her mind at ease, but we were too far out of range for that.

Mike had his binoculars out as we crested the last valley top.

"Down," he whispered, pointing towards the truck. "There are some guys around the truck.

"Stay here and keep down. No movements from either of you," he said. "I'm going to circle 90 degrees to the north. I want you two to be out of the line of fire if it goes wrong.

"Cover me," he added, "but don't shoot unless I go down, all right?"

"Mike, you don't have to do this alone," I told him.

"Yes, I do. Now protect your boy."

I watched as Mike got within 100 yards of the truck undetected, crouching low and moving from bush to bush. I had an eye on him and the truck through my binoculars.

The men looked confused as to why the truck wouldn't start. There was another old gray truck next to Lonnie's, belonging to them, I assumed.

Every couple of minutes, one would grab a beer from the bed. "Where are the guns?" I asked, forgetting for a second that Mike was out of earshot. I counted five men and no visible weapons.

"Thanks for being quiet, buddy," I said, looking down at Hendrix, who I now realized was fast asleep on Mike's pack.

Mike yelled at the men without giving up his position. "Get away from my truck!" he said, loud enough for them to hear.

They were now all pointing in different directions and looked confused.

I smiled as I saw two of the men holding what looked like kitchen knives.

They're in for one heck of a surprise, I said to myself, as I breathed a sigh of relief.

"Crack! Crack! Crack!" came the rapid-fire from Mike's direction, as the back window of their truck exploded. Bullets riddled the roof and tailgate as I watched through my binoculars.

I scanned the area back and forth and watched the men pile into the truck when Mike stopped shooting.

The driver stomped the gas, sending a dust cloud high into the air.

With one more binocular scan and Hendrix now wide awake, we headed toward the truck and met up with Mike.

"That was fun," said Mike, giving Hendrix a wink. "Don't worry, buddy. They're all okay. Just a little scare is all."

"I'm surprised you didn't shoot out the tires," I commented.

"Nah, they're just scrounging around, like everyone else. I wanted to give them a chance to get away.

"Did you see the butter knives they had?" asked Mike, now laughing so hard he was doubled over.

"I bet they pooped their pants," added Hendrix, laughing at his own joke.

Replacing the distributor wire, we headed north, back to the group. Mike took it a bit slower, at nearly 45 miles per hour, and that was fine by me.

Hendrix was asleep again, this time in my lap. I had us both buckled in.

"A couple of weeks ago, I would have pulled you over for no car seat," said Mike with a grin.

"Yeah," I agreed, and added, "thirty years ago, and I would be riding in that truck bed!"

* * * * * * *

Chapter Five ~
Headed to Amarillo, Texas

Lonnie and Jake ended up going into the hospital. Nancy gave them clear instructions on what to locate for Vlad's leg.

They agreed to keep an eye out for any pain meds but knew it would be a long shot.

Entering the hospital, they kept their rifles pointed down but visible to the dozen or more people running around the halls.

Passing the pharmacy, pill bottles lay strewn across the floor. "We're a bit late to the party," Jake said aloud.

"It's about what I expected," replied Lonnie. "Probably like this all across the country by now.

"Let's find what we need and get out of here," he suggested. Searching room by room, they were able to find most of the items on Nancy's list.

Exiting the muggy hospital, Jake couldn't help but wonder where the critical patients ended up after the power went out. He guessed there were a few still left inside somewhere.

Nancy carefully inspected the items they had found and agreed they would do for now.

"Here they come!" screamed out Joy, pointing towards the truck heading towards them.

Mike flashed the lights and gave two honks on the horn. I reached my right hand out the window and gave a thumbs-up.

Joy was sobbing. "Thank you, Lord, for hearing my prayers and bringing my sweet little boy back to me."

Everyone in the group was smiling and cheering. I felt a little like a rock star coming out on stage to a cheering audience, but I knew it was Mike they owed their gratitude to, and so did I.

Hendrix was now wide awake as he jumped into his mother's arms. He was the center of attention, talking a mile a minute about his experience, and loving it. Hudson and Jax ran to hug their brother. "We missed you!" they both kept saying.

I took the opportunity to pull Mike aside. "You saved my son," I told him. "I'll never forget that."

"It turned out better than I expected," he replied. "Glad I could help.

"Do you mind if I ride in the truck with you?" Mike asked Sheila, as she got in the passenger's side. "This day keeps getting better," Mike said to me, with a grin.

As we planned to head out again, Lonnie initiated what would now be known as the Hendrix Plan.

A headcount would be taken at the end of each stop and before we headed out each day by Joy and Lucy for the remainder of the trip.

My heart was full as we pulled out once again, heading north. Hendrix gave me the monocular look, and all seemed right with the world.

I made a mental note to call David tonight and tell him we were having some more delays.

"We won't make Amarillo tonight," I told Jake.

"Fine by me," he replied. "I'm just glad you got your boy back safe.

"How was Mike?" he asked.

"Complicated" is all I could think to say. "But he really saved the day!"

It was late afternoon, and it felt like the day had been a week long.

"Hendrix isn't going to be out of Joy's sight anytime soon," I told Jake.

"You can count on that!" he replied.

"We'll head north for about an hour and find a suitable place to camp for the night," Lonnie called out over the radio.

Looking at the map, Jake and I spotted a river about 30 miles north. I radioed Lonnie to keep a lookout for it, just in case it wasn't too overrun yet.

We were once again making good time. My mind wandered from my boy to Mike and back again.

I wondered if Sheila was going to ask Mike what happened to her boyfriend. Or did she already know?

Just over an hour later, Lonnie stopped the caravan. We could see the river off to the east a few miles. Mike and Jim were tasked with scouting out a safe spot for the night.

With Sheila back in the car with Joy and the other ladies, the conversation was anything but tame. Men were the topic of choice today. Some discussion was in code and other words having to be spelled out in front of the kids.

It was clear to Joy that Sheila was moving on with her life, and Mike would somehow be a part of it. She couldn't wait to talk to Lance about it tonight and get his input, having spent most of the day alone with Mike.

The guys came back 15 minutes later with a thumbs-up on the river campsite.

It wasn't as good as the lake, Joy told me, but it was better than the open terrain, like the first night.

With the tents set up, Jim was trying to get hold of David on the radio. After an hour with no response, he scanned the channels for any government updates. Although there was nothing official at the moment, there was a lot of radio chatter to be heard.

The religious nut from earlier was gaining followers and picking up steam. They seemed to be marching across the countryside, giving honest folks the choice to join them or die.

I'm sure most decided to join the cause, being promised the basics of food, water, safety and shelter, and the rest only wanting to live one more day, I thought.

"It's hard to amass a large group of followers quickly who share your ideology, but I think that guy just recruited a few killers and the rest are given no choice," I told Steve.

I sat with Jim for over an hour, listening to the preaching of this man. "Sooner or later," I told Jim, "they are going to come up against a FEMA camp or the military, and it's going to be a defining moment for one side or the other."

"You've got that right," replied Jim. "The only difference now is that the military has air support, training and superior firepower."

Thirty minutes later, Jim made contact with Raton, New Mexico. Beatrice was on the line.

"Hi, Beatrice," I said, in a jovial voice. "It's been a long time. How's the family?"

There was a long pause when she finally answered. "Lance, we've had some bad things happen here today, and David can't talk right now.

"We are still expecting your group and will make the necessary accommodations when you all arrive. When can we expect you?"

I wasn't sure how to respond to my old buddy's mom, not having any details but fearing something terrible had happened.

"We have been delayed," I told her, "and are still three to four days out, as far as I can tell."

"Let us know when you are a day out," she said soberly. "I have to let you go," she added.

"I will, Beatrice, and I hope everything with your family…"

"She's off-air," said Jim, before I could finish.

I said a quick prayer for David, hoping Mark was okay.

Supper tonight was leftovers. "Fish and venison again," I told my boys. "I know it may not seem like it," I added, "but we've got it much better than most other folks around this great country now."

"We know, Daddy," replied Hudson. "You keep telling us that. Can we try to catch some fish tonight?"

Yo-yo river fishing wasn't quite as easy as lake fishing, I learned. We set ten reels and caught two small sucker fish that no one was willing to eat. Even Ringo passed on these little guys.

Joy and the other ladies kept an eye on Sheila after what had happened to Kelly just a couple nights ago. A couple of hours after dinner, she disappeared into Mike's tent.

"I guess that settles it," said Joy. "Nothing more to see here."

Settling in for the night, Joy had a slew of questions about what happened with Hendrix, and of course my day with Mike.

I decided it best to keep confidential what he had told me, not even telling my wife, and new best friend Jake.

These things can spread quickly, even in close confidence, I thought, *and with a group this small, it could only take a matter of hours to filter through*. Besides, I had plenty to tell about our story finding Hendrix.

That night was the best sleep I had had since everything went dark.

"Let's go! Let's go!" called Lonnie early the next morning, as he ran around, shaking each tent.

"Lance, Jake, Mike and Steve. I need you out here now!" he shouted.

I jumped out of my sleeping bag, nearly tripping over Jax as I stumbled out of the tent.

"What's going on?" I asked, realizing that I was the last guy out.

Lonnie, Steve and Mike were all pointing back down the road we drove up just a day ago.

"What the hell is that?" I asked, just as the answer hit me like a ton of bricks.

"It's them, right Steve?" I asked.

"Them who?" asked Jake.

"That guy we've been following on the radio," said Steve. "It's him or something like it."

I was in shock, not believing what I was seeing.

Hundreds of people were walking on the road, still a few miles away but consuming the distance like locusts. Joy, overhearing us, handed me my binoculars and my stomach dropped as I saw men, women and children marching behind two men riding in a jeep.

All were staring straight ahead with blank stares and carrying weapons, from shovels to pitchforks and pickaxes.

"Is that who I think it is?" I asked out loud. "Look at the lead guys," I told Jake, as he looked through his binoculars.

"No way!" he remarked. "Is that Ronna?"

"It can't be," said Lonnie, reaching for my binoculars.

"I thought he was dead," said Mike.

"Me too, but we never actually saw him," Lonnie added. "Could have been anyone falling out of that helicopter, I guess."

The marchers were flanked on either side by men with rifles. The entire procession was backed up by twelve vehicles that we could see, with most pulling trailers.

"The vehicles," Jake called out, "they're military."

Getting my binoculars back, I observed an elderly man fall out of line and on to his knees. One of the guards shot him in the back of the head without missing a step.

The rest of the walkers were not even phased. No one stopped to intervene or look; they all stared straight ahead and marched.

"That's not good," said Jake, watching the commotion.

"Where do you think they're headed?" I asked.

"I don't know," said Lonnie, "but I damn sure don't want to be in their way."

Everyone helped, even the kids. We were crudely loaded up in 15 minutes. Not the best pack job we had done so far, but it would have to do until we could fix it.

Joy and Tina initiated the Hendrix Plan and got a full count.

"We're going to head north for about an hour to get some distance between us. Then we'll take another look at the map," announced Lonnie.

Jake and I discussed the marchers as our caravan headed north.

"Is Ronna working with the military?" I asked him, already knowing the answer.

"The group is three times the size it was just a couple days ago. How did they get this far?" he asked.

I didn't have any answers but replied that we need to spend some more time on the radio and see what we can find out.

Lonnie stopped our group about an hour later to repack from the morning and decide the route forward.

* * * * * * *

Chapter Six ~ Saddle Ranch Loveland, Colorado

Mac headed back up to the Ranch with a permanent smile. He hadn't felt this way in a very long time. He hoped John and Bill would understand and approve of his feelings for Sarah.

He had planned to wait a few days to discuss it with them, when he saw Bill walking just up ahead.

Maybe I can detour, he thought, just as Bill spotted him.

"What's the story?" asked Bill, with a slight grin and raised eyebrows as Mac pulled up.

"There are only two things that make a man smile like that. And I'm pretty sure you didn't just win the lottery," he continued.

"Well, it's Sarah...I mean...Dr. Melton," said Mac. "I showed her around the property, as you know, and I may have had some lunch with her up on the hill earlier."

"I appreciate your honesty," remarked Bill, "but this is a situation that could have consequences down the road. Does Samuel know?"

"Sarah said he knows and is okay with it," Mac replied.

"I'll check on that," said Bill. "No more lunch dates or anything besides your medical visits until I get back with you. Are we agreed?"

"Yes, sir," replied Mac.

Bill was headed down to see John and thought it best to find Samuel and get this out in the open before it caused any issues between the groups. Samuel was in the machine shop, checking on the new mechanics he had recently acquired.

He had been in the shop for more than an hour, and it was evident that one of the new hires named Jimmy was an asset to the group. He was observed to be a hard worker and fell in with the others like he had been there for years. The other recent hire was not.

It took all of five minutes for Bill to observe that this man was lazy, argumentative, and didn't fit in with the other mechanics.

"Well," said Samuel when he saw Bill. "We hired two and got one good one.

"Ralph!" called Samuel in a stern voice that Bill had never heard before. "Let's talk over here for a minute."

"When I'm done!" yelled the man, without turning around, as he continued hammering a piece of steel.

The other mechanics stood in amazement as he ignored Samuel.

"You had better get your butt over there, and quick!" said one of the veteran mechanics to Ralph.

"Or what?" he replied in a sarcastic tone. "He can't fire me. I'm not even getting paid."

"Ralph!" Samuel said in a loud voice. "Let's talk outside *now*!"

Ralph turned, beat red, his face contorting from smug to rage. He was walking fast, with his hammer tightly clenched in his right hand, towards Samuel and Bill.

As he neared the halfway point across the garage, Bill could hear his mumbling voice saying, "Nobody talks to *me* that way," over and over.

"Samuel, please step outside and close the door," said Bill. Samuel hesitated but did as he was asked.

Bill was talking calmly to Ralph as he advanced, raising his hammer over his right shoulder.

Thirty feet, thought Bill, as he attempted to calm the man down…

Twenty feet, as Bill drew his Glock 17 from his holster, leveling it at the man.

Fifteen feet, as Bill clicked off the safety and yelled, "Stop!"

The man with the hammer didn't seem to hear or care about the orders given.

"Ten feet…nine…last chance!" yelled Bill. "Don't make me do this!"

Ralph was shouting an inaudible cry, like he was going into battle on the front lines.

Everyone in the shop was focused on Ralph and didn't see Jimmy coming up behind him at a full run.

Bill saw him at the last second and held his fire as Jimmy jumped on Ralph's back, wrapping his left forearm around Ralph's throat, arching his back and blocking the swinging hammer with his right arm.

Bill watched in slow motion as Jimmy squeezed the man's neck. Ralph dropped the hammer and was frantically clawing at his throat, while Jimmy slowly lowered him to the floor without any sound or emotion.

"Just tell me when," said Jimmy to Bill, as Ralph stopped struggling.

"Now," replied Bill, "let him go."

Jimmy did as instructed and slowly released his chokehold on the now-unconscious former mechanic. Samuel burst in the back door with two of the new doctors he had just hired. He wanted to know everything that happened while the doctors tended to Ralph.

"He's breathing," one of them called out.

"Let's be real careful with him when he comes to," instructed Bill.

A minute later Ralph was awake, as his hands and feet were being bound with electrical tape.

"You'll untie me right now, if you idiots know what's good for you," he spat out.

Everyone ignored him, and Samuel pulled Bill aside. He wanted to know everything that happened after he left the machine shop.

When Bill was finished, Samuel stated bluntly, "Now I'm down two mechanics."

"What do you mean, two?" asked Bill.

"We are not a violent group, as I told you before," Samuel continued, "so they both have to go."

"Do you mind if I give you my two cents?" asked Bill, as more of a statement than a question.

He continued, "With all due respect, Samuel, neither of our groups condone violence, but it's here on our soil. Jimmy is a hired hand, and I'm guessing he does not practice your beliefs.

"He just saved someone's life, maybe Ralph's...maybe mine, or even yours. He seems like a good man to have around, if you ask me.

"Jimmy could have easily killed Ralph, but he didn't. He neutralized a potentially deadly situation without a weapon, and stopped when told to do so.

"I think you should keep him around, but if you decide not to, I'll talk to John about keeping him on with us at the Ranch."

"I'll think on it," said Samuel, as he asked for Ralph's wife and 10-year-old boy to be brought to the machine shop with their belongings.

Twenty minutes later she walked up with her son and their belongings in a wheelbarrow, escorted by two of Samuel's men.

When Ralph saw her crying, he began swearing at her. "What did you tell them, you ungrateful woman? And where's the rest of our stuff?!" he yelled, realizing only his belongings were in the wheelbarrow.

"Samuel, can we talk over here?" his men asked, pointing to the side of the shop out of ear reach of the others. "You too, Bill?" they asked respectfully.

When Bill and Samuel reached the woman and her boy, her crying was uncontrollable as she fell to her knees in front of them.

"Please, please don't let him take us," she begged.

"Ma'am, you and the boy are his family, and that's not any business of ours," said Samuel sternly.

She stood without a word, and her crying all but stopped. She proceeded to lift her shirt to just below the bra line, revealing a bruised and battered torso. Dark black bruises appeared recent and were intertwined with pale yellow ones from previous encounters.

Bill and Samuel shared a look that was both sympathetic and concerning.

"Son," Samuel asked her boy, "do you know anything about this?"

The boy said nothing, staring at the ground. He was shaking, and a dark stain ran down the legs of his jeans.

"It's okay, son," he continued. "I know you're scared, but you can talk to me."

"Joshua," said his mother, "please stand up straight and pull up your shirt."

He did as he was told and revealed bruises much the same as his mother's.

"Did your father do this to you and your mother?" asked Samuel.

"Yes," Joshua replied. He was still looking at the ground. "He…" the boy started to say, and then said, "Never mind."

"It's okay," said Bill. "Go on, we're listening."

He looked at his mom for approval to continue. "At first," he said, "he used to hit her in the face, but he got in trouble. Now he hits us where nobody can see."

"Doesn't anyone hear you?" asked Bill.

"No, sir," he replied. "We used to scream, but no one ever came, and it just made my dad even madder. Now we…me and my mom…stay quiet."

"Son, listen to me, because this is very important. Your dad is leaving this place very soon," said Samuel, "and I need to hear from you if you want to go with him or stay here with your mom. Once he's gone, you won't see him again."

"I know he's my dad," said Joshua, "but I hate what he does to us. I only want to be with my mom," he said, looking Samuel in the eye.

"Okay, you both go on back to your house and I'll send Dr. Melton up to check on you in just a bit," said Samuel.

"Thank you so much," Joshua's mom said. "My name is Patty, and this, of course, is Joshua. I know you weren't expecting to take in two extra people, but I can contribute as a chef or anything else the group needs to be done."

"I'm sorry we didn't meet before this. It's good to meet you, Patty, and you, Joshua. My name is Samuel. And we could always use an extra chef in the kitchen. If you need anything, you ask for me."

"Mind if I help you take care of this?" Bill asked Samuel.

"Sure, old friend," Samuel replied. "I have some other matters to attend to."

Bill radioed Mac. "I need you down at the West property right away."

"Uh," replied Mac in a panic. "You already talked to Samuel?"

"Not yet," replied Bill. "It's something else I need your help with. Meet me at the machine shop with a couple of your guys."

"Be there in ten," said Mac.

Mac gathered two of his best men and headed down the road. All he could think about was Sarah. *Bill said he hadn't talked to Samuel, so it can't be about that*, he thought.

Pulling up to the machine shop, Mac was calmed by the image of the 250-or-more-pound Ralph, bound by his hands and feet. *This I can deal with*, he thought to himself.

Bill filled him and his guys in with the details and tasked them with removing the former mechanic from the property.

Before Bill left, Mac pulled him aside and asked, "Please let me know when you talk to Samuel. I'm real nervous about it."

"Ha!" said Bill. "You're tough as nails, Mac, but I get it. Can't promise anything, but I'll try to get it done while you're escorting this man over here off the premises."

"Thanks, Bill."

Mac glanced over toward the hospital, about 30 yards away, and saw Sarah standing outside. She gave a quick wave and walked back inside.

"Okay," said Mac. "Let's get this done."

Without having Ralph try to walk, all three men lifted him into the back of Samuel's pickup truck.

"Sorry, boys, that I couldn't help much, but I only have one good arm for now," announced Mac.

From the start of the short trip down the valley, Ralph was swearing and threatening everyone…from his wife and boy to Samuel, and now Mac.

"Let's put one piece of tape over his mouth, so he can hear my exit instructions clearly," said Mac.

Once the tape was secured in place and Ralph quieted down, they were at the south perimeter. The very place they had recruited him from just a day earlier.

"Okay, Ralph," said Mac. "Here's the deal.

"The kind of man who beats his wife and boy has no place in this valley. You will be leaving without them, and you won't be back.

"Truth be told, I'm the last person who would want to split up a family, but yours needs splittin'," he said, as he ripped the tape off Ralph's mouth.

"You're just trying to get to my wife," Ralph spat out.

"I can assure you," replied Mac, "that is the furthest thing from my mind." He fought hard to hold back a grin, as he thought about Sarah and the best date he had ever been on in his life just a couple hours ago.

"We're going to cut you loose in a minute, but I want us all to be on the same page here.

"You ever watch Steve Irwin, the Crocodile Hunter, Ralph?" asked Mac.

"What's that got to do with shit?" asked Ralph.

"Well, when they get a hostile animal that they are about to release, there is a proper way it's done. Now, the interesting thing is that the animal always runs away when released and doesn't turn back.

"Can you imagine," Mac continued, "if that animal were to turn on the very people who released it? I'm sure that particular scene would not make it into the next episode.

"So, to be perfectly clear, my guys are going to cut you free, and you will walk away from here with your belongings, never to return. Is that clear?" Mac asked.

Ralph gave no response. "I'll take that as a yes," said Mac.

Mac drew his pistol and pointed it at the ground. "Okay, boys. Feet first, then hands."

As the last tape was cut, Ralph began to spew a long list of threats, including "You haven't seen the last of me!" and "I'll be back!" reminding Mac of the old *Terminator* movies. This time he did grin just a bit.

"I'll be back!" he said to his boys in his best Austrian accent. Mac briefed the men on the southern border about Ralph while on the radio with the men from the north. All agreed to keep an eye out for him in the future.

Bill caught up with Samuel and asked what he knew about Mac and Sarah.

"Everything there is to know, I suppose," replied Samuel. "She is a prominent member of our community and she is family. What are you asking, Bill?"

"Well, it seems like they are getting to be something of a thing. They had a date earlier today."

"Yes, I know," replied Samuel. "I gave Sarah my permission; I assumed you did the same for Mac."

"Well, we are working on that," replied Bill. "So, you're okay with it, Samuel?"

"So far, I am, but I would like a word with both you and Mac before this goes any further," stated Samuel. "When's a good time?"

"How about now? Mac should be free soon."

"All right. Let's meet at the shop in 30," suggested Samuel.

Bill radioed Mac. "How did it go with Ralph?"

"It's done," Mac replied. "He's off the property and unharmed."

"Great! Now I need you back here at the shop right away. And Mac, this time it's about Sarah. No need to panic, but you need to bring your a-game."

"Yes, sir. I'll be right there."

No need to panic, Mac thought. *It's just the most important meeting of my life!*

Thirty minutes later, all three met in the far corner of the shop.

"We have a lot of things going on right now, so I'll keep this brief," said Samuel. "Sarah has kept me informed about your budding relationship. As you know, she is a crucial asset to our group here. You may not know that she is my adopted daughter, and she even grew up here."

"I didn't realize that," admitted Mac.

"Both of our communities help each other out," Samuel continued, "and we all are wanting to protect this valley. However, we are still separate groups.

"With that being said, we have never had a crossover like I see starting with you and Sarah. I'm not sure what that looks like, but Sarah is our primary doctor here and this is her home. So, the short of it is, I want you to think hard about what you want out of this before we get any further down this road."

"Yes, sir," replied Mac. "I'll do just that."

As the three of them parted, Mac pulled Bill aside and asked, "What do you think?"

"Well, I think you have already thought hard about it and choose to move forward. Is that about right?" Bill asked.

"Yes, sir," replied Mac. "I didn't want Samuel to think I was taking it lightly. I'll get back with him soon."

"For the record," said Bill, "I agree with Samuel on this, and I think John would too.

"Remind me to tell you the story of the male deer," Bill added, and walked away to check on John.

Mac got back on his four-wheeler and drove slowly by the hospital, hoping to get a glimpse of Sarah.

Lucky I am, he said to himself, as he saw her standing just outside the front door. At 30 yards away, she was too far to talk to. He waved, and Sarah turned her hands up in a well-what-happened gesture.

Mac smiled, gave a thumbs-up, and gestured with his right hand to his ear that he would call her.

She laughed, met his smile, and blew him a kiss before disappearing back into the hospital.

"If I knew you would say yes, I would already have asked you to marry me," he said out loud as he rode away.

An hour later, Dr. Melton checked in on Patty and Joshua. After a thorough exam, she ordered an immediate chest X-ray on Joshua, due to pain in his front left rib cage when he breathed deeply…

A few hours after that, Dr. Melton reviewed the X-rays with the two new doctors, and they all agreed on the findings. There could be a hairline fracture and intercostal muscle strains or tears, not visible on an X-ray, that was causing him to have pain when breathing. They all concurred that there were multiple healed fractures across the entire chest, demonstrating years of likely abuse.

"How did this continue without medical personnel reporting it?" Dr. Melton asked Patty.

"They did more than once," she replied, "but Ralph always had a good story, and Joshua was so scared he always told the same story as his dad.

"I should have done something, said something," added Patty, with tears rolling down her drawn face for the second time today.

"I'm truly sorry this happened to you and your son," said Dr. Melton, "and it's not your fault. I believe you will be safe now."

"Is he gone?" asked Patty.

"Yes, he's gone for good," replied one of the other doctors. "At least that's what we've heard."

* * * *

Samuel caught up with Jimmy, after thinking for a while.

"I owe you a debt of gratitude, Jimmy," he said. "Bill told me what happened, and I understand why you did what you felt you had to.

"With that being said, we don't condone violence of any kind here, and I'll have to ask you to leave our group."

"Yes, sir. I'm familiar with your group's beliefs, and I understand your position. Thank you for giving me the opportunity, and I'm sorry I let you down, Samuel."

"No, son, you didn't let me down. It's just how it has to be. I can tell you are a good man and a real asset for the right group," he added.

"Stay here for a few, and let me talk to Bill," said Samuel. "Don't quote me on it, but they may have a position for you in their group."

Samuel found Bill talking to John and informed them both on his position.

"We understand Samuel," said John, "and Bill has told me the rest. I think we could use a man like him up at the Ranch…if you don't mind him staying in the valley, that is."

"Not at all," replied Samuel. "Not at all."

Bill laughed out loud. "What's so funny?" asked John.

"Well," Bill replied. "This would be the third time today I'll be calling Mac down here!"

With that, he got on the radio. "Come on down one more time," he told him.

When he arrived, Bill introduced Jimmy to Mac for the first time.

After shaking hands, Mac said, "I heard what you did. Where did you learn that?"

"Besides working as a mechanic, I had a fight school in Fort Collins called "'The 13.'"

"That sounds familiar," said Mac… "Wait a minute," he added. "You had that DVD—*13 Ways to Terminate Your Opponent.*"

"But only if you have to!" they finished saying together.

"No offense," said Mac, "but that Ralph guy was still kicking after your little altercation."

"Well, that wasn't my call," said Jimmy. "But even if it was, the situation didn't call for deadly force, in my opinion."

"But you could have if you absolutely had to?" asked Mac.

"Twenty more seconds and he would not have walked out of here," replied Jimmy.

"Okay. John and Bill say you're in with our group, if you choose," offered Mac.

"Absolutely," said Jimmy. "Thank you."

"Okay, let's get you packed and moved. You will be on my team as security," said Mac, "but we may need your mechanical expertise from time to time. Agreed?"

"Yes, sir. You can count on me!"

* * * * * * *

Chapter Seven ~ Saddle Ranch Loveland, Colorado

Mac got his new security guy settled in and briefed on the basics. "We'll take the four-wheelers and I'll show you the perimeter area we protect," said Mac. "It takes about an hour and a half for a full loop."

Jimmy couldn't believe his new luck. Just a couple hours ago he was leaving a group, headed alone into the unknown, and now he was part of a new group he felt even more comfortable around.

With a quick tour of the machine shop and a sign-up for night-watchman duty next week, Jimmy felt right at home.

* * * *

Bill was up early, with Dr. Melton on the radio.

"Bill, it's John," she said. "Can you come down here when you get a chance?"

"What's wrong?" asked Bill in a concerned voice.

"It's okay," Dr. Melton said. "Everything is just fine. We've been working with John, and he thought you should be here for his progress report."

"Yes, great! When should I be there?"

"As soon as you can," she replied. "John is excited to hear what's next."

Bill met with John, Dr. Melton, and the new doctors an hour later.

"John, your prognosis is good," said Dr. Melton. "I don't mind telling you that I was worried that first night we saw you. We have an excellent little hospital here, but you were in bad shape and I just wasn't sure we could save you.

"You worked hard," she continued, "and fought to stay alive. I believe that had the most significant impact on your recovery thus far.

"I know you're ready to get home and back to work, so here is my proposal:

"You can go home with one of your nurses providing round-the-clock care.

"Maybe Mac could bring me up once a day to check on you. Or you can stay here if you want and eat all the hospital Jell-O you can stand."

"As much as I love the Jell-O," said John, "I'll take door number one! Thank you, Dr., and all of you here for taking great care of me.

"Can we do the transport about noon today, with a quick stop at our Pavilion so I can give a short speech?"

"I think that's okay," said Dr. Melton.

"It's not good to be away from your people for too long. I want them to see I'm still alive and kicking," said John.

"I'll get everyone together for lunch, and we can plan your speech for noon, if that works," said Bill.

* * * *

At noon John addressed the entire Ranch population, minus a few of the older folks, from his wheelchair.

"Thank you all for being here today. As you can see, I am on the mend. I want to thank Bill for doing a great job running the Ranch in my absence, and Mac for keeping up security measures and fixing our generators and freezers.

"I would also like to thank the elder's council and all of you here for coming together to ensure our prosperous future.

"I am now home, thanks to Dr. Melton and her staff at the West's hospital.

"I am not 100%, as you can see, but I'm getting stronger every day. Bill will continue to lead our group until I can return, fully healed. He and I will meet daily regarding future plans or any concerns that may arise.

"Are there any questions?" he asked.

A few hands raised, with questions ranging from how long it would take to heal to did they catch the guy who shot him.

John and Bill ate lunch with the group and answered questions as best they could.

* * * *

Mac was excited, as he was planning another lunch date with Sarah tomorrow. He returned once again to Rico's kitchen for a hand with the meal.

"Thanks, Chef, for the perfect lunch last time," Mac told him. "I wasn't too sure about the wine, but it worked out just fine. I've got a couple of people to talk to first but just wanted to give you a heads-up for a lunch."

"Sure, thing, Mac," replied Rico. "This is what I do, and I'm always glad to help."

Now it was Mac's turn to call a meeting with Bill and Samuel.

An hour later, they met once again by the machine shop at the West's property.

"I've only got a few minutes," remarked Samuel, "so let's get right down to it."

"Yes, sir," replied Mac. "I just wanted you both to know that I have thought long and hard about my feelings for Sarah, and with your permission I would like to continue seeing her as long as she'll have me."

Samuel chuckled. "That's about what I already thought," he added. "I know Sarah feels the same.

"John's okay with this, Bill?" Samuel asked.

"Yes, my friend," said Bill.

"All right then, son. You two have my blessings," said Samuel. "And now I have other matters to attend to," he added, as he walked off towards the hospital.

Mac was beaming and asked Bill as they walked back towards the Ranch, "So, what's the story of the Buck?"

"Well," said Bill. "The buck is always cautious, and there's a reason they escape hunting season to add pounds each year. However, when females are in heat, the male deer is wholly focused on her, and he loses sight of his own security. They have been known to walk right up on a hunter and be killed, since their guard is down.

"Do you understand what I'm saying, Mac?"

"Yes, I think so. I shouldn't lose focus on my job as perimeter security while I court Sarah."

"Exactly," Bill agreed.

"Do you mind if I take her to lunch tomorrow?" Mac asked nervously.

"From now on, Mac, you're good to go. Just promise me you'll let me know if there are any significant changes with you two."

Mac was relieved and feeling like the best days of his life were just ahead of him.

* * * *

Mac picked up Sarah at noon in front of the hospital. She greeted him with a smile and a quick kiss. "I've got the whole afternoon off!" she declared, with the excitement of a kid on the first day of summer break.

"Me too," replied Mac, with a slight grin as he made a mental note to radio his men and have them cover for him.

"Where are we going today?" called Sarah over the four-wheeler's engine noise.

"We're headed to the caves on the Rimrock. It has one of the best views of the entire valley," he replied.

The bumpy road up to the top of the Rimrock was slow going for the four-wheeler, navigating large ruts and basketball-sized rocks.

"I've never been up here," admitted Sarah, "although I've seen the caves from the main road."

Mac stepped aside and radioed his guys, asking them to keep an eye towards the Rimrock for anything out of place and informing them he would only be available for emergencies for the afternoon.

The main cave was over 40 feet wide, with a standing height of 8 feet, narrowing towards the back. The depth was only about 50 feet, but the main attraction was the very front of the cave, nestled on the upper part of a hundred-foot cliff.

There was a trick to getting into the cave from the top, requiring help from another person. Mac slowly lowered an excited but nervous Sarah into the opening and handed her the prized lunch basket.

Next, he handed down a large blanket, hoping she didn't take it the wrong way. He jumped down, having been here many times before without any assistance.

Spreading the blanket across the front of the cave, they sat with their legs dangling over the cliff.

"I believe the Ute and Arapahoe tribes resided in this valley. There are arrowheads all over Green Mountain," he said, pointing across the valley. "It wouldn't surprise me if they used this very cave as a lookout point for their scouts."

"I can see almost the whole valley from here!" said an excited Sarah. "The view is just stunning! And a bit romantic," she added, with a wink.

Mac felt flushed and fumbled with the picnic basket. The contents were much the same as the last, but the wine was French today. "Domaine Ramone Montrachet Grand Cru," read Mac. "I'm not sure what it is, but it sounds fancy," he added.

Sarah gasped at the introduction and asked, "Where did you get a $2,500 bottle of wine?!"

"No way," replied Mac. "It's got to be a joke."

Sarah continued: "They raffled one of these off at a medical conference I attended a few years back, in Honolulu. The drug companies always gave out the best gifts to the attendees, and who doesn't want to participate in a conference in Hawaii? Anyway, I didn't win it, but I googled the cost and got to try just a sip."

"Should I open it?" asked Mac, as he pulled the cork. "I can assure you that you're not having a lunch date with a millionaire! I hope Rico didn't put it in here by mistake."

An hour later, as the last drops of wine were consumed, Mac packed up the basket and stood to stretch his legs.

"Do you think you can make it back out of the cave without my help?" he asked her.

"Do you need to be somewhere?" she asked, with a flirty smile. "Why don't you help me move this blanket farther back here," as she pointed toward the back of the cave.

Mac was getting nervous, as he understood where things may be heading.

It had been quite a while since he had been with a woman, and he didn't want to look foolish or clumsy with the prettiest woman he'd ever dated.

They spread the blanket towards the back of the dim-lit cave, and she lay down next to him.

"Don't be nervous," she said, as she took his hand. "It's just us." Taking the lead, Sarah calmed Mac and restored his confidence.

He held her after for what seemed like eternity in a split second. He took a moment to take stock of his new life. *I've never been more needed and appreciated by a group of people, and I've never felt this way about another woman in my whole life*, he thought.

"This apocalypse thing is supposed to be bad," he said, "but honestly, it's the best thing to ever happen to me."

"It hasn't been all that bad for me, either. I'm *in like* with you, Mac," she said as she kissed him softly.

"I'm *in like* with you too, Sarah."

"Mac!" came a call on the radio from one of his guys. "Can you talk?"

"Just a minute," he said, telling Sarah he would be right back.

Hopping out of the top of the cave, he wondered what could be so important, since he was unofficially off for the day.

"I'm here," radioed Mac, when he reached the top.

"It's about Dr. Melton, sir," his guy began.

"What about her?" asked Mac.

"No, sir. The *other* Dr. Melton. He's at the north perimeter with about ten others from the West group. Their mountain community was overrun, and they fled down the mountain."

Mac felt like he'd just had a punch in the gut.

"Do we let them in?" his guy asked.

"That's Samuel's call," Mac told him, knowing full well he would.

A solemn Mac went back to the cave to get Sarah. "Time to go," he announced, as he packed up the blanket and picnic basket.

"Is everything okay?" asked Sarah in a concerned voice.

"I don't know," replied Mac. "I just don't know."

They rode down the mountain, with Mac not saying a word.

"Did I do something wrong?" asked Sarah. "You haven't said a word for the last 30 minutes."

"No, Sarah. This was the best afternoon I've ever had, but you need to talk to Samuel. He has some news you need to hear from him."

Mac rode off without a good-bye.

* * * * * * *

Chapter Eight ~ Saddle Ranch Loveland, Colorado

Mac rode back up to the Ranch, feeling numb. His mind was racing with one scenario after another. *Would Sarah want her ex-husband back? Were they officially divorced, or even separated?* he wondered.

Heading straight to the kitchen, he wanted to talk to Rico first.

"Thank you for the perfect lunch," Mac told him, "but something has happened." He filled the chef in on the necessary details, not wanting him to talk with others about the lunch he had made them.

"Love is complicated, my friend," Rico replied, with a pat on Mac's shoulder. "Don't worry about a thing. I am discrete in everything I do."

The next stop was Bill. Mac explained what happened, leaving out the wine and romance parts.

"I'm sorry, Mac," replied Bill when he had finished. "I'll talk to Samuel and see what it means, but I think it ultimately comes down to Sarah and what she truly wants."

"I'll steer clear for now," replied a sober Mac.

Bill filled Sharon in on the new developments. Both felt bad for Mac. "It just has to play out," remarked Sharon. "If it's meant to be, it will surely happen."

Sarah met with Samuel at his house at the far end of the property.

"Have you heard?" he asked her.

"Heard what?" she replied, hoping someone hadn't seen her and Mac just an hour earlier.

"Your husband…I mean, Dr. Melton…well, he's back."

"What do you mean?" she asked, confused.

"Men with guns confiscated our property in the mountains, and he, along with several others, are back at the northern border of this valley," explained Samuel.

"Why have you not brought them back?" she asked.

"I intend to, but I wanted to talk with you first. You, Sarah, are my family, my only family, as you know. Your opinion carries more weight with me than anyone else's."

"Are you asking me if you should let them come home?" she inquired.

"No, sweetie. This is their home, and they can stay if they choose. I just wanted to meet with you and let you know that whatever you choose, you will have my blessing. This has always been your home, and I promise to make this place perfect for you so that you may find comfort and peace each day."

"So, whoever I choose is going to be okay with you?" Sarah asked.

Samuel smiled and kissed her on the forehead. "Yes, that is what I am telling you, Sarah. I want you to be happy here."

"Thank you!" she replied, "for always looking out for me and taking my side."

Samuel was on the radio with the northern perimeter as she walked down the dusty road.

"Let them through," he said, "and send them straight to me."

Samuel met with the people from the mountain compound and was filled in on the details.

"As you know, Samuel," started Dr. Melton, "there were 15 of us up there when they came. We were no match for men with guns. They gave us a choice: to leave or be killed."

"I see," replied Samuel. "Why are there only 10 of you now?" he asked.

"Some of the others didn't want to come back here; they headed further into the mountains…"

"How is Sarah?" he asked.

"She is doing well, Doctor," replied Samuel. "I always keep an eye out for her.

"We'll get you settled in and fit you with your old jobs. It's good to have you all back, and I'm sorry for what happened to you up on the mountain."

Dr. Melton headed straight to the hospital, hoping to find Sarah.

"Hi, Sarah," he said, seeing her disinfecting the hospital floors.

"Hello Bradley," she replied. "I'm sorry to hear about you having to return here."

"Thank you," he replied, "but maybe it was for the best. You look good, Sarah. I mean…you look happy."

"I am," she replied, with a grin and a nod. "A lot has changed here recently," she continued. "Now, if you will excuse me, I need to finish these floors. This is my afternoon off, and I need some time to myself."

"Sure, honey. I understand."

"No, Bradley. You can address me as Sarah or Dr. Melton," she replied.

When he was gone, she took a break and thought about Mac. *What must he be thinking?* she wondered, hoping he wasn't scared off for good.

Mac and Bill met with John to discuss the new information and other matters concerning Ranch security.

"I know I'm supposed to bring Dr. Melton here once a day to check on you, but..."

"Don't worry about it," said John. "I'm sure Samuel will bring her by, if needed."

"I'll bring you down some dinner," Bill told John.

"That would be great! I'm getting an appetite back. Getting shot is an effective way to lose a few stubborn pounds, but I still don't recommend it." They all laughed at that.

Dinner tonight was spaghetti, with turkey meatballs and homemade garlic bread.

* * * *

The night was restless for both Sarah and Mac. He had an appointment to see her the next day to check on his arm. He thought about just not showing up for it and avoiding a potentially awkward run-in with her former, or maybe even current, husband.

He consulted Bill early, asking how he should proceed.

"Yes, it will be a bit awkward, no matter what happens," Bill agreed. "I'll come down with you, since I need to talk to Samuel about what happened at their mountain property. I want you with me, Mac, since you're head of security here. The last thing we need is something like that happening here. There's nowhere to run."

"I know, Bill, and don't worry about me. My job is to protect our group, first and foremost."

They headed down to the hospital about 9 a.m. to find both Sarah and Dr. Melton inside.

There were more patients today than Mac had seen before. "What's all this, Dr.?" he asked Sarah, waving his arm towards the other patients and forcing a smile.

"They are from our mountain community," she replied. "A few of them got a bit banged up getting out."

"You remember Dr. Melton?" she asked, as he stood beside her.

"Sure, I do," replied Mac, reaching out to shake his hand.

Mac was always a straight shooter, and it was killing him not to ask what the deal was.

Maybe he doesn't even know, Mac thought, just as Sarah said, "Okay, Mac. You're in room number two," pointing down the hall. "I'll check on your arm in a few."

Okay, this is a little better, he thought. *At least I'll get to talk to her and see where I stand.*

Minutes later Sarah opened the door to the examining room, closing it behind her.

"Mac," she said in a low voice. "I want you to know…"

There was a quick knock on the door as it opened.

Great, thought Mac, as he saw it was Dr. Melton.

"I'm with a patient," she said, matter of factly.

"Oh, sorry. I just thought I would get back up to speed on all the patients here, now that I'm back full time. So how is that arm doing, Mac?" he asked, taking a closer look.

"On the mend," he replied. "Sarah…I mean, uhm…Dr. Melton, has done an excellent job fixing it up."

"I see," he said, leaving the room abruptly.

"You meant to do that!" said Sarah, punching Mac in his good arm.

"Ow!" he exclaimed, pretending to rub his arm. "I'm not sure what you mean." He smiled.

"It was wonderful…our time on the Rimrock, I mean," she spoke softly. "Things are just a bit more complicated now."

"I know, Sarah, and the last thing I want to do is make things harder on you. That's the truth."

"You're a good man, Mac. Don't give up on me just yet," she replied, as she kissed him on the forehead… Okay, let's check this arm," she said.

Dr. Melton was furious at Mac's comment, as he realized there was something going on between him and his wife.

He found Samuel and Bill talking in the machine shop and began hurling questions at them both.

"Bradley, I need you to calm down now," said Samuel. "This is not how we treat our guests," as he gestured towards Bill.

"You're both a part of this," he continued, angrily.

"A part of what, Bradley?" asked Samuel.

"The plan to steal my wife," he answered.

"Dr. Melton," said Bill in a calm voice, "there is no such plan, I can assure you."

"Thanks, Bill," said Samuel. "I'll take it from here, if you don't mind."

Samuel pulled the doctor aside, and in a near whisper that could pierce the calm, he said just four words. "*I run things here*. Do you understand me, son?"

"Yes…sir," Bradley replied slowly.

"So that we're clear," continued Samuel, "I always have two top priorities. Number one is leading our group and caring for this property. Number two is looking out for my adopted daughter, Sarah, and it's not always in that order."

"I… I…," Bradley stammered. "I didn't know that… I mean, how did I not know that?"

"I guess you never asked," said Samuel, with his eyes fixed on Bradley.

"One more outburst towards me, Sarah, or anyone else in our or their group," he said, pointing to Bill, "and you will be leaving us, not to return. Is that clear?"

"Yes, sir. It is," Bradley replied, as he left.

"Thank you, my friend, Samuel," said Bill as they walked towards the hospital. "There's never a dull moment now, it seems."

Mac and Bradley exchanged stares as they passed each other near the front door.

"Sarah," asked Samuel in front of all of them, "would you mind joining me for dinner tonight? After all, I believe you have the afternoon off."

"Yes, I would like that," she replied. The two walked down the road, not looking back.

"Time to go, Mac," said Bill, putting a hand on his shoulder.

Mac rode back towards the Ranch, wishing he had more answers. *At least there is still a chance, even if it's small,* he thought.

"My dear," said Samuel, as they walked the dirt road to his house. "You know I always want the best for you. I always have."

"I know, father," she replied, squeezing his right hand.

"How are you holding up with all this?" he asked.

"Well, I'm surprised he's back from the mountains, but nothing else has changed."

"He is still your husband, and he's back for you," said Samuel.

"No, father. He's back, but he didn't come back for me. He had nowhere else to go. Nothing else has changed," she stated again.

Samuel smiled and chuckled just a little. "I see your point, sweetie. It's hard to argue when you put it like that... So, what do you want to do?"

"I want a couple of days to collect my thoughts is all."

"We can do that," he assured her. "I'll make sure the hospital is covered, and you can take a much-deserved break."

Samuel and Sarah shared his table in the common dining room and invited a few of the old-timers to join them.

* * * *

Dr. Melton had kept his cool as much as possible in front of Samuel, but the thought of something happening between Sarah and Mac was too much to keep inside.

Reaching into his medical bag, he pulled out a revolver from the very bottom, wrapped in a small gray towel.

He knew how Samuel felt about guns, and this would surely get him kicked out of the group, but he was now determined to take his wife back from that traitor on the Ranch.

When she sees how much I care now, she will want to leave with me, and we can start a new life somewhere down the road, he thought.

Bradley was feeling powerful and thought he would stay put tonight, instead of hunting down Mac immediately.

There were no more patients in the hospital, and he cracked open a half bottle of Jim Beam whiskey. Drinking straight from the bottle, his blood boiled with each swig.

He juggled the .38 special revolver from one hand to the other, back and forth, occasionally checking to make sure he had all five rounds loaded.

It would be dark soon, and he daydreamed of getting rid of Mac and walking off into the sunset with his girl.

With the bottle nearly gone, he changed his mind about going out, stumbling to his feet.

Returning the pistol to his medical bag, he headed the 3/4 mile up to Saddle Ranch.

Jimmy was on security and was now one of Mac's favorite guys. He was easy-going, took directions well, and never slacked off.

Jimmy was the first one to spot the doctor coming up the road through his night-vision goggles.

"Mac, are you there?" he called on the radio.

"Yeah, Jimmy. What's up?" he asked.

"The doctor guy from the mountain group yesterday…well, he's walking up the road toward me with no flashlight."

"Is he carrying anything?" asked Mac.

"It just looks like some sort of medical bag, like you would see on the *Lone Ranger* episodes. He seems to be stumbling a bit as well…maybe drunk or sick. I'm not sure.

"He's close now. What do you want me to do?"

"Tell him to stop where he is. I'll be there in five," said Mac.

Ten more steps and Jimmy yelled, "Stop!" The startled doctor stumbled and fell to one knee, dropping his bag.

"Stay right there for me, Doc," said Jimmy, shining a flashlight into his eyes.

Bradley scooped up his medical bag and stood, using his free hand to shield the light from his eyes.

"What are you doing up here tonight?" asked Jimmy.

"I need to see that coward they call Mac," he replied, stumbling again as he stepped forward.

"That's far enough, Doctor. Stay right where you are."

Mac pulled up on the four-wheeler minutes later. "What can we help you with, Doc?" asked Mac, getting off his vehicle.

"You can start by telling me that you will stay the hell away from my wife!" he spat.

"I'm sorry, but that's not my call, Doctor. It's Sarah's, and it's up to her to decide what she wants."

"I'll bet you were surprised when I came back for her," Bradley hissed.

"Actually, I heard you came back at a full run from the mountains, chased off like a scared rabbit," Mac replied. "You just came back here when you had nowhere else you go. Is that about right?"

"I have something for you," Bradley said, reaching into his bag.

"Easy does it, Doc," said Mac. "I don't want to hurt you."

The doctor pulled out the revolver, pointing it in Mac's general direction and waving it from side to side, as he accused Mac of trying to steal his wife.

"I've got him covered," said Jimmy, pointing his AR-15 rifle towards him. "Say the word, and it's over," he added.

"No, not yet, Jimmy. Let me try to calm him down."

Mac then addressed Bradley. "Doctor Melton, let's take a minute and talk this out, okay?" Mac held his hands out in front of him. "I know you don't want to shoot anyone, and neither do we."

"That's where you're wrong," he replied, putting the revolver to his own head.

"I'm sorry, Sarah," he whispered as he pulled the trigger.

The shot was heard by everyone in the valley, setting off a slurry of radio chatter from both the north and south perimeter, including John, Bill and Samuel.

It was Samuel who had to break the news to a distraught Sarah.

"How did this happen?" she asked him. "What was he even doing up on the road?"

"I'm so sorry" is all Samuel could think to say. "I'll find out what happened; you can count on that."

Samuel and Bill met with Mac and Jimmy on the road, with John on the radio.

"Sir, I would like to tell you what happened, if that's okay, since I was here the whole time," said Jimmy.

"Okay, let's hear it," said Samuel.

Jimmy relayed everything that occurred.

"Is that what happened, Mac?" asked John, overhearing the story on the radio.

"Yes, sir, it happened just that way," replied a saddened Mac.

"I'll send a couple of my guys up here to bring Bradley back," said Samuel, getting back in his truck and driving away.

"All right, Mac," said Bill. "Let's have you go home tonight. Jimmy and I will get this cleaned up. We can talk tomorrow."

Mac's mind was going a hundred miles an hour. This was the last thing he expected, and he wondered if Sarah would ever talk to him again. *Even if they weren't still together, he was her husband,* he thought, *and I guess it's my fault.*

Mac wished he were back down on the road with Jimmy and Bill. The nights he spent alone were the longest of all. The nightmares continued years later of his father locking him in the basement while arguing with his mother. He was 8 or 9 years old when he remembered it starting.

In the beginning, it was just every once in a while, that they had a fight. By the time he was 12, it was almost every day. That's when he knew his father was abusing his mother. He hated that more than anything, sitting at the bottom of the damp basement, hearing his mother's sobs and calls for him to stop. At first, he tried to force the basement door open, but it was always locked from the outside. Eventually, he just stopped trying.

Mac was 14 years old the last day he ever saw his father. This day he went down to the basement without being asked, as was the new normal in the house.

His father was drunk and had just lost his job as a construction foreman. Mac knew something was different this time, as he heard the banging from upstairs. His mother was hysterical and called his name for the first time ever.

"Mac, please help me!" she screamed over and over. He tried the door and it was locked, but he wasn't a little boy anymore. He wasn't the scared kid he always used to be. With a single right kick, he broke the basement door open and faced his father.

"We're done with this," Mac spoke in a shaky voice, holding his mother. "We're done with you."

His dad raised his fist towards him and laughed. "You two deserve each other" was the last thing he said as he walked out the front door.

Mac would remember that day as the best day of his life. He would also recall it as his worst.

From then on, he did everything he could not to be alone. He was thankful for his dog, Bo, who always stayed by his side.

"It's just you and me, buddy," he said, trying to force a smile. Bo barked and laid his head on Mac's lap.

* * * *

Sarah was glad she was alone tonight. The last two days had left her exhausted, and she wondered what Mac did to make Bradley end his life.

She wasn't interested in getting back together with Bradley, knowing full well he had come back to escape the violence on the mountain, and not for her. He had been her husband, though, for several years, and he was a good man.

Running each possible scenario through her mind, she wasn't sure who was to blame.

She fell asleep crying softly.

* * * *

Samuel's men retrieved the body later that night, without discussion, leaving both Jimmy and Bill thankful they could go home and get some sleep.

Samuel talked with a few of his men about burial plans set for later the following day. *Gone are the times of waiting until Saturday or Sunday to bury someone who died a week earlier on an inconvenient day*, he thought.

The service was set for noon, just 14 hours after his death.

Both Bill and Sharon were in attendance, with John on the radio, all representing Saddle Ranch.

Sarah looked for Mac in the small gathering and wasn't surprised to see him missing.

"O Lord," said Samuel, as the body was laid in the freshly excavated ground. "We give you one of our own to watch over until we may all be reunited in your kingdom."

A few of the West members spoke, as Sarah looked on. The funeral service in this next world was less than 15 minutes.

Sarah, still technically off duty, slipped away to her favorite spot on Green Ridge. She came here often to soothe her soul.

Being a little older than Samuel's daughter, Kayla, Sarah watched out for her. At only four years old and with no mother around, the little girl loved the attention.

It was a late October night, on the 26th, 1975, to be exact. Every Sunday a group of people from the West would take the van into the neighboring town of Fort Collins and go to the newly built Foothills Fashion Mall. Sarah loved going to the mall but had stayed home sick this Sunday.

Her parents were looking for a special gift for her upcoming 8th birthday, and Samuel suggested that Kayla go along.

They failed to return that night. Samuel was briefed by the Fort Collins Police the next morning. The van had been heading home when struck by a semi-trailer truck, whose driver had been on the road for more than 25 hours straight. The truck driver was the only survivor.

There were just two things the officer had from the van—a pink elephant belonging to Kayla and a wrapped gift with a music box inside. The tag read: "To our dearest Sarah. May you keep this close to your heart. Love, Mom and Dad."

Samuel officially adopted Sarah over the next few weeks and treated her just like family. He made her a metal waterproof trunk so she could keep her music box safe in her favorite place on the mountain.

Now, once again facing tough times, she pulled her music box from the trunk and wound it fully. Tears rolled down her cheeks as she thought of her parents, Kayla, Bradley and Mac.

Samuel met her there sometime later. He didn't say a word but held her tightly as she wept.

Mac met Bill following the service for Bradley, wanting to know what happened.

"Do you want to know about Sarah?" Bill asked directly. "Well, there's not much to say. Sarah lost someone she was once close to and is probably trying to find answers. You may want to leave her be for a while, Mac."

"Yes, sir. I was thinking the same thing."

"We'll get one of the nurses here to look after your arm for a while," replied Bill.

* * * * * * *

Chapter Nine ~
Raton Pass, New Mexico

David was having fun joking around with Mel, but truth be told he was lonely. It had been a few years since his wife died, and until now he hadn't even thought of settling down again.

Mark and his parents were his only concern. Now he was responsible for a growing group of families, and he missed his. Well…the way it used to be.

Mel stayed over on the couch, and he and David agreed to spend one more day scouting the area and defining their territory.

"Last day, buddy," said David. "Tomorrow we will all get together and define our roles as the official Raton Pass Militia.

"Better keep your eye out for the ladies today," he told Mel.

"You know I will be," replied Mel, "but I think I'm good. I've got a hot one on the line who loves coffee. What more could I ask for?"

"Well, it's not like she has a lot of choices!" said David, laughing.

"Keep it up, buddy, and I'll find myself another best man!" said Mel, jokingly.

"Nope," replied David. "I'm your guy—you know that, right?"

"Yeah, man. I'm just messing with you."

* * * *

The last three houses they visited didn't pan out.

One lady, easily in her 80s, wanted nothing to do with any group, and the other two houses were empty, probably summer homes.

"This is our group then—at least for now," David told Mel. "We're more spread out than I would like, but I guess it's okay at this point."

"I almost forgot," said Mel. "I've got more than a few walkie-talkies in my stash, with plenty of batteries. Maybe we could give at least one to each household and see how many we have left for individual carry. The range could be a bit spotty up here, but it's still a good idea to have them."

With the new group now formed, it was time for inventory and job duties.

Everyone met for lunch and discussed the bylaws for the newly formed Raton Pass Militia. It was agreed that all major decisions would be put to a majority vote. David's dad, Dean, would alone have the final vote, as well as veto power.

Dean, having lived up here for years, was known by nearly everyone in the area as a fair and honest man. With his wife, Beatrice, voted head chef, they had clout among the people.

David couldn't have been happier about some of the pressure being off him. He was unanimously voted head of security, and that suited him fine.

Mel oversaw general provisions, since he had the most of those being added to the group.

Other jobs included hunting, fishing, gardening, sanitation, perimeter security, and food processing. "Anything we can eat from the land ensures that our provisions will last that much longer," said Dean.

Mel and Tammy were getting to be a thing, David noticed. He was happy for his old friend and wondered if he would ever find someone for himself. He had spoken about it the other day to his son, Mark.

"Not that there is anyone here, but would you be okay with me dating again sometime?" he asked.

"Sure, Dad," Mark said, with a laugh. "That's what Mom would have wanted."

David was relieved to hear that. *Okay, God now it's up to You*, he thought. *I'm ready when You are.*

David was able to get James on the radio and told him Lance was still good on his deal so far. "As long as they make it here, you'll get your guns. They're a little behind, we just heard, having run into a bit of trouble. But that will happen out on the road," he added.

"Fine by me," said James. "Just let me know when they arrive and I'll make a quick trip up there."

"James, buddy, I have to go," said David, looking out at a large plume of smoke.

"Mel!" he yelled from the other room. "That smoke is in your direction, just beyond your house, if I'm right!"

"That's not good," replied Mel. "Everything I have is in that house!"

"Let's get all abled bodies to your house—no kids or seniors, please," said David.

With the four-wheelers, they made it over to Mel's house in ten minutes, just in time to see the flames heading down from the ridge behind his house.

"Buckets!" shouted David to Mel. "Do you have any buckets? We can draw from the creek and try to..."

"It's too late," replied Mel, sitting on the ground as the first flames came up from the roof of his home.

David, realizing this, sat down next to him. They watched as the flames engulfed Mel's once-formidable house.

"The fire will stop when it hits the lake," Mel said, smiling, as he pointed to the lakeshore. "It shouldn't be a problem for your parents' place or any of our other houses."

"How can you smile?" asked David, starting to realize how bad it was. "Not only are you losing your house, but now we don't have enough provisions to support the Militia."

Mel kept smiling at David. "Do you remember, buddy, when I took you down into my basement and showed you all the provisions I had been hoarding?"

"Yeah, I remember," said David, "and now it's gone." He shook his head.

"Now, wait a minute. Let me finish," interjected Mel. "Do you remember what the walls of the basement were made of?"

David smiled at this, remembering the thick concrete walls. "The floor and ceiling are concrete too, right?" asked David.

"Exactly. Everything underground in my house is fireproof, although the freeze-dried food may have a hint of campfire taste for a while."

Mel's joke made them both laugh.

"But you lost your house, Mel. How can you joke about that?"

"I always expected it. That's why I hired an out-of-state builder to customize the house. I didn't want some local guys doing it and coming back for some handouts when the power went down.

"The structure was always meant to be temporary housing. I've known since we met out on the lake that I wouldn't be spending another night at my home. It too far away to protect and we need to get all the food, firearms and ammo up to your parents' place. Now it's just something we need to do sooner than later."

* * * *

"You're right, Mel," said David, an hour later. "The fire did burn out at the lake. We've got a lot of work to do after this cool-down. We need to watch this place tonight and get everything moved at once tomorrow."

"I don't mind sleeping on the couch for a while," added Mel.

David radioed to his son, Mark, to bring his friends down to Mel's.

"Oh, no," said Mark, as they pulled up. "I'm sorry about your house, Mel."

"Thanks, but it's okay," said Mel, as he explained the situation.

"We need to provide surveillance on this slab until morning," said David. "We'll grab a couple more guys and take shifts. Each two-person team will take one four-hour shift."

"We'll need this," said Mel, grinning as he handed David a wristwatch. *Tick...tick* went the second hand. The watch read 4:26 p.m.

"How does this work and why didn't you tell me you had it?" asked David.

"Well, it was in a Faraday cage, along with some other fun things, so it didn't get zapped. I've also got a few more—one each for your mom and dad, even ones for Mark and Tammy. And to your second question, I didn't show you everything last time. But you'll see it all tomorrow, buddy."

"I can't wait!" replied, Mark, overhearing the conversation.

They explained to the group over dinner what happened. "We need all hands on deck tomorrow for a provision transport," said David.

"Where are you going to sleep, Mel?" asked Tammy.

"Well, it's okay. I've been crashing on the couch at David's parents' anyway."

"Maybe we could get our own place," she whispered. "There are some vacant houses close by in our new territory," she added, giving him a quick kiss on the lips."

"Are you kidding me?" asked Mel in a louder-than-he-intended voice.

"I was only suggesting…"

"No. No, I think it's a great idea. I was just about to say you made me blush, and that's hard to do. I'll talk to David and his dad about it," he added. Tammy had no idea, but this was the happiest day Mel had known in a long time, maybe ever.

* * * *

"Dad? Dad, are you there?" came the call on the radio.

David fumbled around in the dark, looking for his flashlight. "Yeah, I'm here, Mark. What's going on?"

"We're watching Mel's place, and there have been a few guys wandering around over the past few hours. But now there is a small group around the slab, with shovels and picks."

"Son, can they see you?"

"I don't think so, Dad. We're pretty well hidden in the trees."

"Okay, Mark. You guys stay put and out of sight, no matter what. Got it?"

"But Dad, they're trying to get in through the top, and one guy is trying to cut a lock with bolt cutters."

"Are they armed, son?"

"I don't know. I only see tools—that's it."

"Mark, we'll be there in fifteen minutes. Don't try to stop them. Understand?"

"But Dad!"

"No, son. Do you understand?"

"Yes, sir."

"Mel! We have to go *now*!" yelled David from the other room.

Mel was startled and fell off the couch with a thud. "Ow! Crap! What's the problem, David?"

"There are some guys at your house—they're breaking into your slab."

"No, no, no!" exclaimed Mel. "That's all we've got!"

"Let's go," said David, handing Mel an AR-15 rifle. David ran out the front door, jumping on the four-wheeler, with Mel riding on the back.

"What about Mark?" asked Mel.

"He and his buddies are there, but I instructed them to stand down."

* * * *

Mark and his friends watched helplessly as the last lock was cut and a large metal door on the top of the slab was forced open. One by one, the men disappeared down the stairwell, wildly shining their flashlights, yelling and laughing.

Mark counted six men inside, with just one man staying behind, as an apparent lookout. Mark was able to make out a rifle in his hands.

* * * *

David slowed the bike one-quarter mile from Mel's place, parking it in some bushes. He knew Mark's location and didn't want to use the radio unless he had no choice. "We will be coming up behind Mark and his guys. They will be expecting us, but no sudden movements, buddy," said David.

"I hear you," replied Mel.

Their eyes were adjusting to the darkness as they followed the road to Mel's once-formidable house.

"Dad," Mark called out quietly, as they got close to their position. Mark filled David and Mel in on what was going on. Six men inside and one lookout.

Now Mel could hear the men laughing and hollering as they found more and more items to loot.

Mel was furious, raising his rifle towards the man standing guard. "I'm not going to let this happen. I'm sorry, David."

Without a word, David grabbed the barrel of Mel's rifle, jerking it toward the sky.

"What the hell, David?" asked Mel, now confused.

"I've got a better idea," said David, digging into his daypack. "Now it's my turn for a surprise, old buddy," he added, pulling out a black canvas bag from the very bottom.

"What is that?" asked Mark.

"How do you get a gopher out of a hole?" David asked Mark and Mel, now grinning.

Now Mel was smiling as he saw David's bag open. "You smoke 'em out!" Mel laughed.

"Mel, you and I will flank both sides and come up behind the guard. In exactly five minutes," continued David, pointing to the watch, "Mark, you guys make a distraction and stay low. No gunfire, Just a couple of these," he said, handing Mark a pack of ladyfinger firecrackers and a lighter.

Exactly five minutes later, with no men exiting the structure, Mark lit the fireworks.

"Bam! Bam!" they popped, distracting the lookout. With his rifle raised, he seemed confused as to where the noise originated. He pointed the gun back and forth in the direction of the sounds he heard.

David and Mel quietly snuck up behind him. The barrel of Mel's rifle poked his back as David grabbed his weapon from behind. "Quiet, now," instructed Mel, "or you're done."

They could now clearly hear the men inside the house, talking like they had just won the lottery.

"We're set for life," said one, with another excitedly talking about all of the alcohol he saw. The other men were now arguing about how everything would be split up.

"I found it all," called out one man.

"How about I take it from you?" yelled another.

David could hear a scuffle, with one man clearly striking another.

"Now!" called David to Mel, as he lit three of the smoke bombs, dropping them into the stairwell.

David lifted the heavy door as Mel covered the scout. "Latch it!" called Mel. "Right down there," he pointed.

David latched the door and called to Mark and his buddies to come down. There were a few seconds of silence as he latched the door. Following were sounds of yelling, cursing, screaming, and finally coughing. Mark's guys reached the house just as the smoke started to pour out of the trap door.

"I want every rifle trained on this door," called David, loudly enough to be heard by all.

"I have to open this door now, or they will all suffocate. Don't shoot unless you have to.

"One, two, three..." David swung the door open on three. Smoke bellowed from the stairwell as the first man stumbled out and collapsed on the cement, coughing hoarsely.

Three more came up behind him, gasping for air.

* * * * * * *

Chapter Ten ~
Raton Pass, New Mexico

"That's four!" shouted David. "Two more to go."

"Hey, I see something," called out Mark's friend, Jimmy, stepping up to look down into the hole.

"No!" yelled Mel. "Stay back!"

Jimmy's eyes widened, and he froze, paralyzed at the vision of a man wearing a gas mask and pointing a rifle straight at him.

"Crack!" came the sound from inside, as Jimmy's head snapped backward, his body landing on its back with a thud.

"No!" screamed Mark, looking into the still-open eyes of his best friend.

Mark, in a fit of rage, ran to the open staircase, firing his weapon into the hole time after time.

David grabbed his son and pulled him back.

"I can't lose you too," he told Mark, tightening his grip.

After five minutes, with no sounds coming from the stairwell, David and Mel cautiously peeked down the stairway. The man with the mask was in a heap at the bottom of the stairs.

Just one more missing," said Mel to David. "I'll go first, since it's my house. You've got Mark to look after," he said, as he slowly navigated the cement staircase.

The smoke was mostly cleared, giving clear visibility with Mel's headlamp. He reached the bottom of the stairs, recognizing the gas mask he had purchased a few years ago on the face of the now-deceased gunman.

"One more!" shouted David from above. "There's one more. Be careful, my friend."

Mel cautiously surveyed the basement, having spent countless hours here not long ago.

There are four scenarios, he thought. *First, he's waiting to ambush me. Second, Mark got the count wrong. Third, he died of smoke inhalation. And fourth, he found the escape tunnel.*

Mel found his answer as he cleared each room, heading to the back wall. The contractor had a sense of humor and had the word *Margaritaville* stenciled on to the escape tunnel door, referencing a popular '70s Jimmy Buffet song.

It was open for the second time ever after Mel had tested it when the house was first built.

Well, it's better than a shooter waiting to ambush me, he thought, remembering how the long tunnel led to a thick cover of trees and bushes nearly 1/8 mile away.

"All clear," he called out, loud enough for all to hear.

David met Mel at the bottom of the stairs.

"We've got five alive up top, but I'm not sure what to do with them," said David. "We've got to hold them at the very least until we can clear this house."

"Agreed," said Mel, "and maybe we can talk to them and see if we can work together in any capacity."

"I need to check on my son," said David, disappearing back up the stairs.

David pulled a distraught Mark aside.

"Son, you lost a friend and had to take a life. I know it's hard… What can I do, Mark?"

"Nothing, Dad… It's okay… It's all just fine in this screwed-up next world—just another day at the office."

"Mark, my son, no. It's not okay or just another day. You lost your best friend today, and that's a tragedy. He was a good young man. Brave, tough, and a loyal friend. I'm truly sorry he's gone. I'm truly sorry."

"I know, Dad," replied Mark, clutching him close and burying his head in his dad's shoulder. He cried openly, grieving his friend as the new captives looked on without a word.

Mark's other friend, Chad, holding the captive men at bay, spoke up for the first time.

"What now?" he asked in a frightened, nervous voice.

"Mark, you and your friend Chad go back to the house and get some of our group to help us transport Mel's things. The four-wheeler is a quarter mile up the road, on the east side in some bushes. I laid a long stick in the road, so you can't miss the marked spot."

David pulled Chad aside. "I'm sorry for your loss. He was a good kid…I mean, man. Keep a close eye on my boy, will you?"

"Yes, sir. I will," Chad replied.

David called Mel back up the stairs. "Help me cover these guys until Mark and his friend get back." The men were all standing with their hands in the air.

"Okay, boys. One at a time over here," David said, pointing to an open spot on the slab.

With Mel providing cover, David instructed each man to strip down to their drawers.

"Slow and easy," he continued. "Any sudden moves and we will be asking questions later. Understand, boys?" he asked loud enough for all to hear.

"Yes, sir" came a muddled response from the group.

"Mel," David asked quietly. "Where does that tunnel come out?"

"Over there," replied Mel, pointing to the south. "About 1/8 mile down. He may be back, and I damn sure don't want to get ambushed," he added.

"Crack!" came the sound from the south. "Crack! Crack!"

"I'm hit," yelled Mel, falling to the ground, holding his right knee.

David dropped to the ground beside him, returning fire in the direction of the shots.

He was relieved, knowing Mark had gone the other direction.

"They're getting away!" called Mel, pointing towards the scattering men they were supposed to be covering.

"Let them go," David called out.

"Where are you hit, Mel?"

"Just in the knee, I think, but it hurts like hell."

"I'm coming, Dad," Mark called over the radio, after hearing the shots.

"No, son. You guys go back now and get help. I need every man in our group that can shoot down here. We're running out of time, and we're not going to lose everything now."

"But Dad, is it worth dying for?" asked Mark.

"Yes, son, it is. Now go and don't look back."

Mark and Chad raced back to the house. The sunrise was coming up from the east, over the trees. Mark stared in amazement at the sheer beauty of the dawn, praying for the safety of his dad and Mel.

"You can count on me, Dad. I'll make you proud," he called over the radio.

David smiled without picking up his radio.

"You always do, son," he said, while tending to Mel's knee.

Thankfully there were no more shots from the sniper in the bushes. But he knew they would be back. That was one thing they could count on.

David was able to get Mel's knee cleaned and bandaged with the first-aid kit from his backpack.

"It looks like the bullet nicked the top of your tibia and went clean through," David told him. "You'll be down for a bit, but I think you'll recover okay.

"Take these," he said, handing him a couple of pills and his water canteen.

"What are these," asked Mel skeptically.

"Well, they're not cyanide pills or spiked Kool-Aid, so don't worry about it. They will lessen the pain but not make you too loopy. We're going to need your help to get this done quickly. It's a good thing you were shot anyway."

"What are you talking about, David? How's that good? It still hurts like hell," replied Mel.

"Who's a hot medic?" David asked, trying to hold a straight face.

"Oh," replied Mel. "That's good. I see where you're going with this. Do you think she and I could have one of the abandoned houses inside the security perimeter? You know, just because I may need round-the-clock care for a while."

Now they were both laughing. "Let me check with my dad," said David, "but I'm sure there's no problem with that. I'm sure he and my mom can't wait to get you off of their couch," added David, still laughing.

"I'm just bummed you can't show me around down there," David said, pointing down the stairwell. "I was looking forward to it, if I'm being honest."

"Oh no, old friend. I'm not missing out on that," replied Mel. "I'll drop my ass down those stairs myself if I have to. I've got a couple of surprises you must see, messed up leg or not. Those Tic Tacs you gave me are helping with the pain some.

"Here comes the cavalry," said Mel, hearing the sound of engines coming down the road nearly 40 minutes later.

"Let's just hope it's our guys," added David.

As the four-wheelers and two trucks with trailers came into view, he waved at Mark, who was leading the caravan.

All told, there were 15 men and 3 women, including Tammy. David was happy to see that his dad was not here. *He must be holding down the fort*, he thought. He was already worried about Mark's safety; he didn't need to worry about one more.

"Oh, sweetie," Tammy said, as she saw Mel's bandaged leg.

"Did you do this, David?" she asked, pointing to the dressing.

"Yes, Ma'am. I did."

"You did a great job, from the looks of it," she said, smiling.

"Time to get you home, honey," she said, looking at Mel.

"No, not yet, babe," replied Mel. "I've got a few things to show my old friend here down in the basement."

David was getting annoyed at the "sweetie, honey, baby" talk but kept it to himself. *There's nothing more irritating than watching new love when you haven't yet found your own*, he thought.

David gathered up the group to make a plan. He relayed the story of what had happened thus far and tasked eight men with perimeter security. Each would be equally distanced in a half-mile circle around the slab.

"No one gets in," David continued, "no matter what. The men from earlier will be back sooner than later. No one leaves a stash like this behind without a fight.

"One radio stays with me here, and the rest go to each lookout. This may be the only time I say this to you all, but shoot first, and we will ask questions later.

"The future of our group is dependent on Mel's provisions down there," he added, pointing to the stairwell. "We will not be giving that up to anyone. All agreed?"

"Agreed!" they said together.

With the trailers backed up to the slab, the rest of the men, except for David, Mel and Mark, started the long process of hauling the provisions and stacking them on the trailers.

"I thought you wanted to show me some things," David said to Mel.

"I do, buddy. You've already seen everything they are bringing up. But when they are done, I'll show you what's left," Mel said, with a wink and a pained grin.

An hour and a half later, all the provisions were loaded onto the trailers.

"Is that everything?" Mel asked Tom, who was the last man up.

"Yes, sir. That's everything."

"Okay, David. Now for the fun part," said Mel, smiling.

"Dad!" called Mark over the radio. "I've got a guy 100 yards out, coming through the trees. I can't see him clearly, but he's got a rifle."

"Anyone else on the perimeter have an eye on him?" asked David, hoping for a yes.

"No... No... Not me," came the responses.

"Dad, I've got this," said Mark in a calm voice. "You told us no one gets through."

David was now regretting his words, but he knew those men were bound to come back.

"Okay, son. Take him out," David ordered.

Seconds later, the "Boom!" came from Mark's rifle.

"He's down," Mark said in an anxious but excited voice. "He's hit, but he's fumbling with a radio, I think."

"Don't let him get that message out!" called David over the radio.

Mark fired again, missing his target. The third shot hit his mark in the chest.

"I think he's done," called Mark over the radio.

"David," came a low voice over the radio. "David."

"Dad, is that you?" he asked confused.

"David," he repeated. "I've been shot. Please help me."

David nearly fell over as he felt his stomach buckle.

"Hold your fire!" he yelled, as he ran towards the shots his only son had just fired into the trees.

"Dad! Dad!" he screamed over and over as he narrowed the distance with each step and labored breath. As he neared the downed man, slumped over with his face in the dirt, he saw the watch his father had worn for the last 30 years, stained with blood.

"Oh no, oh no, Dad!" he cried.

"It's going to be okay," he cried out, as he held him in his arms. "I'm going to fix this. I'm going to make you better. I'm going to…" David turned his dead father over and stared into his still-open eyes. "Oh, God! What have I done?"

David ran full out towards Mark, hoping to reach him before he could see what happened.

Mark watched the scene through his rifle scope and couldn't believe his eyes. Feeling dizzy, he vomited onto the ground and prayed to God for forgiveness.

Without a word, he raised his rifle, pointing it just under his chin. "Forgive me, Father," he said aloud, as he pulled the trigger.

"Click!" came the sound of Mark's rifle, and David froze, now close enough to see his son. He felt pain in his upper chest, like a python was squeezing him to death. David let out a scream that pierced the forest.

Mark, realizing his gun had jammed, was trying to clear the jam when his friend Chad tackled him. "Get off me!" he screamed, fighting to keep the weapon.

David made it just in time to wrestle the rifle away from Mark. He held his son close.

"Let me go, Dad," he demanded through his tears.

"No, son. I can't do that. It's my fault, Mark," he added. "It's all *my* fault, and I'm not going to lose you too."

David tasked Chad with helping him to get his only son home.

He briefed Mel and a shocked group about what had happened, vowing to return soon to pick up the bodies.

"We'll get everything out of the house," Mel told him soberly. "Take care of your boy."

David rode the four-wheeler, insisting Mark ride on the back. Passing by his father, they both stared off into the woods where he lay.

Neither spoke a word as they headed back up to the house.

* * * *

Beatrice was out front as they pulled up. She had heard the shots, and somehow, she just knew.

The look on her son and grandson's faces told her everything.

"Mom," said David, with tears running down his cheeks… "I'm so…" is all he could get out.

"I don't deserve to live," choked Mark, speaking for the first time since leaving his post.

"No, Mark. We won't be doing that," said Beatrice. "We've lost enough. No more!" she said sternly.

"If you're going to blame someone, don't you dare blame yourselves," she told both of them.

"You blame me. I sent him there to help," she said.

"We are going to talk about what happened, just the three of us right now," she added. "When we're done, we will honor him every day and speak of this no more."

David kept a close eye on his son, forbidding him from carrying a firearm for now.

Beatrice kept a closer eye on both of them, making them promise her they would not hurt or blame themselves for the accident. Mark was reluctant to make the promise, but after a private, nearly one-hour talk with his grandmother, he did.

David knew better than to ask either one of them about what had been said.

* * * *

Mel and Tammie were settling into their new house, which David had approved, taking the reins from his father.

Most of Mel's provisions were stored in the basement but would be divided over several locations in the coming days.

David heard that his mom had talked to Lance on the radio and would try to connect in the morning. He wasn't sure what to say about his dad, but he promised his mother that he would always refer to it as a tragic accident.

For the very first time in his life, David did not fear death. He looked forward to the time he could apologize to his father, face-to-face. His job now was to look after his mother and son.

The service for Dean and Jimmy was quick that afternoon, with everyone pitching in. The newly acquired members of the Raton Pass Militia prepared the grave sites, with all in attendance saying what they admired about them. David and Beatrice kept a close eye on Mark.

David had all but forgotten about Mel's surprise provisions and brought it up casually the next morning over a tall cup of camp coffee.

"So, what did I miss?" he asked his old friend, "about the extra gear?" His voice was still strained from yesterday's happenings.

"First of all," replied Mel, "I want to say that I'm sorry about your dad. He was a good man and we will all miss him here."

"Thanks, my friend," David choked out.

"Secondly," replied Mel, understanding a change of topic was sorely needed, "we were able to recover all the special things I had stored and wanted to show you."

"Ok, buddy, what have you got?" asked David, with Mark looking on.

* * * * * * *

Chapter Eleven ~
Second Chances Ranch
Weston, Colorado

Chance settled in on his first night home, sleeping just inside the front door.

"Okay, buddy," said James, as he got ready for the 6 a.m. chores. "No more leashes. You're free to roam, but you'll pull your weight, Chance."

He barked and ran outside, as James opened the front door, and waited for instructions.

Jason was up early and ready to get started, with his hip mending well. "I can't wait to help you get things done around here," he said to James.

"I know, Jason. For now, just keep your eyes open. Learning how it's done is 90 percent, and the other ten is just execution," said James. "We will work on ranch security this afternoon."

Chance barked as he ran up to the front gate of the property, tail wagging.

James could see an old pickup truck coming down the highway a couple of miles away.

He jumped off the tractor and helped Jason down.

"Locked and loaded, Jason?" he asked.

"Yep," he replied from behind the tractor. "Why is Chance wagging his tail, though?"

"I don't know," replied James. "Wait! I know that truck," he said, as it came clearly into view. "It's Sheriff Johnson."

They met the Sheriff at the gate.

"Hello, Sheriff," said James, as they shook hands just outside the front gate. "This is Jason, the fellow I was telling you about."

"Good to meet you, Jason," said Sheriff Johnson. "And good to see you again, Chance," he added, reaching down to pat the dog's head.

"What happened to your leg?" he asked? "Was that from the other night?"

"No, Sheriff. Just a four-wheeler accident, but it's healing right up," replied Jason.

"Sorry to hear about your troubles with the two men the other night."

"Thank you, sir," replied Jason. "I'm glad it's behind us now."

"Well, that's partly why I'm here this morning," said Sheriff Johnson, now talking to both of them. "Mind if I come up to the house for a cup of coffee?"

"Sure," replied James.

"Honey," James announced, as he opened the front door to the house. "The good Sheriff's here."

"Hi," said Janice, coming out from the kitchen to greet him. "Can I make you some breakfast, sir," she asked.

"Oh no, Ma'am, but I would love a cup of coffee if it's not too much trouble."

"Not at all. I have a pot on already."

"Mind if we talk for a minute, just the adults?" the Sheriff asked.

"Girls, go upstairs and play for a little bit," said Lauren.

"You know, I realized I've never been up to your house, James. Been past it many times but never realized how impressive it is."

"Thank you, Sheriff," James responded. "So, to what do we owe the pleasure?"

"Well, you may remember a couple of months ago when our little town was gearing up for the elections. Judge Lowry was running unopposed, but my post was up for a vote, along with a few city council seats and the Mayor's position. Then, when it all went to hell, everything just got put on hold.

"My opponent, Mr. Grimes, was up in Colorado Springs when it hit; and well, somehow, he's back and wants an election.

"Judge Lowry and I see eye-to-eye on most things having to do with our town, but he thinks we need to have an election for Sheriff, more of a formality than anything else. Wants the townsfolk to have their say and gain their support for the future expansion of our town.

"Speaking with him yesterday, I mentioned there were good folks like you just outside the town limits who wouldn't be able to cast a vote and have your say.

"He's considering extending the city limits by 20 miles in each direction, to become effective immediately.

"In that scenario, would I be able to count on your votes?"

"Absolutely, Sheriff," said James, "and I think I can speak for all here as well." Everyone nodded in agreement.

"I would also ask that you, James, consider a run for a city council seat."

"You've got our votes, you can count on that, but as far as the council seat, I'm not sure I'd be the right man for the job," replied James.

"Just tell me you will think on it is all," said the Sheriff.

"Okay, I'll do that."

"One last thing," said Sheriff Johnson. "Judge Lowry and I both want to make our growing town a place where our citizens can feel safe. The Judge has decided not to waste valuable resources, including prolonged shelter, food, water, and medical supplies on those who choose to commit crimes in our town.

"The two men who attacked you and your family, Jason, as well as the gun thief dressed as a priest, and another man caught stealing chickens from a nearby ranch, will be hanged in the town square in three days' time."

"Hanged?" asked Lauren, with a shocked look on her face.

"Yes, Ma'am, and the Judge is requesting all able-bodied adults to bear witness to the proceedings.

"The structure will take a couple of days to erect. He thought about doing it on Saturday but didn't want to put a damper on the trading.

"I can expect you all to be there, except for maybe you?" he said, pointing at Jason.

"I suppose we could, but we've got the three little ones also," said James, pointing upstairs.

"No problem. We have that worked out. All children under age 15 will be in the schoolhouse with three of our best teachers. They need to be dropped off between 8 and 8:30 a.m., according to the Main Street clock.

"The sentencing will take place at 9 a.m. sharp, and we should be done by 9:30, I'm guessing."

"Who's going to do it?" asked Lauren. "I mean, who's going to pull the lever?"

"That will be me," said the Sheriff. "Thank you, Janice, for the coffee," he said as he stood. "I'll see you all on Wednesday.

"And James, give some thought about the council position. I could use a good man in that post."

They saw the Sheriff off and finished the morning chores.

"What's this about a city council position?" asked Janice over breakfast.

"Sheriff Johnson brought it up, and it's the last thing I want to do right now," answered James. "Let's take a ride around the perimeter of the property after breakfast, Jason. I want Chance to know the boundaries."

"Sounds good, and maybe you could teach me a few things about your gardens. I want to know as much as possible, so I can start pulling my weight around here."

"Sure thing," replied James, laughing. "I think we're going to get along just fine."

After riding the property, James told Jason he had a surprise for him.

On the far east side of the house was a green door, with the letters RT, and a red door with UG stenciled on the front.

"What's in there?" asked Jason. "Some kind of root cellar?"

"Well, yes and no," said James, with a laugh and a childlike grin. "This door here gives access to two of my favorite places on the property. The problem is, both have stairs. May be a while before I can show you."

"Unless you can help me," said Jason.

"Oh, no! Janice would kill me if I took you in there. She'd want your leg to be good and healed first."

"Your ranch, your call," said Jason, "but now you've got me intrigued, and I don't think the girls are expecting us back anytime soon."

"All right. I'll tell you what. We'll do the easy one first and see how it goes," said James, taking the padlock off the red door. "UG is for underground," he said, as he opened the creaking door. "Could use some WD-40," he added.

James shined the light down the stairwell. "Just two flights down, if you can manage, Jason."

"Give me your shoulder, James, and we should be all right."

After ten minutes, they made it to the bottom.

"Ready?" asked James, as he shined the light into the dark room below.

"Wow!" said Jason. "I was not expecting that… Is that what I think it is? Is that a still?"

"It is, and a highly functioning one at that. I had to fly a guy in from Tennessee to help me set it up properly. He used to work for a famous whisky maker you may have heard of before going out on his own. It's not as easy as it sounds to set up, but once it's done, it nearly runs itself."

"I'm surprised, because…well, with all the religious stuff you were telling me about, I mean."

"Janice and I are religious to the very core, and we're also Catholic. Show me a Catholic who doesn't have a drink from time to time," he added.

"What do you do with all this?" asked Jason.

"Well, we've been trading with the locals in the area for years. It's partly how we were able to afford this property and build the main house and barns. We started in a small camper for the first three years, after buying the property. All we had was the camper and this here still. I also worked in town part-time with a guy named David, who lives just up the mountain."

"I never got why people would buy moonshine over going to the liquor store," said Jason.

"Well, it's like this," replied James. "There's one liquor store in town, and when you go there, everyone knows your business. The city of Raton is not too far but still the same.

"So, do you head all the way up to Trinidad, or even Pueblo, to stock up or just come over here to our place? We've got better quality, prices, free taste tests like those fancy new micro-breweries, and complete anonymity."

"I see your point," said Jason.

"It's just simple economics," said James.

"Did you sell any at the swap meet yesterday?" asked Jason.

"Not a chance. I'm not sure how the Sheriff would like it, since things are getting pretty serious in town."

"Can I try a taste?" asked Jason, hoping he didn't overstep his bounds.

"Tell you what. If we can get you through the green door and up to the roof in one piece, I'll bring some up for us both."

"RT is rooftop?" asked Jason.

"That's it, and it's the best view in the valley. That's the God's honest truth. The only problem is it's three sets of stairs, plus the two we just came down."

"I'm game if you are," said Jason, with a grin.

Twenty minutes later, they were at the top of the stairs. James opened the door onto a rooftop patio, complete with 360-degree views of the property and surrounding farms, a barbecue grill, three lounge chairs, and an American flag flying at half-staff.

"This is incredible!" said Jason. "I've never seen anything like this view."

"Be right back," said James, disappearing into the stairwell.

Five minutes later he returned with an unmarked bottle, half full, and two glasses.

"Look who I found?" he said, pointing to Chance, who had followed him back up. "You know, Jason, ranch work is hard and it's good to take a break now and then. Truth is, I haven't been up here in more than two months.

"Look around. What do you see, Jason?"

"Well," he replied, "It's the only place so far that I can see the whole property. I'm guessing it's a good vantage point for a security perimeter."

"That's right," replied James. "It's the most peaceful spot on this property but may save our lives one of these days."

"I can drink to that!" said Jason, taking the full glass James handed him.

Two hours later came a voice from the front of the house. "Time for lunch!" as the bell was rung on the front porch.

"That may be a problem," said Jason.

The boys had got to talking, and James made two more trips down to the UG over the last couple hours.

"I'm kind of drunk," Jason added, "and it was hard enough getting up the stairs sober with my bad leg."

"I'll go down and get us some lunch to eat up here," said James. "I'll let the ladies know we're talking. I won't lie to Janice if she catches wind about it, but if she doesn't ask, I'm not volunteering to get my head chewed off!"

"Well, good luck," said Jason, as James disappeared down the stairs.

Fifteen minutes later, Jason heard loud footsteps on the stairs. *This can't be good*, he thought, as he reached for his shotgun.

Janice and Lauren stormed out from the top of the stairs and looked at Jason, with their arms crossed, not saying a word.

Chance, at Jason's feet, laid his head down and sighed deeply.

"Where's James?" asked Jason, just now realizing he was slurring his words.

"He would be the one passed out on the couch in the living room," said Janice.

"It's noon, and you're drunk?" asked Lauren, clearly upset.

"Lauren, honey, I'm sorry. I just got carried away and…"

"And *what?*" she asked sharply.

"This is my fault," Jason replied. "James didn't want me to come up here with my bad leg, and I asked him for a sample of his alcohol."

"What do I tell the girls?" asked Lauren. "Daddy's stuck on the roof because he got drunk before lunch?"

"No. I don't want them to see me like this."

"They're upstairs eating lunch. Let's get you into the house. Janice, can you help me get him down the stairs?"

"Sure, Lauren," she replied.

They got him off the roof, without much help from Jason.

"You may as well take the other couch over there by James, so you boys can sleep this off," said Janice. "We will talk about it later today," she added.

Jason had that sense of panic a child has when they are waiting for the punishment to come at a later time.

As he laid his head down and fell asleep, he knew one thing. He would cover for James and take the blame, no matter what.

Hours later, Jason awoke to see James sitting across the room from him on the other couch.

"I'm sorry, Jason. That never should have happened."

"No. I started it by asking for a taste right after breakfast," replied Jason. "Who does that?"

James laughed. "You know we're in deep with the ladies, right?"

"Yeah, I know. I got an earful as they were helping me off the roof, with a promise of more to come. Weird, though… I don't have a hangover!" said Jason.

"Another reason I have so many loyal customers," replied James.

"Can we find the ladies?" asked Jason. "I want to get this over with as soon as possible."

"Yeah, me too. It's the waiting that's hard, as Tom Petty once said."

"Okay. Here's the deal," said Janice as she and Lauren came out of the kitchen, overhearing our conversation.

"What you boys did was stupid and irresponsible. It can't happen again."

"Agreed?" asked both Janice and Lauren.

"Yes, ma'am," they both answered.

"You're both on duty tomorrow night," added Janice, "while Lauren and I get our break on the rooftop. I'm guessing you would rather have wine, though?" she asked Lauren. "Me too," said Janice, as Lauren nodded her head.

"I don't believe we will be passing out, so you guys can rest easy," added Lauren.

"We made a mistake, Jason, and things like that will happen now and then... I guess we're on dinner duty," continued James.

"At the very least, I'm sure," replied Jason, with both chuckling. "Seriously, though, the rooftop is a high vantage point. Is there anything we can do to secure it, in case we need to mount a defense?"

"I'm glad you asked," replied James. "Remind me to show you the plans I've been drawing up."

* * * * * * *

Chapter Twelve ~ Second Chances Ranch Weston, Colorado

"Woof! Woof!" was the sound at the front door, with a low growl. Chance was crouched down and fixed on the front door.

"Rap! Rap! Rap!" was followed by a loud "Bang!" on the front door.

"Janice, get Lauren and the girls upstairs *now*," said James in a low but firm voice. He looked through the peephole but could only make out shapes in the dark.

"Okay, Jason. I need you to cover the front door. It's reinforced and should hold if they try to break in… I'm going around the side of the house," he said quietly. "Whatever happens, don't open the door."

"Okay," replied Jason, "but be careful."

James slipped out the side door with his night-vision goggles on. *Careful*, he thought. *They got here in the dark, so they either have night vision or a flashlight.*

As he came around the side of the house, he kept close to the outer wall, walking in complete silence. Rounding the corner, he saw that the two men were armed, both with deer rifles.

He raised his twelve-gauge slowly, hoping he wouldn't have to use it. He secretly wished they would go away but knew it would not happen.

Okay, talking to himself. *Let's get this done.*

"How can I help you, folks?" James asked, shining his flashlight into their faces.

One of the men and the woman raised their hands to shield their eyes from the light. The other man ducked down, raising his rifle.

"Lower your weapon," yelled James, "so we can talk."

"You won't shoot?" the man asked, pointing his rifle to the ground.

"Why are you here?" asked James.

"Well," the man replied. "We heard you are the man with the moonshine, and since the liquor store in town won't take any cards or money, we're ready to buy."

"Where did you hear that?" asked James, skeptically. Over the years, James had limited his customers to a select group that he trusted to keep his operations confidential.

"The old guy, Winters," he said.

"No, it was Whitters," said the woman, still crouched down.

James knew him well, having been a loyal customer for years. He also knew there was only one way his old friend would give up information about his business.

"You have been misinformed," said James bluntly. "Please get off my property."

"No, we're sure," said the woman. "It was the last thing he said."

"Now, you'll be giving us what we want, or you can join the old man…and his wife," added one of the men.

That was enough for Jason, as he heard the conversation through the front door.

He swung the door open quickly, shotgun raised, and fired on the trio as Chance charged out.

James added fire from the side of the house, without a return shot from the intruders.

Seconds later, there was only silence. Then came a whimper from Chance.

"Cover me," said James to Jason, as he approached the downed trio.

Shining his flashlight, it was clear they were no longer a threat, and no medical intervention would help.

"I'm sorry, ma'am," he said out loud. "I never meant for this to happen…"

Chance lay by the front door, panting, with blood under his hindquarters.

"Oh, boy. I'm sorry, Chance," said James. He kneeled to check his new companion and was met by a lick on his cheek.

"Hold on, buddy. We're going to get you fixed up."

He lifted the dog, with Jason's limited help, and brought him into the kitchen, calling for Janice to bring her medical kit.

She ran downstairs with her medical bag in hand and saw their new addition whimpering in pain.

"Hold him, James, while I check him," she said.

An hour later, she had Chance stable. His right back leg had been cast, and nearly 30 12-gauge pellets were pulled from his hindquarters.

Even the girls pitched in to help. "You won't find a tougher dog than him," said Janice.

"Or sweeter," added Candice, petting him on the head.

It had been a long day, but James didn't want to leave three bodies at his front door for the girls to see.

He pulled Jason aside. "I'll get the tractor and get them off the front stoop," he said. "They will keep in the barn for now. Tomorrow we will decide what to do with them."

The ladies and girls went to bed, with Jason and Chance waiting up for James.

* * * *

"Let's keep your girls inside tomorrow," said James, as he returned. "They don't need to see any more blood."

"Thanks, James. I agree," replied Jason. "I'll help with anything you need in the morning to get things cleaned up."

Both men spent the next half hour answering questions from their wives.

Thankfully, thought Jason, *the girls have gone to sleep quickly.*

Morning came before long, with the girls being informed that this would be an inside day.

After morning chores, James told Jason he would be taking a short trip with Janice to old man Whitter's place. He was pretty sure what he would find but had to see it for himself.

"All right, Jason. You're on duty. Don't go opening that front door again. There's too much to lose in this house," he added, pointing up the stairs at the girls' room.

"I know," replied Jason. "I'm sorry about that. I just panicked, I guess."

James and Janice headed out on the four-wheeler for the short two-mile trek to the Whitter ranch.

"Is Mr. Whitter's wife still alive?" asked Janice on their ride out. "I haven't seen her in a while."

"Well, I was up here a couple months ago, and she was still alive at that point. He just said she had some trouble getting around on her own."

They turned off the road and through a wide-open gate to the Whitter Ranch.

"Real slow, honey," said Janice. "I've never seen the gate open before and I don't see his dogs out."

Cautiously pulling up in front of the house, James could see the front door halfway open.

"Cover me, Janice. I'm not sure who's in there."

As he approached the door, he was taken back by the sickening odor coming from the house.

Quietly, without calling out, James walked the main house, clearing each room. His bandana covering his nose was barely enabling him to continue. There were cans, jars, snack wrappers, and empty bottles of various kinds of alcohol scattered across the floor of the living room and kitchen. Pill bottles were lined up on the fireplace mantle, all empty, with the first one reading Hydrocodone/APAP/ Quantity 60.

He noticed four moonshine bottles, which he had sold the farmer not long ago, laying empty on the floor. *They didn't get any information off those bottles*, he thought, since he had not ever marked a single jar with his or his ranch's name.

James hesitated as he reached what he thought was the master bedroom. He still couldn't tell where the overwhelming smell was coming from.

The master door was shut. He slowly turned the knob and found it unlocked. Opening the door, he gasped, staring at an old antique bed with its white duvet cover nearly completely covered in dried blood.

More stains were plastered across all four walls of the small room. There was no sign of his old friend or his wife.

This is the last room in the house, thought James, feeling sad for them.

"Think!" he said out loud. "They wouldn't have buried them and left a mess like this, would they?"

He was silent, hearing only the sound of his rapidly beating heart.

A low, almost inaudible buzzing sound was coming from the kitchen. *I must have missed that before when I cleared the space*, he thought.

He approached cautiously, fixed on a small white door just off the side of the kitchen.

The smell was getting stronger, and the buzzing sound was coming from behind the door.

He raised his flashlight, not having to turn it on thus far. Shotgun at the ready, he slowly turned the knob. With the door opening outward, he was nearly overcome with the smell of death.

He shined his flashlight down the short staircase and was promptly hit in the face and torso by a swarm of large black flies, knocking him back and unintentionally causing his shotgun to discharge.

Without a word, Janice came through the front door, crouching low.

"I'm okay," said James aloud, knowing Janice would be coming in behind him after hearing the shot.

"The house is clear," he added, shining his light into the basement. "Janice, honey, I don't think you want to see this."

"Yes, I need to, if only to make sense of what happened last night."

Now with each shining their flashlights into the basement, they saw their friend and his wife in a pile at the bottom of the stairs, with what appeared to be the bodies of their four dogs. The flies still there were mulling about, with no desire to escape the dark room.

"I have to take a closer look," said James, as he walked down the stairs. "It looks like they had their throats cut, but I'm not sure about the dogs. I think they have been here for a while, at least a week."

"So those people that came to our house killed them and just stayed here until the food and liquor ran out?!" asked Janice, in disbelief.

"It appears so, honey. I know my old friend wouldn't tell them about us unless it was life and death for him and his wife."

"What was the shot for?" she asked.

"Sorry, it was an accident," James replied. "I got hit by the flies when I opened the basement door."

"I'm so sorry for those two," replied Janice.

Kneeling together, they said a prayer for their dear friends.

"Let's go home and talk with Jason and Lauren about the next step," said James. "We need to all be on the same page before we go into town in the morning.

"I want to give these two a proper burial," he continued, pointing down the stairs. "I'm just not sure how to approach it all with Sheriff Johnson."

They left the house, closing both the basement and front door behind them. James was happy to have the wind blowing in his face on the ride home.

* * * *

Reaching the ranch, James and Jason cleaned the front porch.

Filling him in on the scene found at the Whitters' house, he added, "You did the right thing last night, Jason. May have saved my life. Let's get a plan together, so we're ready next time.

"I'm sorry to get on you about the front door, but I spent my time and a bit of money to make it formidable for any attack. If we open it, we've lost that defense."

"I know," replied Jason. "I get it, and it won't happen again.

"Chance woke up while you guys were gone."

"Janice checked on him every couple of hours last night," said James. "She said he looks good and should recover soon."

"He ate two bowls of food this morning," said Jason, "so I guess that's a good sign of recovery."

The front porch was scrubbed with soap and water. While it wouldn't pass a DNA test, it was clean to anyone just looking at it.

Lunch was served, and it was decided that Janice and Lauren would have their little wine party inside and not on the roof tonight, as previously planned.

The adults were able to talk in the afternoon, as the girls played hide-and-seek throughout the house.

It was agreed that they would bring the three bodies to town tomorrow to show the Sheriff. James didn't want him looking around his ranch if he could help it.

The story was simple. They came up with rifles, looking for food, and threatened us after eluding to killing Mr. Whitter and his wife.

James and Janice would relay the story of their trip to the Whitters' house, citing what they had observed, and ask how to proceed.

The night was quiet, with the ladies getting their time to relax upstairs while James, Jason and the girls read stories from the Bible.

Chance was happy, with the girls barely leaving his side all day.

* * * * * * *

Chapter Thirteen ~
Weston, Colorado

James was up early to load the three intruders into the back of the trailer. Covering them with heavy tarps, he hoped to conceal them from both the girls and anyone in town until he could tell his story.

"I don't like leaving the ranch unattended, but the Sheriff will want us all there.

"Chance should detour anyone hoping to come into the house with a good bark or two. Plus, everyone in and out of town now knows about the hangings, and I can't imagine they would be trying to loot while that was happening," he told Jason.

They all loaded on the tractor and trailer at around 7 a.m., near as James could tell, judging by the sunrise. "I'd rather us be early than late," said Janice, and all agreed.

The road this morning was the busiest James had seen it since the lights went out.

"It seems the good Sheriff got the word out to all the out-of-towners," James said.

"Well, I'll bet that also comes with a lot of extra votes in the upcoming election," added Janice.

"Do you think the judge will expand the town limits?" asked Lauren.

"Honestly," replied James, "I think it's already been decided and only he and the Sheriff knew about it. I want to wait until after the proceedings before I talk to him about these guys," he added, motioning to the back of the trailer.

"About us?" came a voice from the trailer. "No, sweetie," said Lauren. "Not you."

"What are we going to do in town?" the girls wanted to know.

"You're just going to spend an hour or two at the school, so you can meet some other kids your age," said Jason.

"That's fun! I miss reading in school," said Carla.

"Not me!" replied Jenna.

"Well, maybe we can try and find you girls some books at the next swap meet on Saturday," said Janice.

"Just because you're not in school doesn't mean you can't learn," said Lauren. "That would be wonderful, Janice," she added, with a smile.

James was now in a long line of tractors, with a few old trucks and ATVs, all heading into town.

"I'd say this trip is pretty safe so far," James commented, as he waved to a few people he knew.

"There's safety in numbers," said Janice. "I guess that's the Sheriff's point." All nodded their heads.

The one-room schoolhouse was bustling with children of all ages. Sheriff Johnson and his opponent, Mr. Grimes, were both greeting families as they arrived, each wearing their voting pins on their shirt. It was becoming apparent to most that Mr. Grimes was the underdog in this race.

"It's hard to beat a sitting Sheriff," James said quietly to Janice, "and I'm guessing his opponent is just now hearing about expanding the city limits."

"All is fair in politics, even now," she replied.

"Great to see you," said the Sheriff, shaking hands with the adults. "I can assure you your little ones will be safe here," he said to Jason, pointing at his three deputies in front of the school. "No one's allowed in but the teachers and children."

"Could I get a word with you after the…well…the..."

"The hangings?" asked the Sheriff.

"Yes," replied James.

"Sure. About the council position, I hope?"

"It's another matter, sir."

"Okay," said the Sheriff. "Stop by the station about 9:45 and we'll talk."

James, Janice, Jason, and Lauren made it to the square by 8:30, according to the ticking town clock. Last preparations were made to the gallows and hanging platform.

The convicted men were not in sight, and Lauren was uneasy about seeing the men who attacked them. Would they speak to her or just stare? She was starting to sleep a little easier. Well, until a couple of nights ago, that is.

"Will they be covered when they come out?" she asked out loud. "I mean, will they have those black hoods on?"

"Not at first," replied James. "They will be sentenced first and may even be allowed to say some last words, but I can't be sure about that."

At 8:50, Judge Lowry and Sheriff Johnson climbed the stairs to the hanging platform. The crowd of nearly 500 quieted as they reached the top.

"Thank you, good folks, for coming out today," started the Sheriff in a booming voice, needing no microphone. "We understand it was a bit of a trip for some of you.

"Our great Judge Lowry," he said, gesturing to the man beside him, "and I want nothing less than the safety of our townspeople in this new and unforgiving land we were handed only a couple of weeks ago.

"As most of you know, our Federal Government has declared martial law, giving the power to the US military. And in their absence, it is passed down to local law, including judges and law enforcement."

"I know the military rules during martial law, but I'm not sure it gets passed down to local law enforcement in their absence," James said quietly to Jason.

"They don't know, either," replied Jason, waving his arm across the crowd.

"The four coming before you today," continued the Sheriff, "have been tried and sentenced by our good Judge here for various crimes. Our town is sure to be safer when they are gone. Judge Lowry would now like to say a few words."

"Thank you for coming, folks. I'll talk as loud as I can and hope you all can hear me," called out the Judge.

"First, most of you I see are from town, and the rest have been outside the town limits. By order, I declare our town borders to be expanded by 20 miles in all directions, effective immediately. This expansion will give most of you previously outside the limits added protection by our law enforcement and the ability to vote in our upcoming town elections.

"Second, I have asked for you all to be here today to bear witness to today's proceedings, as I hope it will become known far and wide that we do not condone criminal acts of any kind in our town.

"And last, but certainly not least, I want to invite you all to our second swap meet, commencing this Saturday and every one after—weather permitting, of course. The times and rules are posted on the front door of the courthouse.

"Let us begin," he announced, and the four men shackled by their wrists and ankles were brought out from the jailhouse, walking single file.

Flanked by deputies, they were led up the stairs slowly. Two of the men needed help when their knees buckled. Reaching the platform, they were placed across in a line.

Judge Lowry stood on the ground in front of the platform and addressed the sentenced men in a loud voice that most townsfolk could hear.

"You four have been tried and convicted in my court. After careful review of all available evidence, I find you guilty of crimes ranging from assault to thievery against citizens of our fair town.

"The sentence for each of you is death by hanging until you are dead.

"We are a God-fearing town, and as such you are each granted one minute to pray or make amends to your Maker."

No man spoke out loud, but one moved his lips, apparently in prayer, with his head bowed and eyes closed.

Lauren had been staring at the man who attacked her, as she could never forget his face. He seemed to be scanning the large crowd over the last couple of minutes. Their eyes met, and Lauren jumped as the man smiled and blew a kiss with his still shackled hands in front of him.

Jason saw this, his face turning red.

"You son of a bitch," Lauren said under her breath. She looked at Jason, but he was gone.

"Excuse me. Pardon me, ma'am," said Jason, as he made his way to the front of the crowd on his crutches.

Most of the crowd had their eyes on him as he reached the platform, now looking up at his wife's attacker nearly ten feet above him. "I'm as close as I can get!" he yelled up at the man.

James had followed Jason up front and put a hand on his shoulder. "Okay. We're okay," he said. "Justice will be served."

James met the Sheriff's eyes and nodded, indicating he had this under control.

"Blindfolds," called the Judge to the deputies. Each man was fitted with a black hood, with each noose tightened securely on their necks.

"May God have mercy on your souls," said Judge Lowry, as he nodded to Sheriff Johnson.

The Sheriff, with his hand on the drop lever, said a quick, silent prayer. "Forgive me, Lord," as he swiftly pulled it down, felling the four men.

They fell about five feet. *A standard drop-hanging*, thought James, having studied the various hanging techniques a while back. The standard drop was long enough to ensure the neck was broken, but not so long to risk decapitation and turn off the large crowd of potential voters. He had spent nearly a week's full of nights after dinner researching this, after a chance Google search when looking for "hanging plants."

Two of the men were motionless, and the other two were struggling. Jason's man took longer. "That could be me," he whispered to James, as he turned and headed back to Lauren.

James followed him back, and they all headed for the rear of the crowd.

"We're done here," announced James, as they walked away. The ladies picked the girls up from the schoolhouse, as James and Jason waited outside the Sheriff's office.

Nearly thirty minutes later, Sheriff Johnson walked into his office. James and Jason followed him inside.

"Well, how did we do?" the Sheriff asked James.

"I'm not sure what you're asking, sir," James replied.

"About the hangings. It was our first one, and the Judge and I had to do some research on it. Turns out there are a number of traditional ways to hang. There's the short drop, the standard drop, the long drop, and the suspension hanging. Each has a different set of criteria for the gallows or platform. Drop heights and body weights must be carefully calculated to ensure the final result.

"One of your guys took a full 15 minutes to die, according to the town doctor."

"I had done some research on that a while back," said James. "I was searching online for 'hanging plants,' and it autocorrected to 'hanging plans.' Interesting read, though."

"Well, the Judge and I had to do it the old-fashioned way, so it took a bit longer to find the books on the subject."

"Do you think there will be more of those in the future, Sheriff?" asked Jason.

"I believe so," he replied. "Now, what can I help you gentlemen with today?"

"Well," started James, wanting to do most of the talking. "We had an altercation at our property a couple of nights ago." He went on to explain how the three had threatened them, wanting food (leaving out anything to do with the still). He told him about he and Janice's trip to the Whitters' place and what they had found.

"I always liked those folks. Didn't make it up to their place the other day, but sounds like it wouldn't have made a difference, from what you're telling me. I was counting on their votes, though.

"It's a shame about those two. I'll run it by the Judge later today, but I think we're okay on this. You're not the first of your neighbors to run into something like this, you know.

"Let's get the bodies dropped behind the station and I'll figure out what to do about old man Whitter and his wife. It would be good to have them up here in the town cemetery, but from the sounds of it, cremation may be a better way. Can't have a contaminated house getting people sick around here."

The talk all the way home this time was from the girls. They were so excited to meet some other kids their age. Even Candice was now apparently eager to learn.

"And the teachers said they were all welcome to come back each Saturday to the school for learning," explained Jenna in an excited, high-pitched voice.

"Can we, Mommy? Can we?" they all asked, with hopeful faces.

"We'll see, girls," replied Lauren.

"Wouldn't be too much trouble," whispered James to Jason. "I'm quite sure the Sheriff will make the schoolhouse the safest place in town."

"I don't doubt that, but I'd hate to put you and Janice out, if you weren't going to be trading, that is."

"Rest assured, we will be trading every week, so no worries there," Janice piped up, overhearing the conversation.

They paused just outside the locked gate to their property, and both James and Jason observed the property for several minutes before pulling in.

"All good, Chance?" asked Janice, petting him on the head as they opened the door. He barked once and stretched as only a dog will do after a long nap.

Early in the afternoon, with the girls playing outside under careful watch, James saw Sheriff Johnson's truck pass by the property without slowing. He could make out one passenger up front and another two in the bed.

"Guess they're checking out the Whitters' place," said Janice. "Think we should meet them up there?" she asked James.

"Naw. I'm already getting cozier than I'd like with the good Sheriff. The last thing I need is him and his deputies wanting to spend the weekend on our ranch. I'm sure he'll let us know if they need any help."

"Mr. James!" came a worried voice from Jenna an hour later. "Look at all the smoke!" she said, pointing down the road.

"It looks like we have our answer," said James out loud, to no one in particular. "Cremation it is... Rest in peace, old friends. Rest in peace."

Sheriff Johnson and two of his men stopped just outside James' gate on their way back from the Whitter place. James walked down to meet them, hoping they wouldn't ask to come in.

"Well, it's done," said the Sheriff as they shook hands. "I was hoping to bring them back to the cemetery," he added, "but it was too much of a mess.

"It looks like the killers hung around for a while, don't you think, James?"

"That's what it looked like to me, sir."

"We found a lot of things strewn about the floor," continued the Sheriff. Some cans, wrappers, pill bottles, and a few of these," holding up a mason jar he pulled from a plastic Ziplock bag.

James felt a knot in his stomach, recognizing the jar from his still.

"It smells like some sort of moonshine," said the Sheriff, as he put it up to his nose. "But we didn't find any equipment in the house or the basement. Doesn't that seem odd?" he asked.

"I don't know," replied James. "Everything seems odd the last couple of weeks."

Sheriff Johnson laughed out loud at that. "Well, I guess you're right, old friend. Have a good night," he said, tipping his hat to Janice as she sat on the porch.

James walked slowly back to the house as they drove away.

"Upstairs girls," called Lauren, as James climbed the porch stairs.

"What was that about?" asked Janice, with Jason and Lauren looking on.

"I don't exactly know, honey, but he had one of my jars in a plastic bag and was asking questions about it."

"Do you think he knows?" asked Jason.

"I don't know. But either way, it's not good," replied James.

The night was restless for James, as he found his way to the kitchen after midnight. He wasn't too surprised to see Jason at the dining room table.

"Guess I'm not the only one who couldn't sleep," said Jason.

"We need a plan. How about a glass of Scotch?" asked James.

"Maybe just one," replied Jason. "We need a plan. How about a glass of Scotch?" asked James.

"Maybe just one," replied Jason.

James poured two generous glasses and took out a pen and paper. With his flashlight on dim, he made two columns: best-case scenario and worst-case, separated by a line straight down the middle of the page.

"All right, Jason. I'll start," he said.

"Best case, the Sheriff is just fishing, and that's as far as it goes.

"Worst case, he ties the bottle back to me.

"Your turn."

"Okay," replied Jason, "assuming the worst from yours.

"Best case, he does tie it back to you but doesn't think it's a big deal in this next-world.

"Worst case, he considers it a crime committed in his town."

"That's what I was thinking," said James. "Guess we didn't need a tally sheet, after all."

"James," said Jason. "Lauren, the girls and I owe everything to you and Janice. You have our unwavering support, whatever you decide."

"I know, and we appreciate that. I'm just not sure if we should tear the whole thing down tomorrow and bury it, or see what happens.

"Maybe we could take a trip into town tomorrow and talk to Sheriff Johnson. He's got an important election coming up, and maybe there's something we could do to help him out," he added.

"Janice can stay here with Lauren and the girls. She's a crack shot, and with her and Chance around, I'm not worried about being gone for a few hours."

"It sounds like a plan to me," said Jason. "At least we will know where we stand."

The girls were up early to check on Chance. He was improving every day, and it was apparent that he loved the attention.

James dressed, and as he descended the stairs caught a glimpse of the three petting Chance. He took a minute to give thanks in prayer.

Lord, this is everything Janice and I ever wanted. Please watch over her, Lauren, Jason, their girls, and Chance.

After breakfast, Jason and James headed out on the tractor for town.

The Sheriff's office was quiet this morning. James and Jason found the door open, with the Sheriff and Judge Lowry talking inside.

"Hello, James," said Sheriff Johnson, standing to shake his hand.

"I'm sorry, I forgot your name," he said to Jason.

"It's Jason, sir."

"That's it! And you both remember Judge Lowry?"

"Of course," answered James for them both.

"We were just talking about you, James. Isn't that a coincidence?"

"Well, Sheriff, I guess it is," James replied, not wanting to appear uneasy.

"Sheriff Johnson filled me in on the goings-on up at the Whitter place. It's a damn shame what happened to those folks," said the Judge. "It sounds like they left quite a mess behind," he added, reaching for the bottle James recognized, still in the plastic bag.

"No sign of any equipment, the Sheriff told me. How about you, James? Did you see anything when you were up there?"

"No, sir," he replied. "Just the same senseless killings…and quite a mess, I'm afraid."

"You two were neighbors, isn't that right?" the Judge continued.

"Well, sir, they were up the road a couple of miles from our ranch."

"As you know from the other day," the Judge said, "we are very interested in things that are happening in our town here," gesturing with his right hand in a semicircle. "And we get concerned if it appears there may be something out of the ordinary happening here," turning the jar from side to side, studying it. "Especially now, as I have increased the city boundaries by 20 miles in each direction. I believe that would now include your ranch, James."

"Yes, that's correct," replied James, now more than a little uneasy.

"I've never been up to your place, but the Sheriff here says it's quite impressive. Must have cost a pretty penny to build and keep it running before the lights went out."

James made a point not to look in Jason's direction.

It's not often that one gets interrogated by a sitting Judge and acting Sheriff at the same time, he thought. The slightest misstep could prove disastrous, and he was glad he was the only one doing the talking.

"We came this morning to see if we may be able to help with the upcoming election," said James in a Hail-Mary attempt to change the subject.

"Funny you should bring that up," said Judge Lowry. "I hear you are considering a city council position. Is that correct, James?"

"Yes, sir," he said quickly, now wishing he could take it back. "I mean, the Sheriff asked me to consider it."

"Funny you should bring that up," said Judge Lowry. "I hear you are considering a city council position. Is that correct, James?"

"Yes, sir," he said quickly, now wishing he could take it back. "I mean, the Sheriff asked me to consider it."

"I see," replied the Judge. "And what did you decide?" he asked bluntly.

"That's just it, Judge. I need to talk it over with my wife. We've just been so busy around the ranch lately."

"Would you boys give us a minute?" asked the Judge as more of a statement.

"Sure, we'll be right outside when you're ready," replied James.

As they walked outside, both men had a pit in their stomachs. "What is going on?" asked Jason in a low voice.

"I think I was playing some chess here," replied James. "At least I hope so."

"Should we go back to the ranch?" asked Jason.

"No. We need to find out what the angle is. If we leave now, we will be looking over our shoulders every day," James replied.

Nearly ten minutes later, the call came. "Come on back inside, gentlemen.

"It seems the excellent Sheriff here finds you trustworthy and like-minded. We would like to have you run for Mayor of our fair town.

"The position would put you third in command, once the elections are official and the Sheriff here retains his second place in our hierarchy.

"I think you should talk it over with your lovely wife and give us your answer tomorrow," he exclaimed, setting the moonshine jar back on the table.

James' head was spinning, and he was feeling nauseous. Jason put his arm on James' shoulder and spoke for the first time since they had arrived.

"We will see you back here tomorrow," he said, shaking hands with each of them.

They were halfway home when James finally spoke. "Time for another list, I guess. Except this time the stakes are sky-high."

* * * * * * *

Chapter Fourteen ~ Weston, Colorado

James and Jason pulled into the Second Chances Ranch just before lunch.

Janice and Lauren were waiting anxiously to hear about the meeting in town.

"I need a minute, Janice," said James, as he told Jason to fill the ladies in on what he knew.

"What's wrong with my husband?" asked Janice. "I've never seen him like this before."

Jason did his best to fill them in on the meeting with the Judge and Sheriff. When he finished, Janice knew why her husband was conflicted.

James emerged from the back of the house with a confidence Janice hadn't seen since the lights went out.

"I'm going to do it," he announced. "I'm going to be the Mayor of Weston, Colorado. It's the only way forward for us now. I'll be third in charge, and I don't see as I have much choice."

Janice was both shocked and pleased, knowing things had changed and that laying low was no longer an option.

"Won't there be an election?" she asked, confused.

"I suppose so, honey, but I'm sure it would only be a formality. Unless Jason here wants to run against me," he said, joking.

"No, sir," Jason replied, laughing. "I'm quite sure you're the best man for the job."

"I'm sorry I didn't consult you, honey," said James, reaching out his hand to Janice. "But it's the way it must be. The only alternative is to run for the hills, and I like our chances here far better," he added.

"That's true," she agreed. "We ran once and it's not an option anymore," pointing upstairs towards the girls.

"I guess I've got my first Deputy Mayor," pointing at Jason.

"Yes, sir," he replied, while Lauren pulled at his arm. "We're in this together," he said aloud but looking squarely at her.

Chance barked, and the girls ran downstairs, wanting to know everything about the trip to town. After a brief explanation to the girls, all they wanted to know was if Daddy and Mr. James were going to get a gold badge, like the Sheriff.

"I don't think so, honey," their father replied, "but I'm sure we will get some kind of pin or plaque, at the very least."

With a return trip planned for tomorrow, the adults let the girls play out front under watchful eyes.

"I'll have some conditions," James announced…"about the position, I mean."

"I thought you might," added Janice, smiling.

"Number one," he continued. "We will be staying here, since we are now technically inside the town limits. I won't have us watched over every move we make.

"Number two: I'll only be in town no more than three days in a week, which will include our trade day on Saturdays.

"Number three: Chance gets to tag along whenever he wants. Right, boy?"

A woof and tail wag came from a still-worn-out dog.

"Sound good, Jason?"

"I think it's a small price to pay to keep everything you have here. And, like I said before, we're here to support you and Janice 100%. Right, honey?" It was clear to Jason that Lauren was starting to come around.

He took her aside and whispered, "We're a lifetime ahead of where we were when they found us. I always expected we would need to do more to earn our keep. This is our chance to give back to James and Janice, and I will be someone with influence in the town. Besides, I look pretty good in uniform," he said, smiling and tapping her on the butt.

Lauren blushed just before the girls asked their daddy why he was spanking Mommy.

"I think she had a mosquito on her behind," he replied, now with everyone laughing.

"Yep, I got him, all right," he said, running his fingers together. "Wait! I think I see another one" he joked, now laughing even harder.

He and the girls chased a now playful Lauren around the house, waving their arms.

"Don't you dare!" said Janice, as James held his hand out to the side, doubled over, laughing. Chance was barking and wagging his tail. *All seems right in this next world, at least for today*, she thought. The rest of the afternoon was fun and lighthearted, with everyone relaxing on the front porch.

"I almost forgot about my buddy David and his friend, who was going to deliver the guns," James blurted out, just now remembering that's how they met Jason. No one replied.

Feeling a bit awkward, he continued. "I mean, we may have to take a trip up there before long is all. Guess I can always get them on the radio first."

"If the Judge expanded the city limits just 30 more miles, your buddy David would live in town," Janice pointed out.

"I will keep that in mind," replied James, fanning his face with his baseball cap.

"Still a Bull's fan?" asked Jason, pointing to his hat.

"You can take this boy out of Chicago, but you can't take the Bulls out of me," replied James.

"Never missed a game in all these years on TV. What do you think their chances are this year?" asked Janice, with a well-placed jab.

"Not great," replied James. "Maybe next season.

"It takes a lot to feed a big guy," he added, patting his stomach.

"I'm sure the players haven't touched a ball since the last game. Interesting how all their money won't do them any good now. Can't buy food with worthless credit cards and government cash."

Mountain House beef stroganoff was on the menu for dinner, and of course a huge garden salad.

* * * *

Jason and James headed back into town the next morning to give James' response to Judge Lowry and Sheriff Johnson.

"It's odd," said Jason, as their tractor slowly made the eight-mile trek.

"What's odd?" asked James.

"Well, the Sheriff hasn't even been voted in yet, and he's already making big plans with the Judge for the future of the town."

"Well," James responded, "when the two most powerful people in town hang four men in front of just about every citizen, it doesn't take much to go along with whatever they come up with.

"As long as the people are fed and safe, they'll look the other way. Let 'em be afraid and hungry; then you'll get to know what you're up against really quick.

"I'm guessing our new jobs will be the buffer between the people and the law," added James.

"What if they don't accept the terms?" asked Jason, seeming nervous to James.

"I thought about that last night," said James, "and if we can't reach a resolution, then we'll have no choice but to consider Plan B."

"Didn't know there was a Plan B!" said a surprised Jason.

"Ha! Then I won't worry you with Plan C...or D!" laughed James.

"Plan B," he continued, "would be a move up the mountain to join David's group. They have some firepower, and one Sheriff isn't going to come looking for us up there."

"I guess you've thought about this already," replied Jason.

"Janice and I always have a Plan B. Now it includes you, Lauren and your girls, and Chance, of course."

The town clock read 8:45 as they pulled up in front of the Sheriff's office.

"I hope they're here," said Jason in a low voice.

"I'm kind of nervous," he added, "and I want to get this over with."

"I get it," acknowledged James, "but keep in mind we need to take this slow, so we walk out of here with what we want. We won't get another chance at this."

"I understand, and I'll let you do most of the talking, if that's okay," said Jason.

They opened the front door and found both the Judge and Sheriff sitting right where they were the day before.

James had a thought that they never went home yesterday.

He subtly scanned the table for the moonshine jar from yesterday but didn't see it. *The point was already made yesterday*, he thought.

"Hello, gentlemen," said the Judge without standing.

"Good to see you both," said James, shaking the Sheriff's outstretched hand.

"Well," asked the Judge. "What's the verdict?"

"I thank you for your generous offer," started James, and for a moment almost added, "however I cannot accept it."

He caught the missing jar out of the corner of his eye, on the far side of the room, sitting on the floor just inside the closest jail cell.

The next words out of his mouth put a jab in the pit in his stomach, "Yes, sir, I am happy to serve."

A quick glance at Jason reminded him that he had conditions to be met.

"I have a couple of things I'll need to be comfortable doing my new job.

"First, I want Jason here to be my Deputy Mayor, with us both staying at my Ranch and coming to town three days per week, including trade Saturdays.

"Second, I want to have veto power over all decisions affecting the citizens of our town, barring any criminal activities that would render them in your court, sir."

Jason was feeling queasy and wondered if James overstepped his boundaries.

"Third, I want free trade on Saturdays, meaning I will contribute the percentage to this town as I have been but I can trade what I like, including my homemade moonshine," pointing to the jar in the nearest jail cell.

This statement got a smile from the Sheriff. Judge Lowry was stone-faced.

"And last, I'll have my dog Chance in the office most days."

As he finished, James felt secure and confident; he had proposed his terms and laid it all out on the table.

"You know, that jar over there," said the Sheriff, pointing into the cell, was full when we found it at the Whitters' house. He had it stashed way back in a kitchen cabinet, and the intruders just missed it, I guess."

"I'm guessing you poured it out," said James, pushing the line just a bit.

Jason could feel the tension in the room, and he felt sick.

"Excuse me," he blurted out as he ran out of the room. Outside the front door, he vomited on the side of the building.

"Can you give us a few minutes?" the Sheriff asked James.

"Sure, I'll be right outside."

James met a nervous Jason outside and tried to calm him down.

"Why did you do that?" asked Jason.

"Well, it's simple, really," replied James.

"You see, they've got me by the balls with that jar in there, and it's not going away. I'd like to know where we stand right now and not have to worry about it down the road."

"But what if they arrest us?" asked Jason.

"Then it's a bad day, and I miscalculated the situation. I'm confident, though, that we can come to an understanding.

"They need a Mayor they can trust to be the buffer between them and the people. I'm the best choice, and you're my pick for Deputy."

"Okay. That makes sense," Jason conceded.

Minutes later, they were asked back inside.

"You okay, Jason?" asked the Sheriff.

"Sure," he replied. "Just probably ate something wrong."

"You can never be too careful now," interjected the Judge.

"All right, James. I have discussed your concerns with the good Judge here, and we think it might just work.

"We, of course, cannot give you veto power over our citizens, but I'm guessing you knew that was a stretch. Everything else, though, I think we can work with. Understand, though, you're still number three in command."

"The liquid in the jar wasn't half bad," the Judge interjected. "What would you charge me for a case?"

"First one's on me, sir," replied James with a smile, knowing he just got the upper hand.

"All right," said Sheriff Johnson. "Let's get you ready for an election. We've got less than a week to prepare, and there are a couple of no-good drunks in the running.

"Let's meet here tomorrow…and dress appropriately," he added, gesturing towards Jason in a T-shirt and shorts.

"Good day to you both," said James, as they walked out the front door.

"Man, that was crazy," said Jason. "I wasn't expecting you to tell them about the moonshine."

"I didn't have a choice," replied James.

"They were using it against us, and I was not going to have that hanging over my head. Now it's in the open, and it looks like we can stay at the ranch a little while longer."

James headed back to his ranch with his head held high. He was determined to make the best of this situation and had negotiated for everything he really wanted.

"Did you expect them to give you veto power?" asked Jason.

"Nope," replied James. "I just always heard that in a big negotiation it's best to add something huge so they can shoot it down and hopefully agree to the rest of the terms. That's exactly what happened there today."

"How long will it take to make Judge Lowry's case of moonshine?"

"It's already done. I've got ten cases just waiting to be delivered somewhere.

"I guess eight will be going with us to market on Saturday, and one will be staying at the ranch with us."

Both men smiled, and relaxed just a bit on the trip home.

"Today was a good day," Jason announced, as they walked in the front door of their home.

"Tell us everything," said Janice, noticing a change in the two men standing before her and Lauren.

* * * * * * *

Chapter Fifteen ~
Second Chances Ranch
Weston, Colorado

James had two suits to choose from and Jason just one.

"Let's get you handsome men ready for an election," said Janice.

Lauren and Janice did their best to press Jason's pants and jacket that had gotten wrinkled in the move. James was lucky enough to have two pressed suits that he hadn't touched in years.

Offering one to Jason, they quickly agreed it would be too big for him, and hopefully pressing his suit would be easier than doing alterations on another.

Heating some water to boiling on the small camp stove, they carefully poured it, steaming, into an iron. Heating the bottom of the iron on the stove was tricky to get hot without leaving burn marks that could be transferred to clothing.

"I only hope they don't have to wear suits every day," said Lauren.

James and Jason did some work on the still and gathered the Judge's case of liquor.

"Should we bring one for the Sheriff?" asked Jason.

"Only if he asks," replied James. "I don't want us to appear too eager to please them. And mark my words, the next case for the good Judge will be paid for in coin or favor."

"Last day of freedom, ladies," announced James. "What shall we do?"

The girls all raised their hands to answer.

"Okay, Candice. Let's hear it."

"We want to have a picnic on the roof of the house with all of us." The other girls nodded in agreement.

"Think you can make it up there, Jason?" asked James.

"I'm sure he can," said Lauren with a smile. "I seem to remember him doing it once before," she added, as she poked her elbow into his side.

"Ow!" exaggerated Jason, as the girls laughed.

"I'm sure I can manage," he stated, "but I think Chance may have to sit this one out," pointing to the dog, yawning and rolling onto his side.

"Let's make a trip up there ahead of the group and stash some firepower," James whispered to Jason. "I'd hate to get stuck up there if someone came on the property unannounced."

This time Jason navigated the stairs with ease, stopping only a couple of times. Stashing the weapons outside the view of the girls, they headed back to help with lunch.

"We've got this, boys," the ladies announced. "It's been a long couple of days."

"Maybe you should relax with a glass of Scotch," said Janice, with Lauren nodding her head in agreement.

"Did that just happen, James?" asked Jason, both across the house from the kitchen.

"Is that a joke?" Jason started to ask, as Janice walked over with two large glasses full.

"Relax, boys. You've got a big day tomorrow."

"Happy wife, happy life," Jason said, toasting James. "To our new positions."

"It's going to be a wild ride," replied James, touching glasses.

James gave a grin and raised an eyebrow to Jason, as Janice walked back to the kitchen to continue making lunch. Jason held his hands out in an I-don't-know-what-just-happened-but-it's-okay gesture. The men relaxed on the couch and discussed what might happen tomorrow.

Lunch was a Wise brand freeze-dried hearty Chili Mac with Beef, picked out by the girls.

The view was spectacular from the rooftop, as always, and James realized he hadn't been up there in a while. The afternoon was light and fun, as was getting to be the norm lately.

Janice and James stayed up on the rooftop for a while to give Jason, Lauren and their girls some time alone in the house.

Janice stood on the rail, as James stood next to her with his arms around her waist.

"Funny how it took the end of electricity to give me everything I ever wanted," said Janice, smiling, with the wind blowing through her hair.

"Yeah, Mama. I feel the same way," he replied, kissing her on the forehead. "Our life will be different starting tomorrow, for better or worse..."

"I know, sweetie, and you need to keep a good eye out for Jason. I don't want the Judge and Sheriff getting over on him."

"What about me?" asked James jokingly.

"When a man has his back against the wall by two powerful men who just recently hung four people and he asks for veto power over most town decisions, and then proceeds to gain a new moonshine customer—who happens to be the Judge—then I'm not too worried about him," Janice continued.

James laughed out loud at this. "No, I guess you wouldn't worry much at all about a man like that.

"I love you, Mama. I knew the first day I saw you in the pizza parlor back in Chicago that you would be my wife forever, and you haven't disappointed me yet."

"Oh, really?" she replied. "Not yet?

"You're the lucky one James, that I found you." she added, twisting a classic Tom Petty song, this time turning the words around on her husband.

"I surely did, Mama. Yes, I surely did."

They stood looking out over the quiet new land, mostly in silence for another hour, James sipping his Scotch and Janice nursing a glass of Merlot.

"Today is a good day," whispered James, holding her tight.

"Here comes the storm," announced Janice, as she pointed to the east. They could see the streaks across the sky and smell the rain.

"There is no better smell in the world than a coming storm," James replied. Rain poured down just as they reached the front of the house. It rained all that night and into the next morning.

"You boys going to call in sick?" asked Lauren, smiling.

"Sorry honey," replied Jason. "It's not that kind of job."

* * * * * * *

Chapter Sixteen ~ Weston, Colorado

James and Jason packed their suits in large trash bags, opting to change at the Sheriff station.

The tractor was an open-top, and they were already getting soaked just a mile out from the ranch.

"I should have negotiated for an official Mayor truck," said James, this time not joking.

He felt uneasy that he hadn't thought to do that. *The Sheriff would no doubt have access to one somewhere*, he thought.

"You boys brought some extra clothes, I hope!" said the Sheriff, as they walked into his office.

"Yes, sir. It's just that the tractor doesn't have a roof on it is all," said James, hoping for a response about some other form of transportation.

"The Judge will be by soon, and we'll plan out the next few days," the Sheriff continued. "Did you remember the case for Judge Lowry?"

"Yes, Sheriff," replied James. "I'll be right back with it," heading out the door. Jason followed.

"I'm sure he can manage okay, Jason," the Sheriff insisted.

"Yeah, I guess so," he replied.

"So how long has James been operating that still on his ranch?" asked Sheriff Johnson.

"I…um…" Jason stammered. "I don't really know, sir."

"Is that a fact?"

"Yes, Sheriff. I've only known him for a little while. He and his wife took my family in, and it's meant the world to us."

"Hmmm. How did you boys meet again?" came the next question, as James walked back in with the case, overhearing the last question.

"They were neighbors up the road from us," answered James, to the delight of a nervous Jason.

"After it happened, we took an inventory of our close neighbors to see if everyone was okay. The same way we came upon old man Whitters and his poor wife. Anyway, Jason and his wife Lauren needed some help, and we were in need of a couple of extra hands on the ranch. That's about the meat of it, and it's worked out fine so far."

"That's right," chimed in Jason, nervously shaking his head up and down.

The Sheriff laughed deeply. "Well, boys, it looks like…"

"Sorry I'm late, gentlemen," announced Judge Lowry, shaking the rain off his jacket. "I was tidying up the courthouse for this afternoon's proceedings."

"What's happening this afternoon?" asked James, trying to remember if he should know already.

"The two in the back," the Judge said, pointing to the backside of the jailhouse. "Can't see them from here but they're back there, and they're a rowdy couple."

"A couple of guys?" asked Jason, confused.

"Nope. One man and a woman," interjected the Sheriff. "They were caught stealing vegetables from an old lady's garden."

"That's it?" asked Jason, quieting the room.

"Son," replied the Judge, "that's all it takes now to end up in my court."

"What's the punishment?" Jason continued.

"That, I don't know, since I haven't heard all the facts yet."

"Some kind of community service or probation, I assume," continued Jason.

"I believe we have an election to prepare for," said James, putting a hand on Jason's shoulder, with a nod and raised eyebrow that meant no more talking about this.

"We certainly do," Sheriff Johnson chimed in, pulling out a map of the county designating the newly declared town boundaries. "We've got one week until the elections, and we need to secure every vote. We will work north to south and then east to west."

"Are you going around town on that tractor out there?" asked the Judge, pointing to the front of the office.

"Yes, sir," James replied. It's all I've got except for a four-wheeler and a horse."

"I can take them around in my truck," the Sheriff offered.

"All right. That will do for now," replied the Judge, "but I'll see if we can find something more suitable for a Mayor and his Deputy."

The rain let up as they slowly worked the town, trying to spend only enough time as required with each prospective voter.

Both Sheriff Johnson and James were familiar to most citizens. Jason was not.

"We never expected you to run for Mayor" was the consensus James got from most they visited. The third house visited was one of James' longtime customers. The man appeared nervous, opening the door to both James and the Sheriff. He was calmed, hearing the news about the upcoming elections, and said, "We thought Mr. Grimes was running for Sheriff and the other guy with him for Mayor."

"He's been here? Mr. Grimes, I mean," asked the Sheriff, seeming agitated.

"Yes. He told us that you were stepping down and he was the only one left to choose."

Sheriff Johnson's face turned red, his jaw tightened, and he excused himself, quickly exiting the house.

"I'm sorry, James," his loyal customer said. "Did I say something wrong?"

"No. It's just the first we've heard of this," replied James.

James and Jason found the Sheriff in the truck, on the radio with Judge Lowry. The sounds of loud cursing escaped the barely cracked windows.

They waited several minutes until the Sheriff called them to move on.

The next few miles were awkward, as nobody spoke a word. Four out of the next five homes reported similar information when asked by Sheriff Johnson.

He was agitated, to say the least, but kept telling the citizens that there was a misunderstanding and he was seeking re-election as Sheriff in this great town. At each household he praised James, insinuating that they were a package deal.

Nearly ten hours later, they had visited 47 households and James felt good about most of their support.

Arriving back in town, they had about an hour to get home before complete darkness.

"I know we agreed to your working just three days per week, but I need you now," said the Sheriff. "We've got six days till the election, and we must campaign and set the record straight."

"After the election, we're three days, just like we agreed?" asked James, wanting to set the record straight.

"Absolutely. Will you do that for me, James?"

"I think we can help you out on this one," James replied, looking at Jason and getting a nod.

Headed home on the tractor, James' mind was running the possible scenarios.

"Crazy day, don't you think?" asked Jason.

"Yeah, we've got a few things to discuss," James replied. "We need to be cautious about how we interact with Sheriff Johnson and Judge Lowry. They are not our friends and most likely never will be.

"Your questions this morning, although valid, were pushing the envelope with the Judge, and not in a good way."

"I don't understand," replied Jason. "I saw you do that yesterday and it worked out well."

"The difference," replied James, "is that I set ground rules if we were to help them. Basically, they can get what they want if they give us what we want. What you did this morning was to question the Judge's decision on matters we have no control over."

"I get it, and I'm not saying you're wrong, but our first concern is always our families, no matter what," added James.

"You can't fix everything they do, but we can use our positions to ensure that we as an extended family survive and prosper," James continued.

"I understand, James. It's just all screwed up and I'm not sure they have the best intentions for the town."

"They don't, and I wouldn't want to be Mr. Grimes right now, having embarrassed the Sheriff in front of his citizens and potential voters. But we need to keep our eye on what's most important, the only thing more important than any other. Families First, our families first, always, no matter what."

"Agreed," said Jason. "Nothing else really matters."

Getting home just after dark, they filled the ladies in on the day's events and the new schedule for the upcoming week. Janice and Lauren were not exactly pleased with the news, but it was not unexpected either.

"I wouldn't be surprised to see the Grimes fellow suddenly disappear in the coming days," Janice pointed out.

"I would agree," said James. "The Sheriff was both upset and embarrassed by the comments he heard, and that can't be good."

"Did you get a gold star yet, Daddy?" asked Jason's girls.

"No, not yet, girls. We're still trying to get elected. Will you vote for us?" he asked, taking out a pen and paper and writing both their names on it.

"Yes, Daddy, we would love to cast the final votes," said Candice.

"Sweetie, I wish it were that easy, but we need to win by talking with as many people as possible over the next week. Please write your vote on the paper, and we will turn it in to the proper authority."

"Good night, everyone," said James, exhausted by the day. "And thank you, Janice, for completing the chores today."

"No worries, Mayor," she quipped. "Lauren and the girls pitched in, and we had it done in no time."

* * * *

James and Jason arrived in town on the tractor at 8:50 a.m., according to the town clock.

"Would you look at that!" said James, pointing to a bright yellow truck in front of the station. The large writing on the side read "Re-elect Sheriff Johnson." The line below read "James VanFleet for Mayor & Jason Davis for Deputy Mayor."

"It beats a tractor, for sure!" James exclaimed.

"Boots on the street, gentlemen," said Judge Lowry, tossing the keys to James.

"This truck is yours for as long as you are Mayor of our fair town. Now go win an election, so I can let you keep it."

"Yes, sir!" replied James, happy to be out of the Sheriff's truck.

James and Jason stayed in town for the day and talked with nearly 80 residents, introducing themselves and putting in a good word for the Sheriff. They heard much of the same talk as yesterday about Mr. Grimes.

"The Grimes fellow either has balls of steel, or he has no idea who he's messing with," James said to Jason.

Jason drove the truck home that night, following James on the tractor.

A late-night dinner was saved for them, as they showed the family the new old truck.

"Tomorrow is Friday," James announced. "We will work hard on our campaign, and on Saturday we will trade our wares."

"Should Lauren and I start working on a billboard, advertising the moonshine?" asked Janice jokingly.

"We'll be selling it for sure, since that was the deal, but we may want to keep it low profile and just peddle it like the guys at a baseball game for now.

"'Moonshine! Get your moonshine here!'" James called out in a loud vendor's voice.

"Oh, stop it, honey," said Janice, punching him lightly on the shoulder.

The girls were excited to go back to town.

"I hope we can find more books," said the girls.

"Can Chance come on Saturday to the carnival?" asked Jenna.

"He's going to need about one more week to rest up," Janice told her, "so maybe next week."

Chance raised his head, barked once, and rolled back over to continue his nap.

The nights were becoming peaceful, and the gunshots in the distance were less every day.

James wondered if the Judge and Sheriff may be on to something, extending the town limits and demonstrating what happens to lawbreakers in their town.

* * * *

The drive into town on Friday morning was quick. "I could get used to traveling like this," said Jason, rolling his passenger window down. "Wonder if the girls would know how to roll down the window without just pressing a button?" he added.

They were early this morning, not accounting for the time savings the truck afforded them.

Driving slowly through town, the bright yellow truck was getting the attention the Judge and Sheriff were anticipating. They stopped to talk to a few of the old-timers sitting out on the front porch of the only restaurant still in operation. "Weston Grill and Tavern is still open after 52 years and one apocalypse," the front window read.

"Janice and I used to come here every Thursday," said James. "I never imagined they would still be open."

"Lauren and I were here a few times last year as well. Do you think they still have their famous chicken fried steak and mashed potatoes with country gravy?" asked Jason, trailing off as he read it on the window. "Trade days special: Our World-Famous Chicken Fried Steak with all the fixins every Saturday," the billboard read.

Underneath, a smaller sign read "Wanting to buy 1/2 cow."

"We may have to stop by here tomorrow after trade," James told Jason. "Best be getting to the Sheriff's office," he added.

Sheriff Johnson was in a jovial mood, thought James, and the complete opposite of just two days ago.

"Gentlemen," said the Sheriff, shaking both of their hands, with a smile. "I heard you boys talked with a lot of the townsfolk yesterday, and I've been told it went well."

"You heard all that?" replied James, also smiling. "Well, I'm glad it was a good report," now wondering who the Sheriff had following them.

"I've got a surprise for you, James," the Sheriff said, fidgeting like a ten-year-old waiting to open his first birthday present. "Here in the back. Follow me."

Walking past a man and woman in the same cell, seemingly the vegetable thieves from the other day, they stopped in front of the last cell in the building.

A man sat in the corner with a swollen face and blood-stained suit. He was gagged and was trying to speak.

"James, Jason. Meet Mr. Grimes," said the Sheriff, beaming. "We caught him fighting in our safe town, now known for zero tolerance with respect to violence."

The man was trying to stand, and it was now clear his hands and feet were bound.

"Where's the other guy?" asked Jason, now feeling sick to his stomach.

"We haven't found him yet, but we're confident he will be located at some point."

Walking back to the front, the Sheriff said, "Let's keep this unfortunate development to ourselves for now. No use confusing the citizens of our great town right now. We've still got an election coming up, and the townsfolk need to have their say.

"Let's have you boys hit the town again today.

"The Judge and I will prepare for tomorrow's trade days, where I think you'll get a chance to talk to most of the new residents outside the former town limits."

"Sounds good, Sheriff," said James, nearly dragging Jason out of the building.

"Not a word," James whispered to Jason, until we're in the truck and a quarter mile down the road.

"Okay, Jason," he said, after a long pause while driving. "Let's get on the same page here."

"It's obvious," Jason blurted out, "that the Sheriff just beat up his opponent and arrested him. He won't let him speak and can't even come up with the supposed other guy he said was involved!"

"That's true," said James.

"I'm sure he's not just going to let him go before the election," Jason continued. "What about his right to a fair trial?"

"Do you mean the one with the good friend of the Sheriff, Judge Lowry, presiding and issuing the final judgment?" James asked.

"I see your point, James. But if he's behind bars and his running mate for Mayor is a no-good drunk, like the Sheriff says, then why are we even campaigning? I mean, isn't it already in the bag?"

"People are funny, Jason, and it's all about perception. If the Sheriff lets it get out that he's arrested his opponent, then the townsfolk won't have a say in the election.

"If, however, no one sees Mr. Grimes for the next week and only sees the Sheriff ensuring fair trade at the market and making the kid's school safe to learn in, then it's an easy vote. Add a few public hangings of folks who crossed the law, and you're looking at a landslide victory.

"The Sheriff and Judge get the appearance of a fair election, and the townspeople get to think they had a say in it. Everybody wins, and the truth is it's not too far off from the way it used to be.

"Most people thought they had a choice for President, could pick anyone they wanted. When it comes right down to it, we only had two realistic options between what each party had put forward, and maybe an independent billionaire who never had a chance.

"People felt good and powerful, but they were led all the way down the path with promises of the next four years being better than the last, with the newly elected President realizing quickly that their hands were tied and most of their well-meaning campaign promises could not be kept.

"The same is happening here, just on a much smaller scale."

"I don't like it," replied Jason, "but I guess it makes sense. We're the buffer between the Sheriff, the Judge, and the citizens of this town."

"My father once told me a story about a man who suddenly came into a large sum of money from a lawsuit settlement," James said.

"He had advised the man to hire a financial planner, so when his long-lost family members and old friends came to him with a loan request or new business idea, he could say, 'It sounds great to me. Just run it by my advisor, and if they're good with it, then so am I.' It was no coincidence that the adviser always said no, putting the blame squarely on him. Does that make sense, Jason?"

"I'm sorry, James, but I don't understand what you're getting at."

"Well, Jason, you and I are the financial advisors, and the Sheriff is the man with the money. He gets to say yes to townsfolks' ideas and issues, and we have to say no to most."

"So, we're the bad guys?" asked Jason.

"Sometimes it's going to feel like that, I'm sure, but we'll do our best for the citizens here and always put our own families first.

"Just stick close, Jason, and I'll keep us one step ahead of both Judge Lowry and Sheriff Johnson. Let's meet some more townsfolk."

The day was productive, as they spoke with nearly 100 people and likely secured most of their votes for them and Sheriff Johnson. Popping into the restaurant, James was able to secure a now-coveted reservation for seven tomorrow at 4:30 p.m.

Upon hearing the news about him running for Mayor, the restaurant owner gave him and Jason each a small sample plate of what they would eat there tomorrow.

Jason smiled after the first bite, thinking this may be the best meal he'd ever tasted.

"This is incredible," he whispered to James, "but Lauren and I don't have any money to come back here tomorrow."

"Never mind that. We'll be using the money we earn from the trading tomorrow…

"Speaking of that, we've got to get back and start packing up for trade!"

They made it back to the ranch early, around 4:30 in the afternoon.

After chores, they packed up more fruits and vegetables, plant seeds, beef jerky, six jars of honey, four dozen eggs retrieved by the girls, and eight cases of moonshine.

* * * * * *

Chapter Seventeen ~ Weston, Colorado

"I've got half a mind to sell the restaurant that side of beef they're looking for, but don't know what to do with the other half. It won't keep long," said James.

"What if we sold the other half in small 2- to10-pound bags at the market next week? We could take deposits tomorrow and see if enough people are interested before you have to commit," commented Jason.

"Jason, that's a great idea! I like your entrepreneurial spirit. I wonder how much a steer is worth these days?" James pondered.

"We'll stop by the restaurant before trading tomorrow and see what they're willing to pay. In the old days—just a few weeks ago—it was about $1,200 per half, including the kill fee to the rancher," continued James.

"Not many people want to kill their own steer," added Jason.

"Nope," replied James. "Heck, most people couldn't tell you the first thing about harvesting any of the meat they were used to seeing neatly packaged in the grocery store. The only concern they had was the price and the expiration date."

It was an early night, as they got ready to trade in the morning.

* * * *

This time they pulled the trailer behind the truck, heading out early to stop by the restaurant. The other vendors making the same drive pointed at the yellow truck and waved. The girls all waved back, reminding Janice of the floats at the Macy's Day Parade.

Just outside the restaurant, the aroma of bacon filled the air. A small crowd of maybe 15 waited patiently outside.

James and Jason, riding on the trailer with the girls while Janice drove with Lauren up front, jumped off the trailer to speak with the owner.

"Mr. VanFleet," said the restaurant owner, "and Mr....uh..."

"Davis," Jason interjected.

"Yes, of course. Mr. Davis. Welcome, are you here for breakfast?"

"No, sir," replied James, "but we will be back for our early dinner tonight. Have you found that side of beef that you're looking for yet?"

"Great to see you, James," the owner said in a loud voice, adding, "soon to be our new Mayor James VanFleet" to the gathering breakfast crowd.

Taking both James and Jason into a back storeroom, the owner scratched his head nervously.

"No, sir. We've been looking for a week now, and nobody has any beef to sell. I have the customers, as you can see," pointing towards the front of the restaurant. "But I'm afraid we'll be out of beef in just a few days. As it is, we are running out of pork as well."

"What are you looking to spend in trade for a half cow?" asked James—"butchered, of course."

"Well, I'm sure nobody is still taking checks or dollar bills, but I may have some gold coins in 1/4-, 1/2- and 1-ounce Gold Eagles. The trade price was about $1,400 per ounce just a few weeks ago."

"Well, we may be able to help you out," said James. "Half-cow prices were right at $1,200, plus the butcher fee of about $100. So pretty close to a one-ounce gold coin, I reckon.

"If we were agreeable, I could throw in a case of this town's finest moonshine to even it out. I wouldn't know if it could be done until this afternoon, though, since we would have to presell the other half at the trade days."

"If I took 3/4 cow for 1.5 ounces in gold coin, how many pounds of meat is that?" asked the owner.

"Well, you're looking at about 330 pounds of meat off the top of my head," said James, "and that would leave us with about 110 pounds to presell today."

"Mr. James, if you can do the deal, I'm good for it and will pay you 1/3 in advance," said the owner, "if you can deliver in three days."

"I'll let you know when we stop by for dinner," James told him, shaking his hand.

"Isn't gold worth a lot more than that now?" asked Jason, as they walked back to the truck.

"Sure is," James replied, "but so is 3/4 of a cow."

* * * *

They arrived in front of the clock just in time for the Sheriff's introduction.

He went over the rules of trade, just as last time, but then called James and Jason up on to the trailer where he stood.

Speaking to nearly 150 traders, he announced them as the next Mayor and Deputy Mayor of Weston.

"As you all know, our town elections are this coming Tuesday for Mayor, Deputy Mayor, City Council, and of course Sheriff of this great town," he boomed. "I personally endorse James VanFleet for the town Mayor and Jason Davis for Deputy Mayor. Please stop by stand number 49 and give them your support for the future of this town." All in attendance clapped, and a few whistled.

"As you may know," he continued in a voice everyone could hear, "I have an opponent for my position in Mr. Grimes. He seems to be unavailable lately, and we can't be sure if he had a change of heart. Either way, I stand before you as your sitting Sheriff and the best choice for the future of this town.

"Mark my words that you will have your say come Tuesday, and until then you may have comfort that you can trade your wares and let our educators teach your children under the absolute protection of myself and those who serve under me.

"Happy trading and happy voting."

Setting up the trading tables, James kept the moonshine underneath the tablecloth and out of sight.

They prepared to pre-sell 80 pounds of beef, opting to keep 30 for themselves.

"Honestly, with the deal we struck earlier, we could give it away for free and still come out way ahead," pointed out James.

"The Mayor-to-be and the Sheriff give away 80 pounds of beef to the citizens of their fair town," said Jason. "I can see the headline now."

"It sounds like a great idea!" remarked the Sheriff, overhearing the conversation from just behind the booth. "People love free food," he continued.

"We'll need tomorrow off to slaughter the animal," added James.

"Let's do it, James, and double up with campaigning on Monday," the Sheriff added, patting him on the shoulder as he walked down the line of vendors.

The next thirty minutes brought an onslaught of people to James' booth, all quoting Sheriff Johnson on the promise of free beef. The story was retold by each one and ranged from the promise of 1 to 30 pounds of free meat.

Janice reluctantly started a sheet tally of the first 80 people to each receive one pound of meat at next week's trade days.

A massive boom came from just behind one of the vendors stands, knocking an older man to the ground. The Sheriff and his men were no more than ten yards from the explosion, tackling a man holding a backpack in his right hand.

His head was promptly covered with a black hood while being led away towards the police station, to the clapping and cheers of most traders.

The older man slowly rose to his feet and packed up his few sale items without a word and walked away.

"There's your false flag," James said to Jason in a low voice.

"I don't get it," replied Jason.

"A false flag is like a kid saying to look over there while they steal the dessert off your plate. It's a distraction, often scary, where attention is diverted temporarily and there is an option to set the stage for what's to come. It's been used by most governments at some point and can play a crucial role in politics and elections. Did you see how they quickly put a hood over his face, disguising him?" asked James.

"Yes, James, I saw that."

"Was it the bomber or one of the Sheriff's good buddies?" James asked.

"Well, the bomber, of course. I mean, he was right beside the explosion when it happened."

"Was he?" asked James. "Was it Mr. Grimes that did it? Did he set off the bomb that didn't hurt anyone and somehow made the Sheriff look good at keeping the town safe?"

"Well, no, he's locked up. I mean…" Jason paused for what seemed like an eternity but was more like twenty seconds. "Oh, I see now," he said, his face running pale. "I'm not sure I want any part of this," he added, looking sick.

"Hold the fort for just a few, will you, Janice?" James asked. "I'm going to introduce Jason around to the other vendors."

James cut straight across the field, waking slow to talk to Jason.

"There are things going on here, Jason, that are out of our hands. Some are terrible things that we have no control over. I do my best to please God in everything I do. Many times I fall short, but I trust that God can handle the significant issues that are out of my reach. Do you pray, Jason?"

"No…well, I guess I don't really. I think God was with me up on the mountain when we met. But now, after today, I'm not so sure."

"Rest assured, I did worse things than you when I was a young man back in Chicago," said James. "I used to say there is no way in hell I'm ever getting into heaven. But when I read the Bible and started going to church, I realized that there is room for all of us.

"I'm not going to beat you up about this, and you need to understand that we can't fix everything, but we can do our absolute best on the things we can change. Rest assured, sin is everywhere and things happening like today may be out of our control, but they don't go unnoticed."

"I think I understand," Jason replied, with a sigh. "It's just so hard."

"I know, buddy, but everything is still the same. It's Families First, no matter what."

With that, they met each vendor, campaigning for themselves and Sheriff Johnson.

As hours ticked by, they had sold most of the goods on the table, and nearly 65 pounds of beef was ordered.

James didn't bring the moonshine out, waiting for one of his old customers who never came.

Packing up for the day, the Sheriff stopped by for the town bounty. "Sorry about the unpleasant commotion earlier," he said to Janice and Lauren. "Everything in our fair town is safe once again."

"How were the spirits sales?" he asked, as he was leaving.

"None today, Sheriff," James said with a solemn tone.

"That's surprising," commented the Sheriff. "How much for an extra case for Judge Lowry?"

James' mind was running. Should he give it away, knowing it would set a precedent of submissive behavior, or price it sky high to test the Sheriff?

He opted to split the difference, saying, "It's $10 per case, silver, gold and junk coins all accepted."

The Sheriff handed two Silver Eagle one-ounce coins to James, worth $32 in the last world, and said, "I'll take three cases."

"That will work," announced James, retrieving three cases from under the table.

"These ought to last the Judge for a while," commented James.

"We'll see," the Sheriff replied coldly.

Packing up, it was a good day of trading and campaigning.

The restaurant had people lined up around the corner.

"Mr. VanFleet," said the owner, coming to the back of the line to greet them.

"Right this way," he gestured, as they followed him around back and into the restaurant, with their table for seven already set.

"We're not looking for any special treatment," said James.

"Nonsense," replied the owner. "You have reservations!"

The girls were so excited to sit in what could be one of the last restaurants still open anywhere in the country.

There were no menus this day, just the Saturday Trade Special, written out on a large chalkboard hanging on the far wall in front of the kitchen.

James gave the excited restaurant owner the news about the beef, promising to have it delivered in three days from deposit.

"I'm sorry we don't have any pork, though," James added.

"I thought you would be able to make the deal," the owner said, handing James a half-ounce gold coin.

James smiled, as he has seen these many times in the Gold and Silver Depot in Trinidad but had never held one.

With all ordering the Special, the wait was hard. Smells wafted from the kitchen, just like James had remembered the last time he was here, but somehow today it smelled even better.

James placed the coveted coin on the table in front of Jason. "You and Lauren have been working hard and doing a great job on the ranch. Everybody needs some carrying around money."

"Really?" asked Jason.

"I don't think we can accept this," said Lauren. "It's just too much."

"Lauren," replied Janice. "I think it's just right. We can exchange it for an equal amount of silver coins when we get home, if you would like something easier to spend."

"Yeah, that would be great," replied Jason. "There's not a lot anymore that is worth this much in trade, except for maybe a cow."

Everyone laughed at this, even the girls.

"Thank you, James and Janice. Lauren and I feel truly blessed to have you in our lives."

"Me too!" chimed in each girl.

Dinner was worth the wait and served homestyle. A large plate of chicken fried steaks sat in the middle, surrounded by mashed potatoes with real butter and a bowl full of gravy. Collard greens with bacon bits, a hearty garden salad, and "rolls the size of your face," as Jenna put it, rounded out the meal.

"Don't forget to save room for dessert," said the owner, as he served them personally. "The misses has whipped up a peach cobbler with real vanilla ice cream, which may be the best in the country right now!"

The girls were more excited about the ice cream than anything else. By 6 p.m. they were stuffed and joking about doggie bags.

They all sang classic children's songs on the way home. James was caught up in the moment as they reached the front gate of their ranch. Life had gotten easier lately, and he was letting his guard down.

* * * * * *

Chapter Eighteen ~
Second Chances Ranch
Weston, Colorado

"Did you lock the gate when we left?" asked Janice, pointing to the chain lying on the ground at the front of their property.

"I always do," James replied, telling the girls to duck down.

The sounds of Chance's barking were barely heard down the long driveway.

James couldn't see a vehicle from his vantage point but thought there must be one somewhere or why would they cut the lock?

"Okay, Jason. There are a couple of scenarios here. Either we've been robbed, and they're gone, or they parked behind the house or inside the barn and are still here on the property. Until we know for sure, we can't have your girls and the ladies just sitting out here. Let's go to your old place, and see if it's clear. We'll drop them off while we check it out."

"Okay," replied Jason nervously.

Arriving at the old Davis place, a quick sweep revealed nothing out of the ordinary. The last thing Jason had done, as they left with their belongings, was to put a small piece of writing paper in the door jambs that would fall undetected when any one of the three trailer doors were opened. They were all intact, signifying that no one had been there.

Janice, Lauren and the girls slipped into the trailer after a quick sweep by James and Janice and an all-clear sign.

Janice, carrying her Mossberg 590 12-gauge shotgun, posted in the front room of the trailer.

"Be back soon," James said, blowing her a kiss.

Quickly unhooking the trailer from the truck, they headed the three miles back to the ranch.

"It's going to be dark in about 45 minutes, so we've got to make this quick, one way or the other," said James. "They could be parked in the barn, but I'm guessing they are already gone or parked behind the house."

"I hope Chance is okay," added Jason.

"He was just a while ago…" said James, trailing off, and saying a quick prayer for his new four-legged friend.

They drove slowly past the gate, still on the main road to get a glimpse of the back of the house, with James wishing his new old truck was any color besides bright yellow.

"That's it," said James, pointing to an old hatchback parked just behind the house.

With a quick look through binoculars into the front window, James could make out two people rummaging through the living room cabinets.

He didn't see Chance, and he hoped he was still okay.

"They haven't seen us," James announced. "I'm going to drive up just a bit, and we can head to the back of the house, hopefully undetected."

"Then we walk right up and knock on the door?" Jason asked nervously.

"No," replied James. "There's a few parts of the house I haven't shown you yet and you will see one in just a few. It may be the difference in who lives tonight and who doesn't."

James navigated the truck into a deep but navigable ravine, just out of sight of his house.

Jason had the shotgun James gave him, and James had another, plus his Ruger SR40 pistol he wore concealed on his right calf most days.

Ducking low, they made their way to the back of his house, moving slowly with Jason's still-healing leg.

Unlocking the cellar door, they cautiously navigated down the stairs.

James smiled, as he heard Chance barking once again.

Hold on, buddy. We're coming, he thought to himself.

"Why are we down here?" whispered Jason. "I mean, shouldn't we be headed for the front door?"

"Not this time, Jason. We have the element of surprise."

Quietly opening what appeared to Jason to be just a cabinet, James disappeared inside.

"Let's go," he whispered to Jason, who followed reluctantly.

Once inside, they stood in a small room the size of an apartment closet, lit by low emergency lighting.

"Jason," whispered James, "when I pull this lever the wall right in front of us will open from right to left. It's not going to be as fast as I would like, but once it starts, we're fully committed. Understand?"

"Yeah, I understand."

"If we can resolve this without bloodshed on either side, that would be ideal," said James.

"Agreed," said Jason, now feeling as if he were about to vomit for the second time in only days.

"I think there are two at least, but I could only see shapes through the shades with my binoculars. Okay. On the count of three," said James, with his hand on the lever.

"One…two…three."

Pulling down the lever, with a loud creaking sound the wall began to move slowly.

"Get low," James whispered. The fading light from outside made it harder to see.

Stepping through the opening, James faced a large man holding a hunting knife in a hostile stance.

"Drop the knife," said James, "and we may be able to work this out."

His shotgun was visible but pointed at the man's legs.

"You're in my house now," spat the intruder, as he lunged, knife first, towards James.

Raising his rifle, James started to squeeze the trigger, as he heard the Boom just to his right.

Jason fired a second shot, felling the man. All was quiet, apart from Chance barking from another room.

"There's at least one more," said James, quietly looking down at the still man on the floor, just in front of him.

"Daddy! Daddy! Are you okay?" called a high-pitched voice from upstairs.

James looked at Jason, who was doubled over, vomiting onto the floor.

A boy of no more than five years old bounded down the stairs, stopping just short of the bottom, with a fear in his eyes James had never seen in another person. He took a few seconds, scanning the room, from James to Jason and towards his daddy, laying face-up on the floor in a pool of bright red blood.

Nobody said a word. James saw everything in slow motion, as the boy ran to his father's side, sobbing uncontrollably. "What's wrong with him?!" he screamed. "Wake up, Daddy! Please wake up! I'll be good, I promise. Please wake up!"

He grieved his father, not understanding what happened.

"Stay here with him, Jason," said James, as he cleared the house, not expecting to find anyone else.

Chance was locked in an upstairs bedroom and appeared to be unharmed. Once let out, he did his own sweep of both the upstairs and downstairs, sniffing at the man's body but not barking. He licked the small boy on the hand and laid at his feet.

"Jason," said James, handing him the truck keys. "Get the ladies and your girls. We need the trailer too," he added.

"Come in through the front and take your girls straight upstairs. They don't need to see this."

Jason headed back through the wall and cabinet, exiting the cellar as quickly as he could.

"I'm sorry about your daddy," said James in a low, calm voice, as a pit gnawed in his stomach.

"What's your name?" he asked.

"Billy," he answered, not looking up from his dad.

"How old are you," James asked.

"Five and a half," the boy responded flatly. "Is he…I mean, is my daddy dead?"

"I'm afraid so," James replied. "Where's your mommy," he asked, wishing the ladies were already back to help him sort this out.

"She's gone, I guess. I don't remember her, but my daddy shows me pictures sometimes. I have one right here," he said, reaching into the chest pocket of his faded overalls. "Wanna see?" he asked.

"Sure, buddy," looking as the boy held up the picture. "She looks like a good mommy," said James. "Let me show you something over here, Billy," he said, just wanting to get the boy away from the gruesome scene before him.

"This was my mom and dad," James remarked, pointing to a picture on the dining room wall.

"Is your daddy a doctor?" Billy asked, noticing the scrubs he was wearing.

"Yes, he was. He used to deliver babies," James replied.

"Does he still do it now?" Billy asked.

"No. He and my mother passed on some years ago."

"You mean they died?"

"Yes, that's right, Billy, but I still talk to them almost every day," James continued.

"How do you do that?" the little boy asked.

"Well, I pray to God and say nice things to them."

"I don't know what you mean, mister."

"Do you know how to pray, Billy?"

"No. I don't know what you mean… Do I need to learn how to talk to my daddy now?"

"Yes, Billy," James replied, "but we can teach you that when the time comes."

"You and that other guy?"

"No. We have some other people that live here and you will meet them very soon," said James.

"Are they nice or mean?" he asked nervously.

"Oh, they're the nicest people I know."

"Do you have any other family close, like brothers or sisters, aunts, uncles or grandparents?"

"I don't think so; it's always just been me and Daddy," Billy said, starting to cry again.

Running back across the house, he hugged his father tightly and begged him to come back.

James had tears in his eyes for the first time that he could ever remember.

Fifteen minutes later, James saw the headlights coming up the drive, piercing the now-dark sky. The lights blinked twice, signaling Jason was at the wheel.

Janice walked slowly through the front door, having heard the news. She asked Lauren and Jason to take their girls upstairs.

"His name is Billy," said James quietly. "His daddy was the only family he knows."

Janice asked her husband to fall back and approached the grieving boy slowly.

Chance quietly lay at his feet, with his head down.

"Billy," she said softly, putting an arm around him. "My name is Janice. Do you think we could talk over here?" she said, pointing to the living room, "for just a little bit?"

"Okay," he replied, tears still streaming down his cheeks.

"I'm scared," he cried. "I don't have anybody now…" He cried out even louder.

Janice held him tight, rocking him back and forth for the next 20 minutes.

Falling asleep in her arms, she laid on the couch with him. She motioned for James, waving her arm in the air.

Whispering, she said, "Get Jason and clean this up. We don't need any of the children seeing this anymore."

"We will take care of it, honey," he told her, heading upstairs to get Jason.

To his surprise, Jason was sitting on the floor just outside their bedroom.

"Does he know I did it?" he asked. "Does he know I killed his father?" he continued, appearing agitated.

"Please keep your voice down, Jason," James asked him. "He doesn't know what happened. He's only five and didn't even ask. He knows his daddy is gone, but that's all. Be very careful about what you tell him or your girls tomorrow.

"I need your help to get this cleaned up quietly. Billy is asleep on the couch with Janice. We need to do a good job quickly, so no one else sees this. Are you with me, Jason?"

"Yes, of course. I only wish…"

"Let's talk about that tomorrow, okay?" asked James.

Forty minutes later, they had the man wrapped in plastic from the barn, and laid him in a clean horse stall. All traces of blood, to the naked eye, were removed from the hardwood floor where he once lay.

* * * *

Janice stayed on the couch that night, holding Billy, with Chance laying just beyond her feet. She awoke several times when little Billy cried out, shaking but not opening his eyes.

Everyone was up early, except for the girls and Billy.

The adults got a game plan together, to be on the same page with the girls and the new boy fast asleep on the living room couch.

Talk of what to do with the little boy was the topic of the early morning by the adults.

"I'll take a quick run to town," said James, "to tell the Sheriff what happened here."

"Won't he want you to go to work, since you're already there?" asked Janice.

"No, I think we're okay," he replied. "I'll leave Jason here, and I'll show up in shorts and flip flops, just in case.

"Besides, he knows we need to slaughter a cow today to keep his promise of free beef to his new voters. I'm pretty sure he won't want to interfere with that."

James unhooked the trailer from the truck for the second time in 24 hours and headed to town early.

He arrived just after 7 a.m., according to the town clock. He was half surprised to find the Sheriff in the office.

"You're here early," James asserted.

"Well, I was making sure our house guests have some breakfast is all. It's just not right to be hung on an empty stomach," he grinned.

"Are you hanging somebody today, Sheriff?" asked James.

"Oh no. Not yet. I'm just saying they need to appear healthy when we do, assuming of course that the Honorable Judge Lowry rules in favor of it."

James proceeded to tell the Sheriff about the happenings last night and inquired how to find little Billy a new home.

"That's interesting," observed the Sheriff, "and it sounds like you did the right thing. But that's just the start. The way I see it is our future Mayor needs to campaign hard come Monday and Tuesday morning, right up to the election at 2 p.m., ensuring that every man and woman eligible to vote does so.

"The Mayor's position pays a little money each month, and you have just added another mouth to feed."

"Thank you for your time, Sheriff," said James, with his head spinning. "Now, if you will excuse me, I've got a steer to butcher."

"See you boys bright and early tomorrow," said Sheriff Johnson. "Let's start at about 7 a.m. and go until dark."

"See you tomorrow, sir," James replied, not exactly agreeing to the new schedule.

James drove back to the ranch with the windows down. *I guess we have a little boy now*, he thought. James would give his daddy a proper burial on the property, so little Billy could visit him whenever he wanted.

Pulling up to the house, his wife and Billy were on the front porch, sharing a rocking chair.

"Has he met the girls yet?" asked James.

"Not yet. Jason wanted to talk to you first," she replied.

"Do you need anything, Billy?" James asked.

"We're okay," replied Janice, with a wink.

"Okay. I'll find Jason."

James found Jason on the side of the house, sitting with his head in his hands.

"Jason, how are you holding up?"

"Not good, I guess. I've been out here for a while. I can't look the boy in the eye; I just can't do it… Did you find a home for him in town?"

"No, Jason. I did not. I spoke with the Sheriff, and he's not interested in finding him a new home. We can't just give him away at the next trade days."

"I know," replied Jason. "So, does that mean…?"

"I'll have to talk to Janice, but it probably means he's with us now. We won't speak to him or anybody else about what happened. It could just as easily have been me that fired the shot. So that you know, Jason, I had my finger on the trigger when you fired. I want to give his daddy a proper burial on this ranch… So he can visit his grave when he needs to," added James.

"I guess he should meet the girls, then," Jason responded.

Janice brought Billy in and introduced him to the girls.

James pulled her aside, telling her about the conversation with the Sheriff.

"It's a formality really," she replied.

"How so, honey?"

"Well, he's ours to raise and protect. I knew it from the minute I saw him. We can't just go pawning him around town so someone else can take the responsibility."

"That's true, Mama. We'll give his papa a proper goodbye, and I'll make a headstone for him."

"Let's clear out the office upstairs and make a bedroom. I'm guessing he won't want to share one with the girls for too long."

Carla, Candice and Jenna took to their new housemate right away. All wanted him to sleep in their room, but Janice informed them it would not happen tonight.

"He will sleep with us for the next night or two," Janice told James. "I won't have him feeling all alone right now."

"Okay, honey. Let's have you and Lauren keep the kids inside today. Jason and I have a lot of work to do."

* * * * * * *

Chapter Nineteen ~ Second Chances Ranch Weston, Colorado

James and Jason headed out to the pasture.

"How do you pick the steer?" asked Jason. "I used to simply select the biggest one and send them off to the slaughterhouse."

"Now it's an easy pick, since we have one big guy with a bad leg," pointed out James.

"Is it hard to send your babies off to slaughter?" asked Jason.

"Well, I learned a long time ago that you always name your milking cows, but never your steers," replied James.

They coaxed the lame steer into the slaughter pen, a 15x10 compartment gated on all sides, eight feet high.

The steer paced back and forth, both nervous and agitated.

"All right, Jason. It's been a while since I've had to do this, but the process hasn't changed any. I'm going to shoot him between the eyes with my 9mm pistol. A .22 caliber would work as well.

"Next, we quickly need to cut the throat, helping him to bleed out.

"After that, we hang him upside down and open him from bottom to top, pulling the organs out into the garbage can. We will save the heart and the liver."

"That sounds brutal," said Jason.

"Yes, it does, but I can assure you it's much more humane than what they did so you could eat the last burger you had before the lights went out."

"So, what's the difference?" asked Jason.

"We will say a prayer for our steer and honor him for laying down his life to ensure our future. The kill will be humane and quick, and he has lived his life free-range over these 40 acres and not penned up with a dozen other steers his entire life.

"Beef doesn't originate under plastic wrap, as many would like to believe.

"Are you ready, Jason? Once we start, everything needs to be timely to ensure the quality of the meat."

"Okay, I think I'm ready," he replied.

The kill shot was on target, and James thanked the steer for his sacrifice. "You will be feeding our family, and many others," he continued.

Jason stepped up and participated in most of the process. The final preparations utilized the saws and various butcher knives to separate the animal for distribution.

Janice and Lauren prepared the large coolers, having filled 40 one-gallon plastic Ziplock bags with water a day ago and freezing them solid.

The 3/4 cow and bonus heart, tongue and liver would be delivered tomorrow morning to the restaurant owner, a day earlier than promised, and they would keep the rest on ice for the next six days, until trade day. By 3 p.m., all was done and cleaned up.

James thanked Jason for his help and told him about the Sheriff's proposed schedule for the next couple of days.

"We're going to be super busy over the next week, and we won't be around here much at all," James commented.

"Jason," he added, "Billy is our responsibility now. Janice has taken a shine to him, as I'm sure you have noticed. We will raise him as our own, her and me.

"I need you to be comfortable with him, starting today. I will have Janice help with the evening chores, but I want you and Lauren to bond with him. We can't change what happened, and it's not my fault or yours. We do need to protect this little guy and raise him in our family.

"It is important to me that, by tomorrow morning, you can look him in the eyes and see just a young boy in need of a family, and nothing else. Can you do that for me, Jason?"

"I will surely try," he replied, walking back towards the house.

"One more thing," said James. "We need to bury the body and have a ceremony tonight. We will be too busy this next week to put it off. Plus, I want little Billy to say his good-byes, and then start to move forward. It shouldn't take long, using the backhoe on the tractor to dig."

James picked a spot near a large pine tree that was one of his favorite places on the property.

They had the hole dug deep and laid his body next to the grave.

"Jason, listen to me. We have to unwrap this plastic before we put him to rest."

"Can't we just put him in like he is?" asked Jason.

"No. We need to check him first. He may have something on him, like a ring or necklace, that Billy could keep. We won't get another chance at this, so if you help me unroll him, I'll check for any keepsakes for this little boy."

Jason was reluctant, not wanting to see the man's face.

Once the grizzly task was complete, James felt good about his decision, coming up with a few things for the boy.

Laying the man to rest in the hole, they covered him with dirt to the top. James made a cross, tying two sticks together, but vowing to make the headstone over the next few weeks, as he had promised his wife.

The men entered the house to find the girls playing with Billy and sharing their toys.

James made a mental note to find out if the boy's house was close enough to stop by and get some of his clothes and toys.

Jason sat on the living room couch, watching the kids play but not getting too close, continuing for a couple of hours until it was time for chores.

James and Janice headed outside, with Billy not wanting to leave Janice's side.

"It's okay, sweetheart," she said. "We will be just a little while and then come right back."

The girls coaxed him back into the house, with the promise of lemonade and cookies.

Jason sat on the couch with Lauren, talking softly. "James wants me to be able to look the boy in the eyes by tomorrow morning. I'm just not sure if I can."

"By 'the boy,' you mean Billy?" Lauren asked.

"Yes, of course, Lauren. Who else would I be referring to?" he snapped.

"No, Jason. You don't get to do that."

"Do what?" he asked.

"This right here," Lauren continued. "I'm sorry you had no choice but to end a man's life. But it's done, and now that boy you are referring to has a name, and it's Billy. Let me hear you say it!"

"I just don't know if I…"

"Let me hear you say it," she repeated, louder than she should have.

The girls looked over and asked, "Mommy, are you all right?"

"Yes, I'm fine. I'm sorry I raised my voice."

"Billy," whispered Jason. "His name is Billy, and he's just a sweet young boy of five years old that is now a part of this house and our families."

"Say it again," insisted Lauren, "all of it one more time."

Jason did as she asked and felt a little better.

Lauren went to the kitchen and whispered something to Billy, pointing back towards the couch.

Billy slowly walked towards a nervous Jason, stopping just in front of him.

"Excuse me, mister, but do you think you could please help me pour some lemonade?"

Jason paused, frozen, looking him straight in the eyes, and saw exactly what James had said. Just a sweet five-year-old boy, asking for a glass of lemonade.

"Mister, are you okay?"

"Yes. Yes, Billy," he replied, fighting back tears for the first time since the lights went out.

"In fact, I'm better than okay," he replied with a grin, lifting the boy and carrying him into the kitchen.

"You can call me Uncle Jason, if you want," he told him, winking at a shocked Lauren.

Setting Billy on the kitchen counter, he poured a glass for everyone.

Finishing his lemonade, he went out to see if he could help speed up the evening chores.

"Well, that was quick!" said James, looking at a smiling Jason.

"Yes, it was, thanks to Lauren, who nearly had to kick my ass," he replied.

"But we're solid, Billy and me. He's going to call me Uncle Jason. I think he will fit in just perfect around here."

"Well, that's great to hear," replied Janice.

"We're going to keep the burial short," she added, with James saying a few words, and Billy if he wants to.

Janice headed back to the house, switching out with Jason.

"I see you got some lemonade, Billy," Janice noted.

"Yes, ma'am. Uncle Jason helped me get it. I like him. He's nice."

"Well, that's great to hear," Janice replied.

"What should I call you and Mr. James?" he asked.

It took everything in her not to blurt out "Mommy and Daddy."

"We'll think about that," she replied, lifting him and carrying him out to swing with her on the front porch.

"Your daddy, Billy, was a good man, and he loved you very much. He's in heaven now, but you can still talk to him."

"I know. Mr. James is going to teach me to pray, so I can talk to him whenever I want."

"That's nice, Billy. We are going to have a little ceremony tonight, with just us here," Janice said, waving her arm around the property, "so that we can say good-bye to him."

"Okay, but please don't leave me alone, because I don't like to be scared."

"Don't you worry about that, little guy," she replied, squeezing him tight and kissing him on the forehead.

She was reminded of an old Rolling Stones song switching up the lyrics "Twenty untamed stallions couldn't make me leave, no not even one-hundred."

Lord, you sure do work in mysterious ways, she thought.

After chores, they all made the short walk to the gravesite, with Chance slowly tagging along.

"I chose this spot," said James to Billy, "because it's my favorite spot on this whole ranch. Now your daddy can be here always."

James said a few words about daddies and families and asked Billy if he wanted to say anything.

Billy had tears welling up in his eyes but kept his composure, opting to say some words another time.

James knelt next to Billy and opened a white handkerchief, with several items in it.

Billy smiled, picking up the wristwatch that was stuck on 9:03 a.m. Mountain Time.

There was a two-dollar bill and a Susan B. Anthony silver dollar, along with a chain with the dog tag reading:

Jacobs, Bill R.
3765389632
A Pos
No Preference
(ID number, blood type, and religion).

The last item was a custom pocketknife with the initials BRJ carved into the deer-antler handle. James kept this to himself, vowing to give it to him on his 10th birthday.

They walked home just as it was getting dusk.

The men were both exhausted and opted for an early bedtime. Janice and Lauren stayed up a little later, each with a glass of wine, and ironing two suits now.

All the girls and their new cousin were fast asleep on the couch, with Chance lying at Billy's feet.

* * * * * * *

Chapter Twenty ~ Weston, Colorado

Jason and James were up early, loading the truck well before dawn.

The beef was keeping nicely, and James was proud he could deliver a full day sooner than agreed. He was sure the restaurant owner could appreciate the bonus organs.

Heading to town, again opting to change clothes at the Sheriff's, they drove by the town clock that read 5:22 a.m.

"Well," said James, "I didn't want to get here quite this early, but at least we won't be late. Let's try to get the beef dropped off first, if they are open."

Pulling in front of the restaurant at 5:30 a.m., they were surprised to see nearly ten people on the front patio, eating breakfast already.

"I guess they're open," said Jason. "How about some breakfast? This time, James, it's on me!" he added, holding up a silver coin, just one of many he was able to exchange with Janice yesterday for the gold coin.

"That sounds good to me, buddy," replied James. "It's going to be one hell of a day, either way, so we might as well have a good breakfast."

As expected, the restaurant owner was more than satisfied with the early delivery and bonus items.

Handing James a one-ounce gold coin for the final payment, he helped them unload the coolers into their refrigerators and freezers, all hooked up to a hodgepodge of generators.

"That looks complicated," Jason said, pointing to the generators. "It is, and I only know one guy who can make it work," he said, pointing to an old man sitting on the patio, playing chess with a friend.

"We have a deal, he and I, that he keeps my freezers working and I give him free coffee and breakfast. So far, we are both happy."

The owner proudly took down the sign asking to buy half a cow.

"Can I call on you down the road if I can't find anyone selling?" he asked James.

"Sure. I can't promise anything in advance, but I will always consider a request," James replied.

Shaking hands, the owner disappeared into the kitchen.

Jason handed James a breakfast menu from a rack on the wall. Several items from the still-original menu were crossed off, including anything made from pork.

"I guess they are finally out of pork," observed James.

"I was kind of hoping for some bacon," added Jason, "but I can settle for pancakes and still be okay."

* * * *

They pulled into the Sheriff's office around 6:45 a.m. and found it unlocked.

"Let's get changed, boys, and get to work," said the Judge, sitting in his usual spot. "I apologize for that unpleasantness at the trade days."

"You mean the small bomb?" asked Jason.

"Yes, that's what I said," replied the Judge in a serious tone.

"Well, it didn't affect our trading any," interjected James.

"I heard you're giving some beef away to our out-of-town voters?" asked the Judge.

"Yes, sir," replied James. "It was Sheriff Johnson's idea, and it seems to have gone over well."

"I would tend to agree, as I heard about it from more than one trader that day," replied the Judge.

"Howdy, boys," said the Sheriff, coming up from the back of the jail. "I'm about ready to get out there and campaign. I just had to fatten up the cows," he added, carrying three empty plates.

"Speaking of cows, did you get the meat we promised the townsfolks?"

"Yes, sir, we did," replied James.

"I thought about it," the Sheriff continued, "and since all the preorder folks should be here for the election tomorrow, we should give it to them right then. *Cast a vote, get some beef!*"

"That sounds catchy," remarked the Judge.

"We can do that," replied James, now wondering how late he would be up tonight packing individual containers of beef.

"We'll work hard all day and tomorrow, through the election, but we'll be taking off on Wednesday and Friday," announced James, wanting to set some ground rules. "Starting next week, we will be in town on Mondays, Wednesdays, and of course Saturdays."

"Let's get started," said the Judge, not exactly agreeing to the new schedule.

The four men started in the old downtown, walking both sides of the street and talking with everyone they met.

Most everyone knew Judge Lowry and Sheriff Johnson, with a few questioning the whereabouts of Mr. Grimes. "It's too bad he hasn't been around," said one of the older men in a small group playing shuffleboard right on the street. "He's a good man," he continued. "And if he were here, you might have a run for your money, Sheriff," with most others in the group nodding their heads in agreement.

James could tell Sheriff Johnson was not happy hearing this, as he turned red and pretended to get a call on his radio, walking away and down the street.

"This here is James VanFleet and Jason Davis," the Judge told the small crowd, seemingly unfazed by the previous comment. "They are running for Mayor and Deputy Mayor," he continued.

"Howdy, James," said more than a few of the men.

"How's the ranch? Is it still up and running?" asked one man.

James realized that many of the old-timers here were his customers over the years, although some hadn't ordered in a while.

"Yes, sir," replied James. "Everything is running smoothly, as always." The Judge had a slight smile, enjoying the banter.

"Gentlemen, let me be clear," announced the Judge. "We hope you will come out to vote tomorrow and a vote for Sheriff Johnson is also a vote for James VanFleet.

"Well, that was fun," said the Judge, as they caught up with the Sheriff.

"It seems that James is quite popular with the old crowd," he continued, speaking to both the Sheriff and Jason.

Sheriff Johnson pulled the Judge aside, still worked up from the exchange. "I want to kill Grimes," he spat, "right there in his cell."

"There will be none of that," the Judge replied. "Just stick to the plan, and I'll let you hang him in front of the whole town soon enough. Now we still have an election to win." Walking by the Tavern, the window read "Elect James VanFleet for Mayor."

Just underneath read "Re-elect Sheriff Johnson" in smaller letters.

They walked past, with James pretending not to notice.

James was able to get Janice on the walkie-talkie and informed her it would be a late night for him and Jason, now having to divide 80 pounds of meat in the morning.

"Sorry about that, honey," she responded. "We'll have dinner waiting at least."

Having spoken to nearly everyone in town, the four men met at the Judge's office. It was clear that Judge Lowry was already well on his way to a good hangover in the morning.

"Let's have a drink, boys," he said, slurring his words. Pouring four glasses of James' best, he toasted:

"To the future of our town. May God have mercy on those who oppose us."

* * * *

Heading home at dusk, Jason and James discussed the day.

"What do you think about the Sheriff?" asked Jason. "I mean, he looked pretty pissed off today."

"Well," replied James, "he will do anything to win the election, but deep down he would like to win it fair and square. Everyone wants to be liked.

"He knows he can't lose, with Mr. Grimes having left town in the minds of the people, and it's not too difficult for the two most powerful men in town to rig a vote count. But even with all that, he still wants to be picked.

"Judge Lowry doesn't care how it's done, as you heard him talking about a vote for him is a vote for us also."

* * * *

Pulling through the front gate, it was past dark. Only the lanterns inside the house indicated there was someone home.

Opening the front door, Jason smelled beef stroganoff, one of his very favorite meals.

The girls, and even Billy, helped serve them the meal, paired with fresh sautéed green beans from the garden and a glass of Johnny Walker Tennessee Whisky.

"James, if you could make more of this, we'd be in business," said Jason.

"I'll have to look into it," James replied, wondering if it could be done now.

"We have a surprise for you boys," said Lauren. "Close your eyes," she continued, as Janice opened two large coolers filled with meat, individually packed.

"Eighty pounds of beef, boys, ready for tomorrow!" she boasted. "Thanks to the girls and Billy, we got it done."

James, feeling exhausted from the day, was thrilled with the news.

"Thank you all so much," James said. "It means everything to us after this long day, and another to follow."

"I held the bags open!" chimed in Billy, with a big smile.

"That's good, son," replied James, casually, getting an odd look from both Lauren and Janice.

"I mean, that's a great job, Billy! Thank you for helping today."

"You boys get some rest after dinner. Leave us those suits, and they'll be ready for tomorrow," said Janice. "After the election," she added, "I won't be pressing another suit, so let the Judge and Sheriff know you'll be wearing jeans from now on."

"Yes, ma'am," they both replied, nearly crawling upstairs.

James was up early, with little feet jammed into his rib cage. "Who needs an alarm clock when you have a five-year-old sleeping sideways?" he whispered to no one.

He met an already-awake Jason downstairs and suited up.

"It looks like you're ready to go," said James. "Give me just a few minutes, and we'll head out. If we are early enough, breakfast will be on me today."

* * * *

Heading to town, they placed a one silver dime bet on the town clock.

"I pick 4:53," said James, while Jason picked 5:27. The clock read 5:15, with Jason being the clear winner of a silver dime.

"Plenty of time for breakfast," announced James.

Steak and Eggs was the Breakfast Special. Jason was uneasy about ordering it, knowing where the beef had originated. "Just thank the steer for his sacrifice so that we may soldier on," suggested James.

"Not bad," replied Jason after his first bite. "Not bad at all!"

Arriving at the Sheriff's station just before 7 a.m., both James and Jason heard loud banging, sounding like hammers, just beyond the station.

"What's all the racket?" James asked the Sheriff.

"We're reinforcing the gallows for the hangings today," the Sheriff announced.

"Today?" James asked, surprised. "It's voting day."

The Sheriff continued. "The Judge ruled late last night on the three we have in custody."

"Do you mean the Judge who was drunk last night?" asked Jason.

"Excuse us just a minute, Sheriff," said James, leading Jason out of the office.

"That's bullshit!" said an angry Jason when they were outside.

"Yes, it is, so what are you going to do about it?" asked James. "Are you going to bust them out of jail or appeal to the Sheriff's sensible side?"

"I see your point, James, but I don't like it, not a bit."

"Neither do I, Jason, but our focus hasn't changed. We have children that need raising, and that's our business. This is not."

Sheriff Johnson rounded up some men to spread the word of the hangings at noon today.

The town was bustling this morning, with many out-of-town folks pouring in early and everyone wondering who would be hanged.

James and Jason spoke with everyone they could, not addressing any questions about the noon happenings. Many asked about Mr. Grimes and if he would be here for the election.

James reminded Jason not to talk about it, keeping the focus only on the election.

Janice, Lauren and the girls rode the tractor into town, with Billy helping Janice drive. The town was bustling for the first time since the last trade days. The large crowd gathered just behind the Sheriff's station, starting around 10 a.m.

Next-world vendors made their way through the crowd, peddling mostly lunches out of a can. By 11:30 the crowd had swelled to nearly two times the group for the last hanging.

"We've got a voting bunch for sure today!" the Sheriff excitedly told James.

Jason found Lauren, Janice and the kids as the children were being dropped off at the schoolhouse. The girls promised Janice they wouldn't leave Billy's side, even for a minute.

"Who's up on the hanging block today?" Lauren asked Jason.

Jason realized that he had not spoken to his wife about Mr. Grimes. It wasn't intentional with everything happening in the last few days. He pulled James aside, asking if Janice knew about him.

"She does not," James confessed, "but I thought we had more time. I had planned to tell her right after the election. It's going to be an interesting night after all this," he added.

Just before noon, with the crowd both anxious and curious, the Sheriff's deputies led the three convicted people to the gallows. The large crowd gasped, realizing that the second in line was a woman. The third figure was the only one with a hood already on their head.

The gathering citizens from both in and out of town were ablaze with comments and questions about the unlikely trio climbing the wooden stairs before them. Most wondered who the masked figure was, with a few joking that it was the sitting Sheriff's challenger.

"That's one way to win an election!" shouted a large man in a white tank top streaked with sweat and sauce from his canned ravioli lunch.

Sheriff Johnson overheard the comment and smiled, slightly pursing his lips. "I'll make an extra-long drop for you, big boy, at our next hanging," he said under his breath.

As the three people reached the top of the gallows, Judge Lowry spoke loudly to the crowd.

"Ladies and Gentlemen, thank you for being here today to cast your votes in the elections of Town Sheriff, Mayor, Deputy Mayor, and City Council.

"We shall take care of the official business before us, having criminals convicted in my court after all evidence has been weighed. The charges they face range from thievery to participation in violent acts, where there is zero-tolerance for such behavior in our town.

"Each of the convicted will be given ample time to speak with their Maker, if they so choose."

The man and woman Jason knew as the vegetable thieves were mostly quiet. They were both weeping, with trembling legs. Jason could only assume that Mr. Grimes was under the black hood and trying to speak. His hands and legs were shackled, and loud inaudible sounds came from under his hood.

The Sheriff asked James to stand by him, just to the back and right of the gallows.

"Do you want to do the honors?" asked the Sheriff, pointing at the drop lever.

"No, sir," replied James firmly.

"Don't forget," added the Sheriff, "I ensured a win for both of us today."

"I know, but I didn't need it," replied James, walking back into the crowd.

Judge Lowry gave his speech, mentioning again about the criminals being tried in his court and only convicted after all the evidence had been presented.

What a load of crap, thought Jason, pretty sure that none of the three had stepped foot in the courthouse, let alone ever speaking with the Judge.

On Judge Lowry's orders, one couple was executed for stealing vegetables, and the opponent of the Sheriff murdered in front of the entire town, and many of his supporters.

Lowering the bodies of the man and woman, the town doctor declared them dead. The good doctor was turned away by Sheriff's deputies, as he tried to check the third.

Sensing the large crowd was agitated and hot, the Judge announced early voting and gestured where to start the line.

Votes were cast on a quarter sheet of printing paper, preprinted with choices of Sheriff, Mayor, Deputy Mayor, and City Council. Each vote was dropped into a large wooden box, both locked and secured to an outdoor picnic table, and lines formed in front of the three boxes available.

Town volunteers ensured that each voter only cast one vote. There was no checking of IDs or voter cards today. Voting started around 12:30, with the last one cast at 3:15.

Votes were to be tallied under the watchful eye of Judge Lowry in his courtroom, having a neutral stance in the outcome, with his position unopposed. He would have the final say when all the votes were tallied.

The Judge declared that each box would be tallied separately, starting with the first. Nearly 40 minutes later, the votes from box one were counted. One hundred sixty-seven votes were broken down to candidates.

James received 134 votes, or about 80% over his running mates. Sheriff Johnson received 75 votes, or nearly 45% compared to Mr. Grimes.

The second box was nearly the same.

Judge Lowry called for a mandatory 15-minute break before the final box was tallied.

Soliciting a popcorn vendor, he ordered everyone out of his courtroom.

Pulling 30 votes for Sheriff Johnson out of each of the previously counted boxes, he added them to the final box, shaking it back and forth to mix them.

He made a mental note to remember that James needed no help in getting elected.

Forty-five minutes later, with the last box accounted for, the results were handed to Judge Lowry.

Standing on the gallows and without announcing the percentage, as Fox News and CNN would have done in the previous world, Judge Lowry declared Sheriff Johnson, James VanFleet, Jason Davis, and the new town council as victors to serve in the interest of the town for the coming term.

Many cheered, amongst some boos from the now-dwindling crowd.

James and Jason congratulated Sheriff Johnson and the new town council on the win.

James could barely hear the conversation but overheard the Sheriff asking Judge Lowry how close the count was for his position. "It wasn't close at all," replied the Judge, patting him on the shoulder and saying, "Congratulations, Sheriff, on a solid victory today."

James and Jason saw their families off, vowing not to be late for dinner.

"Interesting happenings at the hangings today," said Janice. "Let's talk about it later," she added, with Lauren agreeing.

Janice had brought them both a change of clothes, opting for jeans with button-down shirts and cowboy boots. "Wear these, boys, so the Judge and Sheriff know right away that you're done with the suits."

They did as they were asked and stuck around the main square, talking with their new constituents for the next two hours.

* * * *

"How are we going to tell them?" Jason asked, as they headed home just after 6 p.m.

"You mean about Mr. Grimes, I'm assuming," replied James, as Jason nodded his head up and down.

"Well, my friend, they already know, but we will get an earful for sure since we didn't tell them about the arrest earlier," James continued. "The hanging part we didn't learn about until just this morning, so we might get a pass on that."

"Let's tell them both together and get it out in the open first thing when we get home. It's been bothering me all day, if I'm honest," said Jason.

"Yes, I would certainly agree with that," said James.

* * * *

Janice, having some quiet time with Billy, was able to learn that his home was hours away by car, in southern New Mexico, near Albuquerque. He had been driving with his dad for a few days when they landed here.

Janice considered taking the car they had left to town today, but thought it was too soon for Billy and left it in the barn where James had parked it yesterday.

Arriving home, James and Jason ate dinner and played with the kids. It was monopoly night and the teams were fierce, with Jason and Carla, James and Candice, Lauren with Jenna, and Janice with Billy.

Nothing about the new world could change this game, thought Janice, smiling, with Billy on her lap. James smiled back, never before seeing his wife look so happy. He hoped she would understand about Mr. Grimes.

With the children in bed and Billy fast asleep on the couch, they had the talk.

When James was done explaining how they forgot to mention it, with everything going on, and Jason nodding in agreement, Janice had no expression.

"Well?" asked James as he finished.

"Well," replied Janice, "it doesn't take a genius to assume the hooded person was Mr. Grimes. I'm guessing we weren't the only ones to notice.

"I'm worried about you, both of you," she added. "I'm starting to wonder if we should've just packed up and moved up the mountain when we had the chance."

"We always have that option," replied James to all three. "It's just a last resort.

"Jason and I will do our best to keep the town under control and make our mark on the people.

"Those in charge who have the people behind them can defeat anyone, or two men, if it comes down to it."

* * * * * * *

Chapter Twenty-One ~ Near Amarillo, Texas

Lonnie stopped the group an hour later to look at the map.

"We made great time," he announced, "and got ahead of the marchers, but we don't want to be in their way if we can help it. It's been slow going so far, and we need to make up some time."

Vlad had been studying the map for the last hour and came up with a few alternative routes for travel around Amarillo.

"Let's stick to the side roads and look for campsites near water, if possible," said Vlad, looking pale. "We will need to make another gas run in the next day or two also."

"You all right, buddy?" I asked him. "You're looking a little gray."

"Look! Look!" said Danny and Hudson, as they pointed to the sky.

"Great! More helos," said Mike, shaking his head.

Three helicopters flew high overhead in the direction our group had just come from.

"This is getting interesting," said Mike, grinning like a 6-year-old boy with his first BB gun.

"That's not quite the word I would use," said Jake to Vlad and me.

"What would you use, Jake?" asked Mike, his grin now turned into stone.

"I would say it's troublesome," replied Jake, "seeing as I have a wife and kid to protect."

"So, you think I don't care about our group?" asked Mike, appearing agitated.

"All right, guys," I said, trying to bring the tension down just a bit. "We don't know what this means, but this is not the place I want to be when…"

"Boom!" came the sound from at least 15 miles to the south, followed by rapid-fire, appearing to come from the helicopters.

"What the hell is going on?" asked Steve. "I thought they were all working together."

"I don't believe what I'm seeing," said Lonnie, as we watched a rocket arc up from the ground, taking out one of the birds. More rapid-fire from the other two copters, as another missile was launched, just missing its intended target. The two helicopters headed north and over our group, flying fast.

'So, a couple days ago we meet with a coffee guy named Harry, who was short on firepower, and today his group fends off three military helicopters with automatic weapons?" Lonnie said out loud. "I'm usually pretty good at figuring this kind of stuff out, but I'm stumped," he added.

"Me too," I said aloud.

"One thing we know for sure," said Jake. "There's about to be another shootout in the OK Corral soon enough, and we don't want to be anywhere near it."

We all agreed on that point and headed straight west.

"Look," said Jax, pointing to the side of the road.

"It looks like a raccoon or possum curled up," said Jake. The animal was in a ball but appeared to be alive.

"Can we stop?" asked Jax.

"Now is not a good time," I told him, as the animal raised his head.

"Daddy! Daddy! It's a puppy!" screamed Jax.

I sighed and called to Lonnie on the radio to stop for just a minute. Jumping off the trailer, I scooped up the silver brown dog in my arms and put it on the trailer.

"Can we keep him, Daddy?" all three of my boys asked.

"We'll see," I replied, turning the dog over. "And by the way, he is a she."

"That ain't no mutt," announced Steve. "That there is a Silver Labrador Retriever. They're hard to find and crazy as they come."

"She looks okay to me," said Hendrix, petting her on the head. "I'll call her Mini, since she looks tiny next to Ringo."

Mini drank half a bowl of water and fell asleep on the trailer.

It was now late morning, and the heat intense.

"It's not so bad, as long as we're moving!" Jake yelled to me and Vlad, who was laying down.

"How's your leg doing?" I asked Vlad, as he lay on the trailer. "Hey, buddy, how's your leg?" I asked again, shaking him just a bit.

There was no response. I shuffled over to take a closer look and Vlad looked pale, with sweat pouring from his forehead.

I called Lonnie on the radio to stop and told Nancy we needed her on the trailer *now*.

Climbing on the trailer, she called Tina and Joy for help. "We need something to shade him. And Joy, please bring my other kit," she said, pointing to the far end of the trailer. "It's the one secured by the bungee cords."

Nancy took the temporary cast off and found his leg hot, with long red streaks running from his knee to his groin.

"We've got an infection," she announced, "and it's not responding to the antibiotics I've had him on thus far. We need to get him to a hospital; I mean a *real* hospital, or he's not going to make it."

"I'll take him," said Mike. "Me too," added Steve.

"No, boys. He's my friend and I got him into this, so I'll go," announced Lonnie.

I pulled Lonnie aside and spoke quietly. "I know he's your friend, and we all want to see him get help. You are the lead driver in our group right now, and I need you to lead us to the next safe place for the night. I'll go with Mike and take Vlad to the FEMA camp in Amarillo."

"It's risky, and there's no guarantee you won't be detained or not make it back," replied Lonnie.

"I know, but I pushed for him to join us, and after what happened with Hendrix I need to give something back to the group. Will you keep a close eye on my family?" I asked.

"Just like my own, buddy. Just like my own," replied Lonnie.

Sheila was able to rig one of the cars to pull Lonnie's trailer, freeing his truck so we could make great time.

Lonnie made a point to thank her. "You've impressed us, Sheila, with your work ethic and friendship. I know you were concerned about whether you could join our group. Well, I took a little survey with everyone last night—except for Mike," he said with a wink— "and they all voted unanimously to keep you on as a full member of our group if you so choose."

"Yes, sir…Mr… I mean officer. That's everything I was hoping for," replied Sheila.

"Ma'am, please call me Lonnie."

He pulled Mike aside, saying, "We just officially added your new girl to our group. Don't get bored with her!"

"Ha! No chance of that, buddy," replied Mike. "There's not a lot of choices nowadays, and she's as hot as they come."

Joy and our boys were not happy I was leaving, and I kissed them all as we prepared to leave.

Our radios would be out of range, so we spent ten precious minutes looking at the map. Lonnie mapped out three days' worth of travel, along with potential campsites, just in case we took longer than a day to get back.

Mike drove, while I stayed in the back with Vlad, who was still unconscious.

I was daydreaming about old Western movies. where a man gets shot and wakes up three days later in an unfamiliar house, being cared for by a woman he has never seen before.

We were told there would be a FEMA camp in Amarillo by the soldier we ran into a couple of days ago. *The same one that led us to believe that they threw Ronna out of the helicopter*, I thought. I hoped the information was correct or my new friend would not make it.

I crouched down next to Vlad, not wanting to get tossed out of the bed, as Mike laid on the gas.

"I'm going to need you standing to provide cover once we slow down in the city limits," Mike told me over the radio.

"I'm only stopping for military or the FEMA camp gates."

The miles passed and I tried to talk to Vlad. I had heard before that sometimes unconscious patients could hear and later recall everything that was being said around them, even if they couldn't respond.

"Vlad," I said in a loud voice over the truck engine and wind. "Mike and I are taking you to town to get help." I left out the part about the FEMA camp, knowing full well he wouldn't be happy about it. "The fact that we can make this trip and keep our group safe is because you joined us and gave us the firepower to make it happen. I'm forever grateful to you, Vlad, and for your friendship so far. Just try to hold on for me, and all of us. I don't want to have to drink all your vodka by myself!"

I half expected a comment back, but none came. I looked up to see a highway sign, reading "Amarillo ~ 20 miles."

"Did you see that sign?" I asked Mike over the radio.

"Yeah, buddy, we're close. I'm going to keep up the speed as long as I can, but it won't be long…"

"Hey, Mike!" I shouted, pointing north towards a long line of people off in the distance.

"We will follow the herd," he replied. "They must be heading to the Camp."

Mike slowed the truck to just over 20 mph when he reached the back of the line of people walking, riding bicycles and, to his surprise, there were a few on four-wheelers.

"That's what I'm talking about!" called Mike, pointing towards them.

"What happens when they get to the Camp?" I asked him.

"That's what I was thinking," Mike replied. "If they're going to dump those four-wheelers, we've got room for a couple in the bed."

The line was getting wider, and Mike drove on the shoulder now, only able to go ten mph.

"That's it!" he called out, pointing ahead.

I was able to stand now, looking over the cab, reminding me of much of my childhood.

"I see it," I replied. "Slow and easy. I don't want to get shot today."

Two soldiers near the gate held up a giant stop sign as we approached. Mike stopped idling the engine.

"Cut the engine," one announced with a megaphone.

Mike turned off the motor, and we waited.

Ten minutes went by with no more instructions, and I wasn't sure what to do.

Mike had his driver's side window open, and we could talk without yelling.

I kept Vlad shielded from the sun as much as possible. He was breathing but still unconscious.

Two more soldiers showed at the gates and strolled towards us, rifles at the ready.

"Real still," said Mike to me, not looking back.

At 20 yards out, they ordered us out of the vehicle.

"Hands up, boys," called one, gesturing with his rifle.

We did as we were asked, raising our hands high into the air.

"You guys checking into the Camp?" he asked.

"Not exactly," stated Mike, "but we've got one wounded in the back that needs medical attention."

"So, you just thought you would drop someone off here, and now it's our problem?"

"No, sir," I replied. "We've got a man that has a bad infection from an injury, and he's going to die if he doesn't get help. We've done all we could, and it's not enough."

"Afternoon, gentlemen" came a voice from another soldier, now walking towards us.

"Afternoon, sir," I said, giving Mike a WTF eyebrow lift.

"It's all right," said the soldier. "I know these guys. We met a couple of days ago. Where's the rest of your group from the other day?" he asked.

"They've moved on towards Colorado, isn't that right?" he said, clearly not expecting a reply. "Beautiful country up there, but the terrain can be downright hostile, especially now," he added.

"So, you boys here to take me up on my offer?"

"No, sir. Not exactly," replied Mike. "We've got a sick comrade in the back, and he's going to die if you can't help him."

"Comrade, huh? You mean the wiseass Russian with the bad leg, I'm guessing."

"That's the one, sir," replied Mike, now resigned to being turned away by the soldier.

"Wait here," he said, and walked back to the front, disappearing through the gate.

The minutes ran by in awkward silence, with none of us saying a word.

I felt like I was trying to buy a new car and the guy was taking my offer back to his boss, as I wondered if he was getting a soda and letting me stew.

Nearly 30 minutes later, he returned with a civilian in a white coat, carrying a medical bag.

"We'll take a look," said the soldier, as he lowered the tailgate.

The doctor jumped up on the back of the truck and began to examine Vlad.

"Can't you take him in and get him out of the heat?" I asked.

"I want to make sure he's got a chance at surviving first. I don't need a corpse in our hospital getting other people sick."

It sucked for Vlad, but I saw his point.

"He's got a severe infection," said the Doctor a few minutes later. "He may lose his leg, but I think we can save him."

"What do you think, boys," the soldier asked. "Should we take him inside?"

"Might be good practice for our Medical Team," the doctor spoke up.

"Good point, Doc," he replied.

* * * * * * *

Chapter Twenty-two ~ FEMA Camp
Amarillo, Texas

"Since you boys are here," the soldier added, "let me show you around. First, all weapons in the truck."

Mike and I laid our concealed carry pistols next to the rifles already in the truck.

"Just have to be sure, boys," he continued, as one of his men frisked us.

"Don't worry; no one will mess with your truck here. I want to give you the grand tour, in case your group gets tired of fending for themselves out there in no-man's-land."

The Camp was more extensive than I could have imagined, with people everywhere. Some were wandering about, while most were doing some sort of work.

"Everyone has a purpose here," announced the soldier. "And as you can see, no one wants to leave," as I told you before.

I saw only women and children and guessed Vlad was right about them separating the men.

"Where are the men?" I asked.

"They have their very own Camp just a few miles over there," he said, pointing east. "Keeps things simple...

"Excuse me for a minute, gentlemen," he said, as he veered off to talk to a security guy.

"I don't like this," I told Mike in a low voice.

"Me neither," he said, and added, "Notice how all the guards are men, and the women steer clear of them as they walk around?"

"I saw that," I replied. "I can only imagine what happens here after dark, with all the husbands a few miles away…"

"I want to ask him about Harry, but it's probably a bad idea," said Mike, finishing my sentence.

"Sorry about that, guys. There's always something here that needs my attention.

"We've got running water, and even hot showers," he said, pointing to a building on the far end of the Camp.

"I can't show you those, since the women are showering."

I'm sure it's really private, I thought, as I saw two male guards just inside the wide-open front door, joking and pointing into the building.

"I'm guessing you boys are hungry," he said, opening the door to a large cafeteria.

"Lunch is almost over, but you've got about 30 minutes." He told the guard we were his guests and said, "Dig in, gentlemen. I'll be back in about 30 to finish off our tour."

"Thank you, sir," I said, reaching out to shake his hand. This time he shook it.

Mike was staring wide-eyed at the long line of food, reminding me of the old Sizzler and Golden Corral buffets.

"You're guests of the Colonel, I assume?" asked one of the servers.

"Ah, hell," said Mike. "I didn't know he was a Colonel."

"Everyone is a little less formal here," the server replied, with a smile. "Anyway, you start over here." He pointed towards a large stack of plates and trays. "Then move on down and tell me what you want. We don't waste food here, but you can have as much as you can eat."

Truth be told, I was starved, and since we were guests of the "Colonel," as I now knew him, I was not going to pass up his offer.

The salad bar was impressive, with fresh vegetables, from where I don't know. The sidebar was self-serve, and I loaded my side plate.

Mike skipped this section and went straight for the meat and pasta. He was having his plate loaded with everything from hamburger sliders to French fries, lasagna, and mac and cheese.

I opted for the Italian trio of lasagna, spaghetti with Alfredo sauce, and chicken parmesan with a red sauce that had always been my favorite at the Olive Garden restaurant.

"Look at all this ketchup!" remarked Mike, when he reached the end of the line. "There must be at least a thousand little packets of it!" he exclaimed.

"This is where all the ketchup has been going every time you used to go through a drive-through and they screwed you on the condiments," I joked.

"Man, that used to piss me off," said Mike. "How do you not give out ketchup when someone orders fries? Well, now I know."

We both laughed at that, and even the server smiled just a bit.

"So, what do you think about our little setup here?" asked the server. He seemed nice enough and not at all official. "It's great, right?"

"Not if you're a man, I'm guessing," said Mike.

"We're not allowed to talk about that," the server replied, tightening his facial muscles. "I'm sorry."

"No worries, friend," I said, changing the tone and asking his name.

"Bernie," he said.

"Hi. I'm Lance, and this here is Mike. Who cooks all this great food?"

"I do," he replied. "Well, me and a few other helpers, but it's my kitchen."

"Well, thank you, Bernie, for your hospitality," I said, as we got our drinks and sat to eat.

The Colonel came back just as we were putting our plates up. "Good chow, huh, boys?"

"Yes, thank you, sir," I replied.

"I want to show you our hospital before you leave. But first, there's been a development. Your friend will lose his leg at the hip. It's the only way, the doctors tell me.

"We need to transfer him to another hospital that specializes in these aggressive surgeries."

"Where is he going?" Mike asked.

"To Trinidad, where they have the best surgeons in the country. Did you know that Trinidad used to be the number one place in America to have one of those surgeries?" he added.

"Yes, sir. I remember hearing that somewhere," I replied.

"Their medical staff is spot on with taking things off. We'll have a chopper transport him within the hour."

We took a tour through an impressive tent hospital, where they were already tending to our friend.

"He's still unconscious," said a nurse, realizing we were with him. "We're just getting him prepped for transfer."

"What are his chances?" asked Mike.

"That's not my place to guess," she said soberly.

"Can we talk to someone who can?" I asked, trying to sound polite.

"Wait here," she instructed, as she disappeared behind a heavy gray curtain.

Moments later, a woman in scrubs came out from behind the partition, her white lab coat stained with blood.

"I guess it's bad," said Mike, pointing to her coat.

"No. Oh, I'm sorry. We just delivered a healthy baby boy," the woman said. "The first one of the camps so far," she added.

"I am sure his father will be happy to see him," insisted Mike.

"That's not any of my business," she replied, nervously looking around.

"I'm Dr. Jenny," she said, shaking our hands. "Your friend, he's in bad shape," she continued. "Infections are difficult to manage in the best of conditions, and even harder now.

"He will probably lose his leg, and I can't promise he'll make it through the next few days. We are doing everything we can here, but they are much better equipped for this kind of patient up in Trinidad. He has to want to fight. It's up to him now."

"He's a fighter, for sure," I added. "Can we see him?"

"Sure," Dr. Jenny replied. "I'll give you two just a few minutes," pulling a part of the curtain back. "Right this way, gentlemen."

Vlad was still unconscious but looked like he could just be taking an afternoon nap.

"We're here, buddy," I said, holding his right hand, "and they're transferring you up to Trinidad, Colorado, just above David's place."

"Stay alive, my friend," said Mike from just behind me. "We will check on you in a few days."

* * * *

"You boys are welcome to stay a night," said the Colonel as we exited the hospital. "We've got some room over at the men's barracks."

"Thank you for the offer and your hospitality, sir, but we had better be getting back to our families," I responded. *That's absolutely the last thing I would want to do*, I thought.

"I can understand that," he replied. "Now that you've seen our facilities, give it some thought. We've always got room for your little group."

"Yes, sir," we both replied in an obligatory response.

We found Mike's truck just as we had left it, only filled with gas. I asked the soldier about it, and he just said, "Colonel's orders. There's a cooler too," he remarked, pointing into the bed of the truck.

"Thank you!" Mike replied.

"What are you guys doing with these four-wheelers?" I asked, pointing to three next to the truck and hoping I didn't overstep my boundaries.

"Not sure," came the soldier's reply, as he got on the radio.

Five minutes later, after a chat with the Colonel, he said, "You guys can take two if you can carry them, according to the Colonel."

"No shit!" Mike said, with a grin and excitement of a boy with his first bike. "Let's load 'em up!"

His truck bed was only going to hold one ATV.

"How do you feel about riding?" he asked me.

"I'm not leaving an extra machine here," I told him, "and I'll lead."

Passing the parade of the walkers, all wondering why we were headed the opposite way, we stopped to look at the map.

Now late afternoon, it looked like a few hours' ride to meet our group.

"You up for it tonight?" Mike asked me.

"Let's do it!" I shot back, as Mike opened the cooler.

"That's what I'm talking about!" said Mike, looking at all the food in the cooler.

Reaching for the note on top, he read it aloud. "Thank you, Mike, for talking with me today. I hope you come back soon to see me…" he trailed off, leaving out the "Love, Bernie." He turned a shade of red that was rare, especially for a cop.

I decided to give him a pass on this one, asking him to repeat himself, like I couldn't hear him, as I turned off the engine.

"Nothing," he said. "Just a bunch of food from the Colonel," he called out, quickly stuffing the note into his front pocket. "Looks like he was sweet on you," he added.

"Ha," I said. "Maybe so."

I rode in front at a steady 50 mph, dodging vehicles when needed.

Saying a quick prayer for Vlad, I wondered if God was watching over us every step of the way. Was it a coincidence that Vlad would be headed the same direction as us?

I felt good today. We dropped off a fellow comrade alive to the best facility in the area, snagged a couple of four-wheelers, and have a large cooler full of old-school food.

"I'm coming, Joy!" I called out as loud as I could over the dusty road.

At this speed, we could meet up with them before dark, and I would get to sleep in my own bed, or at least sleeping bag, tonight.

Lonnie was spot-on with his camp calculations, and two hours later we approached cautiously.

Mike, with the truck, took the lead as he radioed that we were close.

My boys were jumping up and down when they saw me. It made me proud that we had raised such good boys, even though I knew they were just getting excited about the new four-wheelers.

"Wait until they see the burgers and mac and cheese!" Mike told me, as we lifted the cooler out from the back of the truck.

Luckily, they hadn't eaten yet, just arriving at camp about 30 minutes earlier.

Mike did the honors of unloading the large cooler, calling out the food as he went.

"Who likes hotdogs?" he asked, holding up a package of 20. "What about hamburgers? Mac and cheese, lasagna, spaghetti, I think with red sauce?"

The hands in the group kept raising as Mike announced more items. "Anyone like Chinese?" he called out, pulling out eight large containers of various dishes.

I knew he was having fun being the guy with the goods. "I only hope you have broccoli beef!" I called out, only half kidding.

"Two right here!" he said, raising large Tupperware containers over his head.

"All is right with the world," I said aloud, winking to Joy.

I secretly wondered when we would get some time alone. *Probably not for a while*, I thought.

Glancing back at the trailer, I saw Sheila hop up and give Mike a hug and kiss. *She has officially moved on*, I thought. "Good for you," I said, giving Mike a nod.

We all settled in for a well-deserved dinner of real food. We shared that Vlad was being flown to Trinidad, where he would receive care at an excellent hospital.

Everyone was asking what the FEMA camp was like and how many people were there. I kept it to the basics, not wanting anyone to equate camp life with hot showers and hamburgers.

"They separate the men from the women and children," I told the adults as the kids played games. "The women's showers are anything but private, and I can't imagine what happens when the lights go off at night."

I wasn't looking to scare anyone, but now everybody seemed to look at our new meal as a once-in-a-lifetime opportunity and not something they would seek out long-term. I, of course, was wrong using the term *everybody*.

At dawn, Ringo let out a low growl, standing and facing south. A group of 12 to 15 people were heading north, just 100 yards from our camp.

Looking through my binoculars, they appeared harmless. I observed a few families strewn together, searching for something better.

A woman from our camp, whose name I couldn't remember, ran towards them, arms raised in the air and yelling, "Take me with you" over and over.

Her husband chased after her, calling her back.

Joy stood next to me, watching the commotion. "What's that all about?" I asked her, keeping a close eye on the passing group.

"I don't know, honey. I think they have been having some problems, but I didn't realize it was this bad."

"If he doesn't go with her, he'll never see her again," I told her.

"You told them both last night what to expect, and that's all you can do," she replied to me.

Minutes later, both the husband and wife fell in with the traveling nomads. "I hope the food is worth it," said Jake, from just behind mem, as I jumped.

"Man, you scared the hell out of me!" I told him.

"Always be aware of your surroundings," he replied. "Even in a safety zone like this," he pointed out, gesturing around our camp.

"Point taken," I agreed.

We packed the camp quickly. It seemed to get easier every morning as we all pitched in and knew our roles.

"Good luck, my friend," I said aloud, hoping Vlad was still alive. "We will be back for you."

Following the Hendrix Headcount, we were back on the road. The two four-wheelers snuggly fitting on the trailers would no doubt come in handy on our still-long journey.

"Amarillo, here we come!" said Jake aloud as we pulled out.

Heading north, we settled in at 20 miles per hour.

What's next, I thought, reminding me of the old days when Joy could ask me about my day and I couldn't think of anything interesting that happened; this sometimes went on for weeks.

Now, in this next-world, every day seemed crazier than the last. I wondered when I would get another boring day, and thought it not likely anytime soon.

"So, what's up with Mike?" asked Jake. "I mean, you two have spent a lot of time together over the past couple days, and he hasn't killed you."

"Ha, I responded," wanting to be careful about what I said.

"All I know," I continued, "is that he's a complicated guy with a lot of baggage. Not a bad guy necessarily, but one to certainly keep an eye on. The more I get to know him, the more I think we need someone like him in our group."

"I wouldn't have expected you to say that," replied Jake.

"I think you two should keep your distance," I continued, "but I'm slightly less worried about you two having a conflict now, if that makes any sense."

"Not really, buddy, but I'll take your word on it for now," replied Jake.

The miles passed, with the wind in my hair reminding me of days now gone by, riding my motorcycle down a country road or running a boat around a lake.

There were small groups of people still meandering about, but they seemed less each day. *Perhaps they made it to one of the shelters or starved along the way*, I thought.

I felt genuinely thankful today, like I should be wearing one of those T-shirts that say "Blessed" on it. I never really understood it until now. I was blessed with my family, new friends, all the food we could ask for, and the firepower to keep it.

I relaxed just a bit, hoping the rest of the trip to David's parents' house would be smooth sailing.

* * * * * * *

Chapter Twenty-three ~
Northwest of Amarillo, Texas

Driving for nearly two hours, I radioed Lonnie to take a break and let the kids stretch their legs.

"Sure thing, buddy. Let's find a spot where we can get off the main road just a bit."

A few miles ahead was a side road that cut across an open pasture. We could see the fence line 30 yards off the road, with posts every 20 feet.

"What is that?" asked Jake, pointing to the fence line.

I looked and saw something hanging from nearly every pole for the next 200 yards. Looking through my binoculars, I could see the carcass of a dog on each pole.

"Those are coyotes," I said aloud, "and it's a message."

"To the coyotes or us?" asked Jake.

"Both, I assume," I replied.

Before I could even radio Lonnie, he was turning us all around. "We'll stop soon, everyone," he called on the radio. "Just not here."

Twenty minutes later, the kids were begging to stop, as most had to go to the bathroom.

We pulled off into the middle of a large field, with knee-high grass in most places.

I was a bit nervous about the hot vehicle engines catching the dry grass on fire. Thankfully the road was open to a small circle in the middle, mostly clear of tall grass.

We circled and let the kids run off to a little steam inside the protected area. I sat up on the trailer, watching the wind sway the tall grass around us. It was peaceful, and I tuned out everything but the wind and the sound of our children laughing and playing tag.

"Stay inside the circle!" I called out to them, feeling overprotective, like Joy always accused me of being.

Lonnie, Steve and Mike were on the trailer now, with Jake and me. Mike and Jake kept their distance, and it was a little awkward.

"You boys friends yet?" Lonnie asked them. Neither man answered.

"Well," he continued, "we're a group here, and a family really."

"Remember, it's Families First," I said jokingly, trying to lighten the mood. It didn't work.

"Hudson! Get back here right now!" yelled Joy from behind us. I looked to my right and saw a head 15 yards off in the tall grass, and then another. I counted four in all, as I smelled the cigarette smoke.

I was pretty sure I knew the only two who smoked were Vlad and Sheila.

I had a flashback of a young me, maybe 16, on the very top of a mountain in the Colorado Rockies, smoking cigarettes with my buddy and cooking lunch over a campfire. Even though we had cleared a three-foot perimeter around the fire, as we always did, today something was different. The wind picked up quickly and took my lit cigarette straight out of my hand and into the dry grass ten feet away.

The fire was immediate, and we had only seconds to respond, as the grass caught fire and bellowed a thick cloud of dark black smoke into the clear summer air.

I quickly grabbed a large tarp and all our water. The fire was now expanded to ten feet and growing every second as the wind kept steady. I said a quick prayer, realizing that another minute would send the fire careening down the mountain towards the nearly two dozen houses only a mile away.

In a panic, we frantically threw the tarp out over the middle and poured water wildly across the expanding flames, breathing in the heavy smoke and coughing loudly.

"It's not working!" I yelled to my friend over the crackle of small twigs and leaves burning.

"We need to get help!" he shouted back.

There was a pause, like the parting the Red Sea, I imagined, and all was quiet. The wind was no more, and the fire was low and contained within itself. We both stood in amazement at this miracle before us.

Without a word, we buried the small flames left under six inches of dirt, using only a tiny garden trowel from my backpack.

We stayed nearly two more hours to make sure they wouldn't spark again.

To this very day, I don't know how we stopped that fire, but I have had a healthy respect for it ever since and I felt it was the hand of God.

"Daddy, where's Hudson and Danny?" came a voice from my left, off the trailer.

Jax and Hendrix were there, as well as the other kids, minus Hudson, Danny, and Lonnie's two kids.

"What going on, boys?" said Sheila, as she approached the right of our trailer.

Lonnie, Jake and I looked on in horror as she put her thumb and index finger on her nearly finished cigarette and flicked it into the grass, towards our kids.

I could see the bright red cherry on the end of her cigarette as she took her last drag and yelled "No!......" as she sent the fire starter flipping end over end towards my boy.

It all was in slow motion, like a car crash, and I watched it land in the grass. There was a pause, and nothing happened. I held my breath for what seemed like an hour, but was only a split second, and saw the first flame. We stood up on the trailer and saw Joy jumping the nearly five feet off the trailer towards the kids. She landed on her right foot and let out a scream, falling hard on the ground.

She managed to get to her feet as Jake, Lonnie and I jumped from the trailer.

"Stay here, Mike," Lonnie called out. "You're our spotter for the kids."

I called Joy to stay back, as she was in the grass, limping towards the kids and straight towards the expanding flames.

Mike had the megaphone and called out instructions to both the adults and children. He had a clear view of the situation from his vantage point.

"Everyone back in the vehicles and ready to move out," he told the others.

I had landed hard, but on both feet, off the trailer. I could see Joy, but no one else.

"Where are they?" I thought, trying to remain calm.

"Get your wife," said Jake, with a hand on my shoulder. "We'll get your boy."

My panic all but disappeared as I believed him, and I concentrated on Joy.

Moving close, I could see her using both hands and one leg while dragging the other.

I grabbed her from behind, and she screamed for me to let her go.

"I'm sorry," I told her. "I'm not trying to hurt your leg."

"Let me go!" she screamed again, grabbing at my hands. "I need to get the children!"

I could feel the heat from the expanding flames, now moving closer to us.

Joy fought me for the first time, as I dragged her back towards the caravan. I told her over and over that Jake and Lonnie would get Hudson. Nancy met me halfway back and distracted Joy just a bit by asking about her leg.

I looked down at her right foot, and the angle was all wrong. Her heel was at a 90-degree angle in relation to her leg. It just looked odd with her neon pink tennis shoe still on.

Dragging her slowly backward towards the trailer, I could see the adults' heads over the grass, running right to left and zig-zagging. They called out three names but not Hudson's.

My mind was racing. *Was he okay? Why didn't they call his name too?*

My thoughts flashed back to the very beginning, in the Kroger grocery store parking lot, when I had to give myself that little pep talk. *Get your shit together, Lance,* I could hear myself saying. *Do your job here and get your wife back safe. Your friends will take care of the rest.*

Mike helped us lift Joy onto the trailer, as Nancy evaluated her.

I turned to run back into the field when I heard the softest voice. "I'm sorry, Daddy," came the familiar voice of my sweet boy.

I turned to see Hudson, with his face covered in black soot, and I could smell the unmistakable scent of his singed hair. But he was alive and talking…

"No, son," I said, tears welling up in my eyes. "I'm the one who's sorry.

"How did you get back here?" I asked.

"Mr. Jake pulled me out of the burning things and told me to run as fast as I could back here."

"What about the other kids?" I asked.

"I don't know," he choked, as he started to cry.

"I saw Danny for a minute, and then he was gone… My back hurts, Daddy."

"Let me see, son." I turned him around and was taken back by the nearly one foot of his shirt missing in the back. His skin was worn black ash, and large blisters were visible. I lifted his shirt to find more of the same.

"Oh, buddy, I'm so sorry," I told him, as he cried harder.

"Daddy, it hurts so bad. I feel like I'm going to die."

I lifted him onto the trailer, calling out to Nancy to get him.

My two are back and alive, I thought, *but her Danny is still out there*.

A guilty conscience I've always had overcame me, as I jumped off the trailer and ran towards the expanding fire.

I ran straight for the two heads I could see.

Lonnie was holding his boy tight but let him go, pushing him to run towards the caravan.

Two more, I thought.

"Danny! Danny!" Jake called out over and over. "Where are you?"

Jake was systematically canvassing the areas around the flames, calling out his name.

I ran towards him, calling Danny's name. The grass was tall, and I couldn't see my feet.

My right foot hit something hard...or was it soft? I couldn't tell, but it sent me sprawling onto my chest in the tall grass.

"What the..." I started to say, as I looked back and saw a child covered in black ash, shaking on the ground.

"Danny? Is that you?" I asked.

"Mr. Lance," came the soft reply. "Please help me. I think I got hurt."

I carefully lifted the now unrecognizable boy from the hard ground, realizing his face had been badly burned.

"Am I going to be okay, Mr. Lance?" he asked.

"Yes, buddy. We're going to take good care of you."

I wanted to tell Jake I had his boy but decided to run straight for Nancy.

Danny needed more help than both Hudson and Joy now, and he had to be the priority.

Lonnie's only daughter was still missing. Dropping Danny off, I ran back to Jake.

"Is he okay?" he asked.

"I don't know; he's hurt bad," I said, cringing with the news.

"Go to your boy," I told Jake. "I'll help Lonnie."

A reluctant Jake made his way back, as Lonnie and I searched for his little girl.

Smoke filled the air, thick and dark black, as we called for her.

Mike called out from the trailer, pointing to the far eastern edge of the flames.

Lonnie was the closest and disappeared as he bent down into the grass. He emerged with a body in his arms. He ran past me as her arms and legs hung straight down. Her eyes were open, I noticed, but she was not moving.

Nancy was at capacity when Lonnie put his little girl up onto the trailer.

As I approached, she didn't appear to be burned but she was not breathing.

"Lance, you're up," called Lonnie in the lead truck.

The field was now ablaze with fire on two sides of our caravan.

"Let's go! Let's go!" called Mike over the bull horn. "Every vehicle back the way we came!"

I was the first truck and got turned around as quickly as I could without throwing the injured around on the trailer.

I could see Lonnie in my rearview, bent over his lifeless little girl. Thirty compressions followed by two breaths, he counted over and over.

"Please, Lord," I prayed. "Not this. Please let his little girl and Danny be okay."

Nancy was calling out instructions to Jake and others, with a lot of movement on the trailer from my rearview.

Joy was holding Hudson, with his head buried in her chest. I could barely make out Jax and Hendrix in the car just behind the trailer.

Once back at the highway, we headed north, wanting to put some distance between us and the expanding inferno. I held steady at 15 miles per hour to navigate stalled out vehicles without jarring the trailer around.

I looked in the mirror and saw Steve put his hand on Lonnie's shoulder, as he shook his head back and forth.

Lonnie pushed it away, forcefully, and kept counting: one, two three, four, five....

"Twenty-one," he counted, "twenty-two…and I heard a gasp as his little girl took a deep breath and began to cough hoarsely. She tried to sit up but fell back into her father's waiting arms.

Lonnie and his wife were both sobbing, holding their still-coughing little girl.

I wished I could be back on the trailer and talk to Joy and Hudson. I called on the radio for Steve to come up and take the wheel.

He was just able to navigate around to my open driver's door and into the cab. The switch was easy at only 15 miles per hour.

Going back the same way, I made it over to Joy and my boy.

"Joy, honey," I called out as I got close. "How are you doing?"

She didn't answer but just looked straight ahead at her twisted foot. Hudson cried softly in her arms. "Joy," I said quietly, touching her shoulder gently.

She jumped. "Huh?" she replied.

"I'm here," I told her. "I'm right here."

"I'm looking at my foot, and something is not right," she said without looking up.

"I'm sorry," she said. "I'm...I feel like I'm in a fog... I mean, my foot hurts but not as bad as it looks. And where's Hudson?"

"Honey, he's right here in your arms," I said, noticing the large lump on her forehead for the first time.

"Do you know my name?" I asked her.

"Of course, Lance. I just feel numb, I guess, and my ears are ringing.

"What happened?" she asked. "Is everyone all right?"

"I don't know. Hold tight, and I'll check."

Hudson was quiet but breathing normally, as best I could tell.

I made my way over to Jake and Nancy, who were tending to little Danny. "How's he doing?" I asked.

"He has some bad burns," replied Jake. "A few on his face and the rest on his chest."

I could hear him whimpering as Nancy tended to him. "Hang in there, buddy," I told him.

I worked my way over to Lonnie, still holding his little girl close. I touched him on the shoulder, and he turned quickly, like he was about to knock my lights out.

"It's just me, buddy," I told him.

His face relaxed. "Sorry, Lance. I thought you were someone else."

"How is she?" I asked, knowing most of it already.

"She's alive," his wife interjected angrily, "and that girl Sheila is to blame for it," pointing her right index finger towards the back of the caravan.

"Hold on," Lonnie told her, lightly grabbing her outstretched hand and lowering it. "There will be time later to see what happened. Right now, we've got injured to attend to, and that's all."

"I know exactly what happened," she spat. "It was her damn cigarette that started the whole thing. Who's smokes a cigarette in the middle of a field of dry grass? And what kind of idiot throws the lit butt into the middle of it, where our kids are playing?"

"That's enough right now," said Lonnie sternly. "Stay here with our girl. I'm going to check on everyone else.

"What have we got?" he asked me.

"Danny has some bad burns on his face and chest. Hudson has burns on his back, and Joy appears to have a broken foot and a concussion."

I grabbed three cold packs from one of the freezers and wrapped them each in a towel. "Hold this on your head," I told Joy, handing her one as I put the other on her ankle.

"This one's for you, my brave boy," I told Hudson, carefully placing it on his back.

"Thank you, Daddy," he said softly, trying to force a smile. "I'm sorry we were playing outside the circle," he continued, and started to cry again.

"Are they going to be okay?" he asked. "My friends, I mean…are they hurt bad?"

"I think they're going to be okay. And son, it's not your fault. As the adults, we're responsible for what happened. It's our job, my job, to keep an eye out for all of you. I didn't do that today, and I'm sorry, buddy."

"It's okay, Daddy. I'm not mad."

"I love you, son," I told him as I kissed his soot-covered forehead.

"How's your head, Joy?"

"I have a headache and feel nauseous, but I'm thinking a little more clearly. If I could just take a quick nap, it might help."

"No, honey. We can't do that. I need you to stay awake for me. I'll sit here and talk to you."

"Why is this so hard," she asked.

"What do you mean?"

"Well," Joy said, "at least at home we were safe, and we knew what to expect. Now every day seems worse than the last. What if we don't make it to Colorado?"

"We will, Joy. We will make it, I promise you that."

"Tell me about our new life," she said, as she yawned deeply.

"Stay with me, Joy, and I'll tell you both about what our life in Colorado will be like in a few short weeks.

"You have both been to the Ranch more than a few times but probably never really saw it in its entirety. I walked every foot of the valley growing up, and I know it forward and backward.

"We will work together, side-by-side, farming the land with many other like-minded survivors.

"The days will be filled with the laughter of our children and the nights with stories of the past.

"No traffic, no bills, bosses or deadlines. No more missing dinner with our kids. Just quiet, slow living, getting to know our children for the first time."

"That sounds nice," she responded, kissing Hudson on the cheek.

"That's what this is all about," I added. "Not just for our family but everyone here. It's a chance to start over, and it couldn't happen in McKinney."

I gazed towards the back of our line of vehicles and could see the smoke in the distance getting farther away. The entire horizon was on fire, but the wind must have pushed it the other way. I wondered how far it would burn with no one to fight it. There would no doubt be many people in its path without vehicles to outrun it.

One cigarette, I thought, *could start its own flaming apocalypse.*

My mind flashed to Sheila casually flicking the cigarette butt into the field, and I knew our group would never be the same again.

"Keep an eye out for a hospital or, even better, an urgent care," called Nancy to Steve over the radio.

Passing through Memphis, Texas, Steve called out: "We've got an ER up on the right. It looks like a clinic and not a hospital."

"It's okay," said Nancy. "There won't be any meds left, but everything we need should still be there."

She was right about the meds, as the front doors were smashed in with the cinder block that still lay on the floor inside the clinic.

Mike and Steve swept the building, finding it empty except for the pill bottles strewn about the floor.

"Big city or small town," said Mike, emerging from the office. "Everyone loves their drugs."

I was surprised to see Mike joking around, after his new girlfriend nearly killed four of our kids.

I didn't say anything, knowing this would all be discussed in the coming days.

Mike's biggest problem right now may be his only real friend, Lonnie, I thought.

"Let's get everyone needing treatment inside," called Nancy.

I helped Joy and Hudson off the trailer.

"You guys stay here," I called to Jax and Hendrix, who were both worried about their mom and brother.

Nancy assessed the children first and told Joy she hadn't forgotten about her leg.

Lonnie, Jake and I were tasked with finding the supplies Nancy was calling out.

The Urgent Care was no hospital, but it still had at least 20 rooms filled with cabinets, most with the doors open.

"It looks like someone checked every room for meds," I said to Jake.

"At least they left everything we need right now," he replied.

"Mike and Steve, cover the entrance!" yelled Nancy. "No one in unless they're with us."

She started working on Danny, who was burned the worst.

I got Joy and Hudson on the same gurney and did what I could to keep them comfortable.

Lonnie's boy seemed fine, just shaken up.

His little girl was still coughing. I wondered how much smoke she, Danny and Hudson breathed in.

I had heard that people could die hours or days after breathing in a lot of smoke, and worried about them all.

The lump on Joy's head was getting smaller, and she seemed much clearer now.

"How are you feeling, sweetie?" I asked, now thinking it was a dumb question.

"A little better since Nancy gave me those pills back at the last stop."

Her ankle was now grossly swollen, and it looked like we may have to cut off her new pink tennis shoe. For the first time since it happened, I thought we should have checked out a mall or two. *How long do shoes last*, I thought? *What about shirts, pants, socks and underwear?*

We had been wearing the same clothes for a few days, between dips in the lake. Our clothes had held up, but what about next year or the one after that? The kids would no doubt need a different shoe size frequently as they grew, as well as everything else.

"We're traveling with firepower and room on our trailers," I told Joy, still trying to keep her distracted from the pain.

"We need to take an hour or so and hit up a Walmart or shopping mall and secure proper clothing for the next few years, until the power is restored."

"Sounds good to me," she replied in a tired voice. "Just don't forget to find some pink tennis shoes."

"I'll get everything in your size, honey; I can promise you that."

With Danny and Lonnie's girl taken care of, Nancy turned to Hudson and Joy.

"Sorry, it took so long," said Nancy. "I'm only one person, and a lot is going on here."

"No worries," replied Joy. "You're doing a great job. Can you tend to Hudson first?"

"Absolutely," Nancy replied, giving him a pill to swallow. "That should help some with the pain," she added. She proceeded to remove his tattered shirt and cleaned his burns.

I held his hands as he cried out, "Daddy, please make her stop."

Mini licked him on the cheek and laid down in his lap. He calmed a little, petting her head.

"I'm sorry, son. I know it hurts, but we must do this to get you better.

"Remember that time," I said, hoping to distract him a little, "when we went to Bolivia to visit your uncle, aunt and cousins?"

"Yes, Daddy. We saw the Dakar Rally, racing across the country with the monster trucks and motorcycles."

"Remember," I said, "when the huge Red Bull truck kicked up sand all over us? It was dusty, and sand flew everywhere. It took Mom almost a whole hour to get it all out of your hair when we got back to your cousins' house."

"Yeah, Daddy, that was so cool."

"It's like we're doing now," I added, only a bit slower. "We have big trucks and trailers kicking up dirt, and two cool four-wheelers as well."

"All patched up," Nancy announced.

"You're next, Joy," she said soberly, "and this is going to hurt bad. Take these," she told my wife, handing her two large white pills.

"Let me know when the pain is low."

Twenty minutes later, a reluctant Joy called for Nancy. "I'm ready," she stated matter of factly.

I asked Tina to take our other boys to play with Veronica and Suzie.

Joy screamed out as Nancy set her foot.

I cringed at the sight, imagining the pain she must be going through.

"Let's go," Nancy called to me. "Hand me that splint over there," she commanded.

I did as she asked, and minutes later my Joy was taped up, with her foot looking normal.

"You were able to save her shoe!" I commented, seeing the pink sneaker now straight and uncut.

"Yes, I guess," she replied, but this still needs to be cast soon.

I gave an exhausted Joy a high five at the news, still vowing to stock up on more shoes and clothes.

Lonnie, Jake and I scoured the clinic for anything we may need down the road. We ended up with 16 large Tupperware-type containers filled with everything medical, except of course meds.

We headed out north again, with everyone patched up as best as allowed.

Lonnie, Jake and I sat next to each other as we pulled out.

"What's next, Lonnie?" asked an obviously agitated Jake.

"Sheila is now an official part of our group, and her reckless behavior threatened all our children. I'm not sure, but we need to address it as a group," Lonnie replied.

"On the one hand, with Vlad down, she's the only one who can fix the vehicles when they break down. On the other, her carelessness could have cost the lives of four of our children."

* * * * * * *

Chapter Twenty-four ~ Clarendon, Texas

I told them about my shopping mall idea, and they agreed it needed to be a priority.

"The only issue," pointed out Jake, "is that shopping malls are in the middle of cities and that's precisely what we've been trying to avoid this entire trip."

"The big-box stores are probably all taken over by now, anyway," said Lonnie.

"I'm sure you guys are right," I replied, pushing the idea to the back of my mind.

We drove in silence for a while, and it seemed odd not to have Lonnie driving the lead truck. It was clear, however, that he just needed some time with his little girl. Mini lay next to her, licking her hand, and her cough seemed to improve with each passing mile.

"That's it!" Jake pointed up the road. "The sign!" he added.

"Clarendon Outlet Stores ~ 10 miles," it read.

"Are you okay for a quick stop?" I asked Lonnie. "It might be the best chance we get for clothes and shoes."

"Sure," he replied, stating that it would have to depend on security.

Half an hour later, we could see the store complex up ahead. Lonnie retook the position of the lead truck driver, in case we had to maneuver quickly.

With a slow approach, the parking lot was nearly full of cars, and if I didn't know better it could have been just another shopping day. Circling slow around the lot, there were no signs of people. Jake and I scanned the stores on either side with binoculars. "Notice something off?" I called out to Jake.

"The doors?" he asked.

"Yes, they're all intact," I replied. "Not a single one broken, except to the food court."

Lonnie stopped us in the far end of the parking lot, while his wife and Tina wrote down everyone's clothing and shoe sizes. Setting expectations, it was mentioned there could be no requests as to brands, styles or colors.

The ladies lobbied for one of them to assist in gathering the items needed. "They don't trust us to make fashion decisions for them?" asked Jake, but not so they could hear.

"Would you?" I asked him, laughing.

We had our first group meeting since the fire. Everyone was present, except Sheila, who stayed in Mike's truck.

"Okay, everyone. Here's the plan," I said, standing on the trailer.

"We will be here for about two hours, if it is safe. I know its lunchtime, and most of you are hungry, so those staying here can get something together for the group.

"Jake and I will clear one store at a time, and then bring Tina in to help gather clothes and shoes. Lonnie and Jim will cover us from here. Mike and Steve are going to refill our gasoline tanks and storage cans with vehicles from the parking lot. If that goes quickly, they can help us with our tasks. Nancy will continue to aid our wounded.

"Let's go and be safe, everybody," I called as we jumped off the trailer.

"How did you decide who had what tasks?" Jake asked me, as we strolled towards the first kids' clothing store.

"Pretty easy," I told him. "I kept you and Mike separated. Then I kept both cops from having to pry a door or smash a business window. And your wife gets another couple hours to do what she does best, helping people."

The crowbar we had previously used at the grocery store wasn't working as well at the kids' clothing store. "It's smash-and-grab now," I told Jake. "It's a first for both of us," I added. "Want me to go first?"

"Sure, buddy," said Jake. "We've got enough stores we need to hit to give us both 3-10 years in the big house just a couple of weeks ago."

I took the first swing and smashed the front door. The tint film held the shards together, making the flying glass I had imagined to be much less dramatic. The door was still intact, just in pieces.

Clearing the film shards took a few minutes, as we wanted to make sure Tina could duck through and not get cut.

Clearing the store was quick, as there was only a front area filled with kids' clothes and a small back office and bathroom.

Tina came inside and gathered us for a meeting. "Thank you, boys, for securing the store. Now it's my turn," she stated with a smile. "I'll pick out the clothes and hand them to you. Just stack them near the front, and this will go quickly. We'll do the same for the other stores. Any issues with that?"

"Nope," I replied quickly, as Jake did the same. I nodded at Jake, thankful I had no responsibility picking out clothes.

We did the same for the shoe store and women's clothing outlet. Tina walked past me with two pairs of bright pink tennis shoes in Joy's size 8 and gave me a wink.

"No special requests, huh?" Jake said, punching me in the arm.

"Not my rules, buddy. Not my rules," I responded, smiling.

"I'm getting my Danny some Air Jordans," he added.

The men's store had a bit of everything, including clothing, shoes, and even a few suits. Tina did a bang-up job here as well. I was just happy to have some boxers, socks and T-shirts.

With the shopping center clear, Lonnie pulled the lead trailer in front of each store. The clothing took up nearly 1/8 of the trailer.

I was happy to be back with Joy and my boys, checking on her and Hudson. Both were in good spirits, with Joy appearing comfortably medicated.

Nancy told us that all her patients were improving, and this was all I could ask for today.

I checked in on little Danny with Jake and saw that his face was wrapped, giving only a small slit for his eyes and mouth. "How's he doing?" I asked Nancy.

"He'll recover," she replied, "but his face will never be the same."

I felt a slow-building tension in my gut, with a flashback to the cigarette butt that changed everything. With my two on the mend, and Hudson's probable scars only visible on his back, I couldn't imagine how Jake and Nancy felt, their boy likely scarred for life; and Lonnie with his wife, so close to losing their little girl.

"This must be addressed sooner than later," I told my half-dazed but almost smiling beautiful wife of ten years, now surrounded by all her boys, even Ringo.

"I can forgive a mistake," she told me, "and even for my boy here," gesturing to Hudson. "I'm just not sure about the other families," she continued.

"Yes, I agree. Now it's up to them to decide what happens with her," I replied.

I called Jake and Lonnie for a quick meeting. "Hey guys," I started. "I know we were all affected by the incident with Sheila, with my family having the least injuries. I was involved in a similar situation a long time ago, where I was the careless one. It turned out okay in the end, but it just as quickly could have been this bad, or worse.

"Joy and I are willing to forgive Sheila for her mistake, assuming that she is remorseful and takes responsibility for her actions. I am not suggesting you two and your wives do the same, as it is your decision to make.

"Joy and I will fully support whatever you two decide, and we will all move forward as a group, with trust and respect once again."

"Thank you, brother," replied both Jake and Lonnie, giving me the all-is-okay nod.

I returned to Joy, not able to give her an idea of what was to happen. "It's in their hands now," I told her, "and Lonnie has more skin in the game with Mike than anybody else."

Mike and Steve secured as much gasoline as we could carry.

I could see Steve in the front cab, but Mike was not in sight. I wondered what he and Sheila may be talking about.

With us stragglers on duty, we were each saved a sandwich and a bag of chips, all nacho cheese. If we hadn't already eaten all the pickles, it would have been the perfect lunch.

I made a mental note to start making pickles again as soon as we reached Colorado, just as I had done in my home kitchen over the past few years with my boys.

Ready to head north once again, Lonnie was struggling with his decision. Mike was his closest buddy, and even though he was a loose cannon, so to speak, he was a friend and former partner.

Lonnie did not doubt that Mike would now choose her side, and if she went, then so did he. *It might be better with him gone*, Lonnie thought, casually looking at Jake but not uttering a word.

Lonnie knew better than to ask Jake's opinion of Mike and his own wife about Sheila. Usually steadfast and straight to the right answer, he was on the fence and hated being indecisive about his decisions. *I'll interview them both*, he thought, *but I need an impartial witness.*

"Lance, you're up," Lonnie stated, "but this time it's not about driving the truck."

"What do you need, brother?" I asked, having an idea of what was coming.

"I need your help sorting this mess out," was all he said.

"I'm guessing he wants to get this over with," I whispered to Joy, as Lonnie called me, pointing to the back trailer, where Mike and Sheila were inside the SUV.

Lonnie slowly opened the passenger side front door, and we heard the wailing sound of a woman in the back seat.

"She's been like that since it happened," said Mike, sitting in the driver's position. "Says she wants to kill herself for the pain she caused."

"She's right," said Lonnie, looking clearly at Mike. "She did cause a lot of pain, and we may have children who are scarred for life, including mine."

I didn't say anything, keeping unusually quiet. I realized this would be more about Lonnie and Mike than anyone else.

They talked over Sheila's crying, with her not hearing a word.

I stood back, knowing I would get the full report soon enough.

Lonnie emerged from the cab nearly ten minutes later. "It's a group decision," he told me, "as we all agreed at the start. I'll be voting for her to stay, even though my wife won't agree," he added.

"Joy and I are okay with her staying," I remarked, "especially after hearing about her remorse for what happened. Vlad has quit smoking, at least for a while; she may want to consider it as well."

"Agreed on that point," replied an exhausted Lonnie. "I can't wait for this day to be over, if I'm being honest."

"I'm with you, buddy," I said, grabbing his right shoulder. "When do we check into the Four Seasons for a weeklong beach vacation?" I asked, joking.

Lonnie gathered the group, wanting to get this done one way or the other right now, I guessed.

Everyone seemed to have an opinion, with some upset and others trying to be logical about the facts presented.

After 30 minutes, a hand vote was taken, and the majority decided to keep Sheila in the group if she personally apologized to each member affected by her actions.

I felt good about the decision, putting the call squarely in her corner. I was not too far away from having to apologize to so many people all those years ago with my careless mistake, and it easily could have been much worse.

Sheila, hearing the news, opted to wait on the apologies for now, inciting some in the group to rethink their positions.

* * * *

We headed back north, with only a few hours until we needed to make camp for the night.

"Keep an eye out on the map," Lonnie called over the radio, "for a suitable site to stop for the night."

Jake and I carefully reviewed the map and found a few suitable sites.

I relaxed just a bit, letting the wind blow through my hair and petting Mini, who was laying just beside me.

Looking at my reflection in the back window of the truck, I caught a glance of my now-scruffy face. I was never much for growing a beard, although I knew I could. It just got itchy is all, and I would need to shave soon, I thought, catching a glimpse of Hudson looking at me. "Should I grow a beard, son?" I asked.

"Daddy, I think you already did," he replied, moving close to me on the trailer and resting his head on my leg.

"I love you, son," I told him, "and I'm so happy you're okay."

"I love you too, Daddy, and I'm so happy you're growing a beard," he said, laughing at his own joke.

Detouring around Amarillo from the south to west, Jake and I looked for a camping spot with a lake or river nearby. We settled on Buffalo Lake National Wildlife Refuge. "I hope it's not overrun with people looking to hunt the wildlife," I pointed out.

"That's what I was thinking," replied Jake. "I'm not quite sure about this one."

Stopping a few miles out from the refuge, it didn't take binoculars to see all the people with makeshift camps strewn about the lake.

"We're going to have to pass on this one, guys," said Lonnie over the radio. "Sorry, but the lake is out for tonight. What's one more day without a bath," he added, his first joke since the fire.

"I was hoping for a lake stay tonight," said Jake.

"Yeah. Me too, brother," I told him, not finding another one anywhere close on the map.

Cutting back up to I-40, we stopped at a small municipal airport, on a whim, in the town of Wildorado.

Jake, Jim and I cleared the area and found seven hangar apartments vacant, still stocked with food and various bar spirits. All told, there were 16 beds, and room for more on various couches and lounge chairs.

We opted for a night indoors, giving preference to families with wounded from earlier today.

After raiding the liquor cabinets from the hangars, the men had a Scotch tasting in plastic cups. We were treated to a long list of great Scotch, including Macallan, Glenlivet, Jonnie Walker blue and black, Glenmorangie, and even some old standby Famous Grouse.

The ladies found some excellent wines, including Silver oak, Mayacamas Vineyard Cabernet, Ken Wright Cecil Vineyard Chardonnay, and Joy's favorite, Kim Crawford Sauvignon Blanc.

The adults got a rare moment to relax, as the kids slept deeply, and the dogs helped keep watch.

Everyone slept inside tonight, even the dogs, except for Mike and Sheila, who opted to sleep in the truck.

"I get that she's upset," I told Jake in a low voice only we could hear. "But if I were her, I would have apologized right away and gotten it over with."

"Yeah, I agree," Jake said. "Lonnie seems pretty annoyed about it, and I'm not sure he won't change his mind soon if she waits much longer."

I slept better that night than every other one since it started. We were in a real bed, and the dogs were quiet all night.

I was sure we slept in but had to confirm it with Jake. "We sure did! It says 7:35," he replied with a grin, checking his pocket watch.

Gathering outside for a headcount, the passenger side door of Mike's truck opened and Sheila stepped out. Mike helped her along, walking slowly as she was unsteady. Facing the group, it was silent, with no one speaking, not even the children.

Sheila stepped forward, stood in front of each child affected yesterday and looked them each in the eye, apologizing for her actions. She did the same for Joy and Nancy.

I was moved by her sincerity, wishing she had done this yesterday.

Lonnie's wife turned away, refusing to bear witness. The rest of us watched without saying a word.

Mike pulled Lonnie aside, out of earshot from the rest of us.

* * * *

I told Jim I wanted to try to get hold of David in Raton Pass this morning. Forty minutes later, he was on the line.

"Hi, David," I said, with a knot in my stomach, knowing I was about to hear some bad news.

"Hi, buddy," David replied solemnly. "We had a tragic accident here, and we lost my dad."

"I'm sorry to hear that," I told him, knowing his dad was a huge loss to him and the community.

Something told me to skip the next logical question, nearly always asked in the old world: "What happened?"

"He was a good man, a good father to you, and grandfather to your son," I told him. How's your mother holding up?"

"Better than the rest of us," he replied. "She's sweet as punch and tough as nails," he added.

"How's your trip?" David asked, hoping for a change in the subject.

"Brother, you have no idea," I told him. "Every day is crazier than the last. I figured we'd be at your place a few days ago, and as it sits we're just northwest of Amarillo."

"That's closer for sure," replied David, "but still a ways out."

"Let James know we're still good on our deal, if you talk to him," I said.

"I haven't spoken to him lately, but I'm sure I will soon, and I'll let him know," replied David. "Remember when you could drive from Dallas to Colorado in one long day?"

"Yeah, we did it just six months ago; now it's weeks, no doubt. Plus, everybody wants to take our heads off!" I added. "I've got some crazy stories for you, my friend.

"You find a girlfriend yet?" I asked him, hoping I wasn't hitting a sore spot about his deceased wife.

"No, not yet," he replied, "but Mark gave me the go-ahead if any suitable ladies were to come along."

"Who knows?" I said. "The right one may show up on your front doorstep one day."

"We'll see," he replied, "but in the meantime I've got a group of good people counting on me to lead them in the coming weeks, months, and maybe even years. I'm just trying every day to be the leader they can trust and respect. It's not easy," he added.

"I know," I told him. "Here we have a few of us who all take turns, depending on the situation at hand. We'll try to give you another call when we're about a day or two out. There's a lot of wide-open country between Amarillo and you guys, so I'm hoping we can pick up the pace.

"Our buddy Vlad, the gun guy, is already in Trinidad, and hopefully alive after an accident, but he got to ride on a chopper."

"All right, buddy. I've got to run for now," said David. "Talk to you soon."

I half wanted to stay in the hangars for another week or two and rest up, but I knew it couldn't happen.

I resolved to keep my eyes open on the map for more small airports on the way.

"That was an awesome night," said Jake, as we headed out. "The airport thing, I mean."

"Yeah, it beats sleeping outside, next to the road," I added.

* * * * * * *

Chapter Twenty-five ~
East of the New Mexico Border

"Let's make some miles today!" said Lonnie. We all gave a whoop, like we were a bunch of cowboys starting a new cattle drive.

I felt good today. Strong, and with renewed hope for our journey.

I had a feeling that we would have a good day. Heading west from Amarillo, we saw a sign for the Big Texan Steak Ranch and Brewery.

"Daddy! Daddy!" Jax and Hendrix called out. "It's the Big Texas place," pointing at the oversized billboard.

Every time we drove to Colorado, this was our stop in Amarillo. They had a contest similar to the one John Candy did in the movie *The Great Outdoors*. Here it was, a 72-ounce steak, baked potato, salad, roll with butter, and shrimp cocktail. Everything had to be eaten in one hour to get the $72 you paid upfront refunded.

The boys loved watching the contest, where we sometimes saw as many as five people competing at once. I remember asking one server how many completed the challenge. She told me about one in ten.

"I'm going to miss that place, buddy," I whispered to Hudson.

"It's okay, Daddy. We can just stop there on the way back."

"Good thinking, Hudson," I replied, and asked, "Where did you learn to be so smart? Didn't I teach you that?"

"No, Daddy. I go to school."

"Ouch!" laughed Jake, overhearing our conversation.

"That does kind of sting," I joked back.

"Today is going to be a good day," I told Jake. "I can feel it in my bones."

"We're going to hit Highway 287 north, then 87 Northwest," Lonnie called over the radio. "It's a three-hour drive to Raton City, New Mexico, from here in optimal conditions. If we're lucky, we could be there by tomorrow or the next day," he added.

"There's not a lot of people up this direction, but we need to be on our toes. We all know what can happen when we relax out here."

I heard Lonnie and agreed with him, but nothing could change my mood this morning. I was relaxed, and it felt good.

Two hours passed, with mile after mile rolling by.

"Time for a potty break for the kids," announced Lonnie, slowing the lead truck. We stopped single file, and the kids took turns using the porta-potty on the trailer.

"Hey, buddy, I called," seeing Jax climb up on the trailer.

"Daddy, can I ride up here with you and Hooty?" Hooty was a nickname we had given Hudson a few years back but hadn't been used in a while.

"Sure, son. Just let your mom know," I replied.

"Eyes open!" called Lonnie a few minutes later. "We've got a couple of guys on bikes from the east."

"Get down, boys," I called, now realizing I was only talking to Hudson and Danny.

"Where's Jax?" I asked Jake. "Did you see where he went?"

"I think he's in the potty," he replied.

The two men on the bikes were headed straight for us at 50 yards out. I couldn't see any clear signs of weapons. Each rode an old Indian motorcycle, with side bags and sleeping bags on the back.

"Cover me," I told Jake, as they approached the east side of our trailer.

"Howdy, folks," the first man said, putting the kickstand down on his bike and shutting off the engine.

"Nice bike," I said, wanting to appear less concerned than I was.

"Thanks," he replied. "It's one of the few machines that still work these days, except of course for all these," waving his right arm in a sweeping motion towards our caravan.

"Must be nice to have all those vehicles and a lot of supplies, I reckon," added the second man, putting the kickstand down on his bike but not cutting the engine.

"Nowadays," he continued, "it's good for a man to have something valuable to trade, don't you think?" he asked, looking squarely at me.

I glanced at Jake, and he gave me the nod, saying, "You're covered. Let's get this done and over."

"Well, sir," I replied, "we don't have anything we need, so we wish you two good luck down the road."

"Everybody needs something," he stated with a grin, as he looked up and down the trailer.

I had my hand near the butt of my Glock 17 pistol, visible to all in my right hip holster.

"I'm sorry, gentlemen, but we're not interested in…"

"Got this here snake antivenom," he said, as he put a heavy black glove over his right hand. "Out here in the wide-open country, it's easy to run into all kinds of things that could kill you. You folks can never be too careful.

"This here antivenom is genuine, through and through. Got eight bottles straight from the hospital, still cold. How much are you boys willing to pay for this?" he stated.

"As I told you guys before, we're not interested in trading or buying anything."

"Show them," said the man who had been the first to talk but was now quiet.

I caught a glimpse of Mike at the end of the trailer, watching the exchange intently.

The man with the antivenom set it on the ground and reached quickly into his side bag, using his gloved hand.

"Is that what I think it is?!" I called out to Jake, as he pulled the three-foot snake out of the bag and threw it end over end onto the trailer. It landed just in front of the porta-potty and immediately curled up. I heard the unmistakable rattle of a diamondback rattlesnake.

We all froze, and I watched in horror as my sweet boy Jax flung open the porta-potty door and took one step out.

The agitated snake struck in seconds, sinking his fangs into my boy's right leg, just under the knee.

Without thinking, I ran to him, stomping the snake as he tried to strike my work boot.

Everything slowed as I thought about tending to Jax. He needed help, but my body was headed the other way. Dropping my holster and pistol on the trailer, I leapt off the trailer at a full run, crashing into the man who had hurt my boy.

I struck him over and over as Joy was screaming at me to stop.

Mike pulled me off, saying "That's enough, Lance."

I fell to the ground, exhausted, and looked at the other man. He was covered in blood but alive.

"On your knees, boys," commanded Mike.

"Not in front of the kids!" I yelled to Mike.

"That was a stupid thing you guys did…" I started to say, as Mike interrupted me.

"Take no prisoners," he said in a low monotone voice, firing a fatal shot into the first man's forehead.

"And leave none," he added, pointing to the second man, the one who had thrown the snake. He said, "I'll give you a head start. Now ride."

The terrified man, still bleeding from his face, fumbled to get his bike turned around and sped away, kicking up dirt and rocks.

"It's over, Mike," I said loud enough for everyone to hear.

"Everyone should learn to shoot a bow and arrow," replied Mike. "Isn't that right, Lance?" he asked, not taking his eyes off the trailing man.

Raising my bow that I had never before shot, he pulled back on the string, letting the arrow fly towards the man on the bike. "High and just to the right," he said, quickly positioning the second arrow and releasing it.

We all watched the man riding away in slow motion, but not able to outrun the arrow. It hit its mark, throwing the rider from his bike.

We heard a scream. We could all hear the screams as he staggered, trying to run away.

Jake looking through his binoculars, could see the man was running with part of the wooden arrow sticking out of his right buttock.

"Run boy!" yelled a crazed Mike. "Run for your life!"

Mike followed him with my bow and the last arrow. His pace was fast, but he did not run.

"Here I come!" Mike yelled over and over.

Joy, Tina, Jake, and even Lonnie, were all yelling at Mike to stop and come back.

He never turned around as he closed in on the now-condemned man. At 15 yards out, Mike drew his last arrow and let it fly. It flew true, lodging into the man's mid-back, just to the right of the spine. He screamed again, only louder this time.

Most on the trailer were shocked by this slow, methodical rundown of the man who had hurt my boy. But not me. I wasn't shocked at all. I had seen it before.

I looked for Jax, turning a blind eye to everything else around me.

As Mike closed in, he found the first arrow he shot, with the bright yellow feathers sticking out of the ground. He stood in front of his prey, casually checking the last arrow for damage, turning it over and over in his hand, like one might inspect a rare coin, as the man begged for his life.

Jake and Lonnie watched through their binoculars as Mike drew back the bow, sending the steel-tipped arrow deep into the man's forehead. Stepping on the body, he withdrew the arrows from his head and back.

Walking slowly back, Mike picked up the motorcycle. Dusting it off, it started right up. He rode up to the side of the trailer, not acknowledging the shocked and scared children and adults.

He looked at Jake, and with a slight smile called out, "She's got a few scratches on her, but she still runs like a top," putting the kickstand down and cutting the engine.

Laying my bow and two blood-stained arrows on the trailer, he looked directly at me. "Lance, I owe you one arrow," he spoke in a casual, monotone voice.

Without another word, he walked back to his vehicle. *And the old Mike is back*, I thought.

I snapped back into focus and saw Nancy, Tina and Joy tending to Jax.

"Lance," yelled Nancy. "Listen to me. I need to see those vials on the ground."

I gathered them up, with bright sticky blood covering a few of them.

She looked carefully at each one and said that they were the real deal.

"Jake, get my small blue medical bag from the car. It's got my snakebite kit in it," Nancy said.

Jax was crying as I held his hand.

"Daddy, why are you bleeding?" he asked, touching my hands.

"Oh, it's okay, sweetie. I just got a few cuts is all."

I realized that Jax hadn't seen what happened, but the shocked faces of both adults and the other children told me that they had.

"Daddy, am I going to die?" asked Jax. "I haven't even ever had a girlfriend," he added.

"I thought all girls had cooties?!" I said, hoping to distract him just a little.

"Well, most of them do, but there might be a few that don't."

"Oh, really?" I replied, raising my eyebrow.

"Daddy, what are they doing to my leg?"

"They're just fixing where you got hurt."

"Do you mean where the big snake bit me?"

"Yes, son, that's precisely what they're doing, and you will get medicine to help you feel better."

"Was it a water moccasin, like in Louisiana?"

"No, son. It was a rattlesnake."

"Like the one you used to have for a pet?" Jax asked.

"Kind of, but this one was mean." Jax was referring to a story I told him and his brothers of a friend and me finding a baby snake when we were just about his age. We kept it in boxes, old crates, and even in the pockets of our overalls for three weeks, always playing with it. It never acted aggressive or tried to bite us, and we thought it was just a common garden snake.

On the third week, we showed it to my friend's very concerned dad. He said it was a baby rattlesnake and wanted to kill it. We convinced him to drive us out of town, so we could let it go unharmed.

"This one today, Jax, was mean, like most of them, and I'm sorry it hurt you."

"I guess it was just my turn," he said, matter of factly.

"What do you mean, son?"

"Well, Hendrix got lost and Hudson got burned, so it's just my turn, is all I'm saying."

"It's not supposed to be like that," I told him.

"Guess it's not going to be a great day, after all," I told Jake.

"I'm sorry, buddy," he said, and added, "Let Nancy take a look at your knuckles when she's done."

"I'll do that," I said, laying down next to Jax.

I stroked my son's head, making sure not to get any blood on it.

"You're going to be okay, buddy. Nancy is really good at fixing people, and even better with kids."

"I know, Daddy. I saw her helping everybody from the fire."

"What's the first thing you want to do when we get to Colorado?" I asked.

"Hmm," he replied, thinking on it. "Well, I would like to go camping!" he blurted out.

I laughed out loud. "Son, we have been camping nearly every night."

"I know, Daddy. But I want to camp just with you."

"Okay, it's my turn," I said, feeling good again after his comment. "I want to go fishing with you. Not like we did back at the lake, but with real fishing poles in the river."

"I feel tired, Daddy," he said, as I noticed he was sweating.

"It's okay. Stay with me."

I looked at Nancy, concerned. "Just keep talking to him," she said. "This is a process, and not a quick one."

I kept him awake, reminiscing about old times in his formidable four years on this planet. We talked more about Colorado and what it would be like for him and his brothers growing up.

I saw Jake, Steve and Lonnie lifting the two motorcycles onto the trailer. "Never hurts to have more running transportation," Jake said, "especially a couple of bikes."

"Let's keep going," Nancy told Jake and Lonnie. "I can work on Jax just the same if we're moving, and a little wind may cool him down."

"You okay, Mike?" called Lonnie on the radio, receiving no reply.

"Let's head out!" called Lonnie.

Today was supposed to be a good day, and I felt guilty realizing that I was the only member of my family not to be hurt or lost on this trip.

Maybe there's a doozy waiting for me tomorrow, I thought, and quickly dismissed the idea.

* * * * * * *

Chapter Twenty-six ~ Saddle Ranch Loveland, Colorado

Mac wandered in a daze for most of the morning, saying few words to anyone.

Bill met up with him just before lunch to see how he was holding up.

"You all right, Mac?" he asked, reaching down to pet Bo.

"I will be," Mac replied. "It will just take a little time."

"Maybe you should take the afternoon off and clear your head," Bill suggested.

"Thanks, Bill. That might just…"

Three shots rang out from Green Ridge, followed by one more.

"That's close," said Bill. "I think your afternoon off will have to wait."

Mac was already on the radio with his guys, shouting instructions.

"Can you watch Bo?" Mac asked.

"Sure," replied Bill, "but be careful. It sounds like the shots were close to one of the houses up there."

Bill made his way to the Pavilion and told everyone to go inside until further notice. "Stay away from the windows," he added.

Bill radioed John and Samuel, who had both heard the shots, informing them that Mac and his guys were assessing the situation.

Mac grabbed Jimmy and two more men, all riding ATVs and headed up the mountain.

Mac called over the radio to his guys. "We're not sure what this is, so let's take it slow and easy. I don't feel like getting shot today."

Mac ran the possible scenarios through his mind. There were two houses up on the ridge, both occupied. But the shots could have come from anywhere on the mountain. Sounds had a funny way of echoing up there. *Maybe some hunters*, Mac thought.

They headed up to the MacDonald place, since it was the closest to the Ranch. The old man was out front on his porch, smoking a classic tobacco pipe. "Must be up here about those shots, I reckon."

"Yes, sir," Mac replied.

"Well, wasn't us. Came from over the hill there, towards the Millers' place."

"Were you thinking about checking on them?" Mac asked, knowing full well the two families had been feuding for years.

"Mac, you know better than that," the old man replied, pausing to refill his pipe. "Those two are crazier than both of my ex-wives," he said, laughing.

"What's that?" called a woman from the house.

"Nothin', darlin'. Just talking to Mac and some of his guys is all."

"All right. We'll check it out," Mac told him. "Have a good day, sir," he added, as they rode east across the ridge.

Mac slowed to a stop a quarter mile down the road.

"Group up, guys," he said over the radio, motioning them to stop and cut the engines.

"These two, the Millers I mean, are a scary lot, and the kids too. We had to stop letting the children on the Ranch interact with them a couple of years back when we found out they were torturing small animals."

"That's sick," said Jimmy. "What kind of animals?"

"Mostly rabbits and chickens, to start, and then some cats, and eventually one of our Ranch dogs. Anyway," Mac continued, "they're all armed to the teeth and could star in the next remake of the movie *Deliverance*.

"Let's go slow, guns down, and be careful. Single file behind me. I did some carpentry work on their place a while back, so they know me."

Fifteen minutes later, Mac rounded the last turn to the Millers' place. A body lay across the driveway, just feet from the front door of the fortified compound.

Mac looked around but saw no one. Cautiously, he made his way to the downed figure, asking his guys to cover him.

The body was a man face-down on the gravel, and it appeared he had been shot in the back.

Mac turned him over slowly and saw it was Mr. Miller. Checking for a pulse, he found none.

There was no sign of anyone outside, and he couldn't see into the house.

Returning to his men, he wasn't sure how he wanted to proceed. Taking his binoculars out of his pack, he scoured the rest of the property and saw nothing out of the ordinary.

No dogs, he thought. *They probably killed them too*, remembering the four that had been here last time he was up.

Walking cautiously to the house, he knocked on the front door. "Rap Rap." After two minutes, he knocked again.

A clearly intoxicated Mrs. Miller, wearing a black silk nightgown torn at the shoulder, opened the door just enough to see out.

"Maaac," she slurred. "What er you wooing here?"

"I'm sorry ma'am, but I found your husband outside. Are you okay?" he asked, still confused.

"I am now," she replied. "It's a new world, and I got tired of him always judging me and calling me a drunk."

"Did he threaten you?" asked Mac, still not understanding what happened.

"Maybe he did," she replied. "Is that what you need to hear?"

"No, ma'am. I'm just trying to understand what happened is all."

"Go home, Mac. My boys will be back soon, and I'm not sure what they'll do when I tell them you shot their daddy."

Mac and his men all heard this last statement, as she slammed the door closed, followed by the sound of two deadbolts locking.

Mac felt his stomach drop. "Let's go. Let's go, boys," he called out, as they raced from the driveway.

"Bill," he called on the radio. "We've got a problem."

Mac's mind was racing as he sped down the mountain.

Jimmy, riding up ahead, pointed to the far end of a long meadow. Mac looked over to see the two Miller boys and only two dogs. The boys were waving for them to stop.

"What's the call?" asked Jimmy on the radio.

"Keep going," commanded Mac, as he waved to the boys.

Halfway home, Mac wondered if he should have stopped and tried to explain the situation.

How do you tell two teenage boys that their daddy is dead, still laying on the driveway, and their mother killed him? "You don't," he said aloud.

Mac met with Bill and John at John's house, and with Jimmy's help informed them about the "misunderstanding," as Mac put it.

"It sounds like there was no misunderstanding," said John, listening to the entire story. "You've got a woman killing her husband, for whatever reason, and telling her sons that you did it. It's straight forward, and they're sure to believe it, coming from her."

"How old are they now?" asked Bill.

"Sixteen and seventeen, I think," replied Mac.

"We'll talk with the elders and see if any of the old-timers have encountered something like this before. In the meantime, let's increase perimeter security on the Green Ridge side," continued John.

"We'll talk tomorrow after breakfast," added Bill. "You boys stay on high alert, just in case."

Mac rode slowly back up to the Ranch. "What the hell is happening?" he asked out loud. "A couple of days ago, I had a perfect lunch with the love of my life, and now everything is turned upside-down. Are you testing me, Lord?" he called out angrily. "What's next? My dog Bo gets sick and dies? I've tried to be good all my life, Lord. Am I not good enough for you?"

Jimmy, following close behind, slowed just a bit, hearing every word. He had never been a religious man, but he did say a quick prayer for Mac.

Mac was exhausted after this very long day. Always calm and sure of himself, he was now questioning everything. "What do you think?" he asked Bo, who laid at his feet.

Mac had never been much of a drinker, telling people who teased him that his father had drunk enough for them both.

Tonight was different, as he cracked open a bottle of George Dickel Tennessee Whisky that he had kept unopened for over three years. He was reminded of a Chris Stapleton song from a few years back, called "Tennessee Whisky."

> He poured a large glass and sang the tune low and slow, with a Country drawl, *changing lyrics as if the song were his own.*

> *You sip like Kentucky bourbon*
> *You age like Tuscan wine*
> *You're as hot as a fireball*
> *I never get tired of your attention and it's all mine, all mine*

"What do you think?" he asked his best friend in the whole world, petting his head. "Should we stay here or try our luck somewhere else? Maybe up in the mountains, away from all this drama." Mac smiled, knowing his friend would follow him to the ends of the earth without question.

Falling asleep after one more glass, he dreamed of Sarah. Bo woke up Mac with a low growl, escalating into a tooth-baring snarl, sensing something just beyond the front door of the small cabin Mac had occupied for several years.

Mac jumped out of bed, tripping over a small end table in the dark, and fell forward with a loud bang on the wooden floor.

Dazed for a moment, he thought he might be dreaming. Bo's continued barking brought him back to the present.

Grabbing his pistol and leashing Bo, he slowly opened the door to more darkness. The moon was small this night, with heavy cloud cover making it nearly impossible to see with the naked eye. "Who's there?" he called, now finding his flashlight knocked over on the floor.

There was no answer, and he slowly crept out the door. He shone the flashlight around in a broad arc, not seeing anything out of the ordinary.

Turning back, he saw it.

The writing covered his front door and most of the front of his cabin.

Bright red letters, with varying threats, were strewn about the walls. "You gonna die, just like he did," read one.

"Kill a man and take avantage of his wife = Deth penalty," read another.

Mac felt nauseous with the new revelations, most assuredly from Mrs. Miller, now playing even more of a victim. This lasted for a moment, as nausea was replaced with anger.

He had been framed for a man's murder, now apparently taking advantage of his widow, and he was being terrorized by two teenage boys.

He was also angry at his night watchmen for letting someone on the property, especially with the increased security just announced yesterday.

He thought about quickly spray painting over the graffiti, not wanting to cause a full-on panic around the Ranch tomorrow or have people thinking any of it was true.

Finding two large cans of black spray paint in the mechanic shop, he covered the words as best he could. They were partially visible still but unreadable.

Mac and Bo returned to his cabin for the night.

The morning was bustling with questions about the paint on Mac's house.

He called a meeting with Bill and John to discuss the new events.

John was concerned that people had entered the property under cover of night without being detected, and Bill commented on the need for increased security.

* * * * * * *

Chapter Twenty-seven ~ Capulin, New Mexico

Nancy took proper care of my boy, and Lonnie called Jake and me to the front of the trailer.

"How's your boy?" he asked.

"I'm not sure," I replied. "I know Jake's wife is doing the best she can for him. I really need to get back to him," I explained.

"I understand, Lance," said Lonnie, "but what do you think?"

"I think," I replied, "that I'm not sure I made the right decision, bringing you all on this death march to Colorado.

"It's been one disaster after another," I added. "I should have stopped those guys from throwing the snake onto the trailer. I mean, I had the chance. I just froze.

"I missed the kids playing outside the ring of safety, and they got hurt.

"I almost lost my youngest boy, leaving him behind. Who does that?" I asked.

"We all did," added Jake. "I never imagined the man would do that, and we let our guard down, with your boy getting hurt. We are all responsible for the fire, and even Hendrix getting lost. We are a family, a large one, but family no less, and each of us bear responsibility for the children."

"Maybe we should have headed for Louisiana or stayed in McKinney," I said.

"No, Lance. We are on the right path, and close to our midway pit stop," said Lonnie. "We're all alive, and hopefully Vlad as well," he added. "Go now and be with your boy," he suggested.

Jax was feeling better, and Nancy gave me a much-needed nod. "He's going to be okay," she whispered in my ear.

Lonnie and Jake looked at the map.

"We're 287 North to 87 West to 64 Northwest to Capulin, New Mexico, about 170 miles up the road. It's home to the last dormant volcano you may ever see," said Jake.

Back on the road, I wondered what would be next. Another killing, more fire, maybe a scorpion bite? How about the Capulin volcano suddenly erupting for the second time, after 60,000 years?

Obsessing about the trip so far, I wanted to see the best parts of the trek. I knew I was getting cynical and needed a rest. Focusing on David's place so close now, I wanted to relax and let my guard down, but knew I could not.

Sitting next to Joy, she was upset about the bikers. "You didn't have to do that," she told me, "and don't even get me started about Mike!"

"I can't explain his actions," I told her, "but for my part, I just saw red."

"What does that even mean?' she snapped.

"It means," I said, "that someone hurt our boy and I just reacted without thinking. I saw red, and nothing else.

"As for Mike," I continued, "I thought I was getting to know what made him tick. I was sure I had him figured out, but I was wrong. He's still as unpredictable as always."

"I know, honey," Joy responded calmly, with a sigh. "I wanted to tear that man from limb to limb for hurting our sweet boy. I just didn't want the kids to see it."

"Me neither," I agreed, "but it just can't be helped sometimes. Their little worlds, all of them, are forever changed. And by the time we get to Colorado, God willing, they will be hardened in a way we can't undo. We will, however, pray with them daily and remind them what it's like to be a kid sleeping safe and sound each night.

"We will all start a new life, slowly erasing the past tragedies from their memories. It will take a long time, and maybe even generations, to feel normal again," I added. "We will persevere and overcome our obstacles. Tomorrow we will be at David's place, and we can rest for a couple, or maybe even more, days. We will be safe there and can relax just a bit.

"I owe you a date night," I told her, kissing her in front of our kids.

"Ewww, that's gross!" said Hudson.

"Smoochy-smooch," added a tired Jax, and Hendrix just covered his eyes, peeking through his open fingers.

"That's right, boys," I laughed. "You will understand soon enough."

Nancy, satisfied with Jax's stability, looked at my hands.

"The first knuckle here looks broken," she said, touching my right hand. I winced but didn't flinch.

"I'm going to wrap this for now," she said, "and we will take a closer look later, probably at the midway stop."

"Thank you, Nancy," I told her.

"I think it will heal up just fine," she replied.

"No. Thank you, Nancy, for what you did for Joy and both of our boys," I continued. "You went above and beyond expectations, and we as a family are truly thankful for you and Jake."

"If you make her cry," said Jake, "I'm going to shoot you with this nerf gun," he chuckled, holding up an impressive nerf gun rifle belonging to his boy.

"No such luck," added Nancy. "But seriously, I'm just glad I could help."

Hendrix quietly handed me his nerf pistol, and I cocked it quickly, catching Jake in the left shoulder with the first shot.

"Oh, it's on now!" he retorted, peppering me with all eight nerf rounds from his rifle.

Everyone was laughing at this, even Joy and Jax.

Miles past quickly, and everyone was tired from the road.

There was nothing, I mean literally nothing, between Amarillo and Raton, New Mexico, besides the two billboards.

"Now leaving Texas, The Lone Star State, and Welcome to New Mexico, The Land of Enchantment."

The rest was God's country, pure and unspoiled.

Arriving at our destination late in the day meant we were only 40 miles from Raton Pass.

Lonnie asked me if we should push through tonight or wait until morning.

I made the call to wait until morning, wanting to radio ahead and not show up in complete darkness.

Capulin, being a national monument, had a Visitors' Center in the front that appeared abandoned.

There were no campsites available, but a few tents were scattered across the area.

Forming a circle around the Visitors' Center, we agreed that the ladies and children, with Mini, would stay inside, except for Sheila, who refused to leave Mike's side, and the rest of us, including Ringo, keeping a close eye this last night.

Jake, Lonnie, Steve, Jim and I all opted to sleep on the trailer with Ringo.

Staring up at the sky, I had forgotten what it was like to see the stars so bright.

I had Jim set up the radio and had a quick conversation with David, informing him we would be there tomorrow morning.

He informed me that they would be waiting for us just across the main bridge, separating the now old territory with the new land that the Raton Pass Militia now claimed.

"Take it slow up here," said David. "We've got you covered on our side, but you've got ten miles of dirt road before you get to our bridge, and we're not sure what's out there."

"We will do just that," I told him.

There were no streetlamps or houses to pierce the pitch-black night sky, only bright white stars as big as Texas, and a few scattered campfires. I fell fast asleep, looking for constellations, with Ringo by my side.

Waking up to stiff backs, both Lonnie and Jake asked me for an adjustment.

Pulling out the makeshift therapy table we found at the Urgent Care Center, I adjusted each of them, with audible cracks that all on the trailer could hear.

"Good as new," announced Lonnie.

"Yep, me too," added Jake. "Thanks, buddy."

"No worries," I told them, thinking it would be good to have one more chiro around, so I could get adjusted too.

Those inside the Visitors' Center poured out early, with my boy Jax looking good as new.

"How are you feeling, son?" I asked.

"Great, Daddy! I don't feel sick anymore, but I wish you could have stayed with us last night."

"Me too, buddy," I told him, "but somebody had to keep Ringo company," I responded, with a smile.

The group took our time this morning, cooking a hearty breakfast of powdered eggs with the choice of chopped venison or fish. Most opted for the meat, with a few sticking only to the eggs.

Today was a milestone for our group, and I wanted to say something.

Tina allotted me four large cans of corned beef hash that I cooked over the Coleman stove, to most everyone's delight. We ate as a group slowly and unafraid for the first time since we left our homes.

With everyone gathered, I offered a breakfast prayer.

Dear Lord, thank you for watching over our children on this great trip West. You are with us at each triumph and every tribulation, never leaving our sides.

Please watch over Vlad, and all of us, as we near our halfway point to our destination. We are families first, and it's in your name we pray. Amen.

All said "Amen" and Mini barked, sitting just under the corned beef hash pot.

"Don't worry, Mini," said Jax, who had taken a shine to her. "I'll make sure Daddy saves you some."

With everything packed up this morning, Jake's watch read 9:23 a.m.

"OK, everyone," Lonnie called out. "We're about 40 miles from our destination in Raton Pass. The road on Highway 64 runs into Interstate 25, which goes straight up through Colorado, south to north.

"We will be on that highway most of the rest of our journey to Loveland. The only problem is that it runs right through some major cities, including Trinidad, Pueblo, Colorado Springs, and even Denver, as well as smaller towns, including Raton, New Mexico, about 30 miles from here. Every one of these towns and cities will require planning and foresight to maneuver safely around.

"I anticipate making it to our next stop by early to midafternoon today, God willing. Once there, we can rest up and plan the next stage of the journey west."

Heading northwest on Highway 64, the terrain was changing, desert giving way to foothills, with views of the mountains beyond.

The air, crisper and cleaner, preceded the coming storm Lucy had warned us about a day earlier. Long bands of rain far in the distance fell like shooting stars, streaking down.

"Do you smell that, Jax?" I asked.

"Smell what, Daddy?"

"The rain, son. Take a good long smell."

Jax laughed as he did, saying, "It smells like a wet dog!"

"Ha! That's funny, buddy. Maybe it does," I considered. "It happens to be one of my favorite smells in the world," I added, "right after coffee!"

"Good day?" asked Jake, patting me on the shoulder.

"Absolutely. I knew it would be. I was just off by 24 hours," I replied, holding up my bandaged hand and shaking my head.

Lonnie slowed to a stop, as the radio crackled. "It looks like we're about to get wet," he announced. "The storm is headed our way, and we can't outrun it. Let's get anything covered with the tarps that can't get wet. It looks like we have about 15-30 minutes before it's on top of us."

Everyone pitched in, securing the tarps over both trailers and cinching them down tight.

"We'll be pulling off in a safe place if we can find one ahead," announced Lonnie.

Getting the children and dogs off the trailer and inside the vehicles, we headed straight for the coming storm.

Lightning streaked the darkening sky, followed by booms of thunder. I counted the seconds between lightning bursts and explosions of thunder rattling the caravan. One one thousand, two one thousand, three one thousand, and then a "Boom!"

"That's what I always heard," Jake agreed. "A couple weeks ago I would have Googled it and we would know for sure in a few minutes. Now our best guess is all we've got."

"I wonder if we will be starting over as a country once again, putting a high value on libraries full of books?" I asked Jake.

"Even if the power is restored, that doesn't necessarily mean we'll get our Internet back. And even then, I can't afford a $600 iPhone anymore," he replied.

"No worries, buddy," I replied. "I kept a few in my faraday cage, just in case."

Lonnie stopped as the rain began to fall. "Off the trailer, boys!" he shouted.

Jake and I squeezed into the SUV with our wives and kids, with Steve and Jim jumping in with Mike and Sheila.

Slowing to under 10 miles per hour, the rain beat down on the vehicles and trailers. Two miles up, we huddled beneath an overpass, each vehicle side-by-side, taking up both the east- and westbound lanes of Highway 64.

The passing storm gave way to the most incredible double rainbow most of us had ever seen. The children begged Lonnie to drive fast to the very end, "to find the money," as Hudson put it.

"What would you do with all that money, Hudson?" asked Lonnie, genuinely curious.

"I would buy a bright red dirt bike motorcycle that runs on gas!" he blurted out.

"Is that so?" replied Lonnie. "Then I guess we will have to keep an eye out for just such a prize," he added, with a wink.

Back on the trailer, after removing the heavy blue tarps, Jake and I assessed the provisions. All checked out, except for some clothes from the strip mall.

"They will surely dry out eventually," I suggested.

"The next stop is I-25 North," Lonnie called over the radio.

"We have two choices here. Either stay on the Interstate, which largely bypasses most of the city of Raton, or cut through Climax Canyon Park. And no, that is not a joke but the actual name, for a reason I don't know. This route is longer, and partially unmapped. but may be safer.

"Either way, we end up back on I-25 for the only way up the steep climb to Raton Pass at the top of the mountain. What say you?" he asked those with radios.

Most votes steered towards the Interstate route, as it seemed the fastest way to a much-needed rest.

"Okay," said Lonnie. "We will settle on the Interstate," he stated, "stopping briefly.

"All children inside the vehicles and all able-bodied men on the trailers, locked and loaded."

Lonnie switched driver's seats with his wife, and Mike did the same with Sheila, as both men stood watch from the trailers.

"Slow and steady, with eyes open all around!" called Lonnie.

Interstate 25 made navigation easier, with both sides of the road passable for the caravan.

"Raton city limits, three miles," called out Jake.

I-25 ran across the east side of Raton, south to north, cutting across the northern fifth of Raton City from east to west.

"Not too bad," Lonnie called over the radio from our trailer.

"We're headed for Raton Pass," I told Jake, asking him if he had been through it before.

"Yes," he replied. "Nancy, Danny and I came through here with our moving truck, headed to Texas."

"It's one way up," I told him, "and probably no way around with the trailers."

"I know," Jake replied, "and I'll be surprised if we don't encounter an obstacle or two."

* * * * * * *

Chapter Twenty-eight ~ Raton, New Mexico

Fifteen minutes later, quickly navigating the city of Raton, Jake spoke again.

"I was wrong," he said, pointing ahead as he looked through his binoculars. "There are no obstacles, but there's a full-on barricade!"

Lonnie called to his wife to stop the caravan, still a mile out from the blockade.

Every man in the trailer looked through binoculars; also Joy and Nancy.

"It's not too late to take the Climax Canyon route," announced Lonnie.

Both Jake and I informed him that the trailers would never make it up the steep grade of fire roads to the top.

"We've got two choices," I called on the radio. "We take the alternate route and likely lose the trailers, or we negotiate a deal at the roadblock."

Joy, Nancy and Tina replied on their radio, saying, "We've got this. We will negotiate the terms of crossing the barricade."

Jake and I were uneasy about it, as Lonnie announced, "You will go with one of us guys as a backup."

"I'll go," I asserted.

"No, buddy. I've got this," interjected Jake.

"I was thinking Mike would be the right choice," said Lonnie.

"Really?" I asked, with Jake agreeing.

With his radio deliberately turned off, he said, "He's violent and unpredictable, but he takes care of this group, especially the women and children."

"Yes, I do," said Mike, overhearing the conversation from the side of the trailer.

"Mike, I'm sorry," said Lonnie. "I didn't mean…"

"It's okay, brother," Mike replied. "I'll make sure nothing happens to the ladies. You can count on that."

Jake reluctantly agreed to the proposal. I, having faith in both Joy and Mike's ability to negotiate a situation, agreed as well.

"Ladies lead," I called to Mike, who smiled and nodded yes without uttering a word.

Lonnie took over the wheel of the lead truck, pulling slowly toward the barricade. "Real easy," he announced. "This is hopefully the last barrier to a much-deserved rest."

Thirty yards from the barricade, Lonnie stopped the lead vehicle, cutting the engine.

"I count four shooters behind the barricade," I announced, looking through my binoculars.

The ladies walked, with both Nancy and Tina supporting Joy's shoulders and protecting her hurt ankle, towards the barrier. Their pistols were hidden beneath their clothing.

Mike followed three paces behind, his AR rifle pointed to the ground.

Jake and I walked ten paces behind Mike, our rifles also pointed down.

A few of the men on the barricade whistled and hollered as the ladies approached. A look from Mike quieted the juvenile behavior.

"I'm not sure about this," Jake said in a low voice.

"It's not my first option," I replied, "but the ladies are top-notch negotiators, and not a lot of people are going to mess with Mike."

"Except for me. I guess that's what you're worried about, right?" Jake asked.

"Yes," I replied. "For a short time, when he and I were looking for Hendrix, I thought it wasn't a big deal, you and him, but I'm not so sure anymore," I said quietly.

Approaching the barricade, Joy asked who was in charge.

The catcalls started again from a few of the younger men on the barricade.

"You're limpy gimpy," said one loudly, an overweight man with grubby clothes and a long beard, "but I can work with it."

"I do," I said aloud, as I envisioned training my AK on his mid-chest.

"Don't do it," said Jake. "Not yet, I mean," with his hand on my left shoulder.

I held my rifle down, stomping down my adrenaline and vowing to take him out first if it came down to it.

"Who is in charge here?" Joy repeated loudly, with conviction.

"I am," said an older man with graying hair and a commanding voice, coming forward from the side of the barricade.

"One more word out of your little boys up there," said Joy, pointing to the barricade, "and we'll see who has the superior firepower. Are we agreed?"

"Yes, ma'am," he said, smiling.

"Stand down, boys," he called out.

"My guys are young and sometimes stupid. Sorry about that," the man in charge continued.

"This is our road, and we control it up and over Raton Pass."

"Why didn't you just block the road into town?" asked Tina.

"Too many ways around the Interstate," he replied.

"Like Climax Park?" asked Nancy, teasing just a bit.

"Yes, just like that breathtaking park with the god-awful name," he replied.

"There's only one way over the pass besides this road, and most vehicles wouldn't make it. It comes down to simple economics. I now own a piece of real estate, and I'm guessing you need to cross our property."

"What then?" asked Joy. "You tax us again on the other side at the bottom?"

"No, ma'am. A deal is a deal, all the way through. I've got the same barrier on that end for folks wanting to come this way. The good thing is that once we are agreed, you get a lifetime pass."

"Pass to what?" asked Tina.

"You can come over the pass front to back or back to front, free of charge, after your initial 'tax,' as you call it," the old man replied.

"Beyond our pass is anyone's guess, but most other roads have multiple detours you could get those trailers across," he added, pointing to our caravan.

"Do you really think you have more firepower than we do?" he asked, as more of a casual question.

"I guarantee it," chimed in Nancy.

Mike stood stone-cold and didn't speak.

He looks like one of those English Palace guards, thought Joy. *The kind people try to mess with, but really shouldn't.*

"Okay, sir," said Joy. "What's the price for safe crossing?"

"Well, ma'am. That depends."

"What's the price?" asked Mike, talking low and slow, making the ladies and the older man uneasy.

"What are you offering?" the man asked, now with a slight quiver in his voice.

Mike looked at Joy, gesturing with his hand to continue.

"Two handguns, brand-new in the box, one 9mm and one 40 Cal with 50 rounds of ball for each," she stated.

"Where did you get guns in a box?" the old man asked. "Never mind," he added, withdrawing the question as he looked at Mike staring a hole through him.

"Let me think on it just a minute," he said, disappearing behind the barricade.

Coming back around, he asked Mike if he could get 100 rounds for each handgun. Mike nodded to Joy to answer.

"Seventy-five rounds for each and guaranteed safe passage up and down the pass. We'll be at the top for a few days, before heading down the other side.

"If you don't fulfill your end of the deal on either side of the pass, or I hear any more sexist comments from your guys, your little tourist trap here is done. Are we understood, sir?"

Mike couldn't help but smile at the negotiations.

"That's my girl," I whispered to Jake.

"Yes, ma'am," the old man answered reluctantly.

"You heard the lady," he called up to his guys. "Not a word or you'll be dealing with this guy," he called out, gesturing to a once again stone-cold Mike.

There was some whispering from the men on the barracks but it was inaudible.

Tina returned to the caravan to retrieve the passage items.

Heading back to the vehicles, Joy gave me a wink and Mike was laughing again.

With payments made, a few trucks were moved aside, allowing for the caravan to pass easily through.

"We're looking at a 6% grade over the pass," announced Lonnie over the radio, as he and Mike resumed driver positions.

"Low gear on all vehicles," he continued. "We should be the only group on this road, at least up to the turnoff just before the Colorado border."

"Let's take it slow and steady," called Jake, "and all radios on, in case there are any issues."

Single file, we headed up the pass. Jake and I were on the lead trailer with the dogs, and Steve with Jim on the back one. The children reluctantly rode inside the vehicles.

"We're headed up to 7800 feet above sea level," called Lonnie over the radio.

"It's going to be cooler up there; and for the kids, keep yawning until your ears pop," he added.

"I love it up here," I told Jake, waving my arm toward the west.

"This is truly God's country," I added, breathing deeply.

"Miss Texas yet, buddy?" asked Jake.

"Not today," I laughed. "Not today."

Nearing the top, I called out to Lonnie over the radio. "We'll be taking a left up about two miles. There's a place to turn off, and I want to radio David. There are ten miles to go, and I want his group to be ready if we need any help."

Lonnie pulled off the highway, just before the Colorado line.

Jim set up the ham radio and was able to get David on the line in minutes.

"Okay, buddy," I said. "We're just off the Interstate at the pass. Any idea of what we're headed into?"

"Sorry, Lance. We've got our side of the bridge covered, but it's been so busy here we haven't gotten around to doing a proper recon of the other side.

"There are occasional shots heard from that side, but it may just be hunters. We have done some reinforcements to the bridge, so your trailers hopefully will have a safe crossing.

"Remember, though, it's a good long drop down the river, and it's running high right now. Let's have you all stop just before the bridge, and we'll have anyone not driving walk over under our protection. Then one vehicle at a time, with the lightest ones first."

Lonnie and Mike resumed their spots back on the trailer.

Lonnie asked all adults to meet up, after a coordinated potty break for the kids.

* * * * * * *

Chapter Twenty-nine ~ Raton Pass, New Mexico

"We've got ten miles of dirt to our halfway point. We will be able to rest up in relative safety for a few days, but all will need to pitch in and carry our weight, so we're not freeloading off their group," I said.

"The next ten miles may be easy, or may not be. We're committed once we start," I added. "With this narrow road, there is no turning around for us, especially with the trailers.

"One way in and one way out, at least for two-wheel-drive vehicles, like ours."

Jake led a quick prayer for the group, and we were off.

The open road disappeared into the trees. Jake looked at his watch, and it read 3:37 p.m.

"You don't still have your nerf gun out, do you?" I asked Jake, elbowing him in the side.

"I wish," he replied, "but I do have a good idea for the kids later today."

"Eyes open, boys!" called Lonnie from the back of the lead truck.

"We've got eyes on both sides," called Lonnie over the radio. Looking closely into the trees, I saw people staring out from the cover of the woods.

"Five miles per hour," Lonnie called out, "but keep moving."

"This could go either way," I said to Jake in a low voice.

"I was thinking the same thing," he said. "We're so close. I just want some downtime."

"Me too, buddy," I replied.

"Stop!" called Lonnie to his wife, who was driving the lead truck.

The caravan came to a halt, and Jake and I jumped on the back of the truck to join Lonnie.

"That's a new one," said Jake, pointing ahead 20 yards to the trench more than ten feet wide and across the entirety of the narrow road.

"We're stuck!" called Lonnie to Jake and me.

Mike and Steve walked up from the rear trailer and hopped on the back of the lead truck.

"We're on our own," I told them. "David's nine miles away."

The caravan stopping just short of the crossroad pit, I could see it was six feet deep.

"Simplicity at its best," I said aloud, hoping this good day wouldn't end badly.

Waiting for nearly five minutes, men and women emerged on both sides from the trees. Rifles were clearly visible but varied considerably, from shotguns to deer rifles and a few BB guns, from my vantage point.

"Off the trailer," called a man, stepping out of the trees to my right.

"What's your name, sir," I asked, staying put.

"The Keeper," he replied.

"Of these woods?" I asked, playing along.

"That's right," he responded, "and we don't need any outsiders coming into our territory."

"We're not outsiders," I told him, hoping I wasn't causing any future problems for David. "Just passing through is all," I added.

"Passing through to where?" asked the Keeper.

"The other side of the bridge," I responded.

"Who do you know over there?" he asked sternly.

"David," I told him.

"How do you know him?" he responded.

"David Jenkins and his parents have had property up here for years," I added.

"You mean Dean and Beatrice?" he asked.

"Yes, they are David's parents," I replied.

"Shame what happened to Dean, getting offed by his own grandson," the Keeper replied, spitting a dip onto the dusty road.

Jake and Lonnie looked at me, brows raised.

"What do you mean?" I asked, still having no idea how we would get past this point.

"My men saw it," he continued. "Looked like an accident. Talk about being in the wrong place at the wrong time," he said, chuckling.

My blood was boiling at this asshole casually talking about the killing of a man I always looked up to and admired.

"What do you want?" I asked matter of factly.

"We're just talking here," replied the Keeper.

"All right. Put up the bridge or whatever you have, and let us cross," I commanded.

Jake gave me a look to take it slow. I looked at Mike, as he grinned and said, "You ready?" in a quiet voice.

More men walked out into the road from the trees, all sporting old hunting rifles.

"And if we don't?" replied the Keeper, half-smiling, with a toothless grin.

"Then we just take it," interjected Mike, raising his AR and firing a single shot into the Keeper's forehead, snapping his head back and collapsing to the ground.

"Who's next?" asked Mike loudly, waiving his rifle back and forth towards the now gathered crowd of nearly 20 men and women.

No one responded, with many laying their weapons on the ground in front of them.

"Who's second-in-charge?" he called out loudly.

"I guess that's me," said a man who had already laid his weapon down.

"What's your name?" Mike asked. "And if you tell me something like 'The Keeper,' I'll kill you where you stand."

"Yes, sir," he replied, stammering and shaking. "My name is Nate, and we don't want any trouble."

"Come over here, Nate," I told him, and tell me what you know about Dean Jenkins.

I got the full story and thought I had a pretty good idea of what happened, now feeling bad for both David and Mark.

"How do we cross with the trailers?" I asked Nate.

"We've got steel beams," he replied, "and I think it will hold the weight."

"You better hope it does," replied Mike, "because I'm done screwing around with you guys.

"In the lead truck," commanded Mike to Nate. "Have your guys lay the steel and you drive us over. We fall short, and you're not going home tonight. Understood?"

"I'm not sure I'm the best man to drive across," he stammered.

"Sure, you are," replied Mike, "unless it can't be done.

"Careful of your answer here. If it can't be done, then you guys have been lying to us all along. And that's what happens to liars," he said, pointing to the former leader laid out on the hard ground.

Nate instructed his people to lay the steel beams across the ditch.

We all got off the truck and trailer, except for Nate and Mike, both in the cab.

Slowly crossing the beams, Nate let out a sigh as they reached the other side, trailer intact.

"Four more to go," Mike announced, standing on the side with his new friend.

"I guarantee this bridge will hold," said Nate.

"If you guarantee it, then it's good enough for me," replied Mike.

"And I guarantee you're going to drive each vehicle and trailer over it to the other side," he added.

One by one, Mike's new friend drove each vehicle over.

"See, I told you it would hold," said Nate, looking relieved.

"Don't worry. On your way back, we'll give you a hand," he added, with just a twinge of sarcasm.

"We forgot to ask you, Nate. Who's third in charge?" asked Joy, loud enough for everyone to hear. "Do you see my point, Nate?"

"Yes. I mean, yes, ma'am."

"Last thing, Nate. Who's now second-in-charge?" Joy repeated. "This ditch had better be filled in when we head back this way. You've got two days to get it done."

"When did your wife go badass?" Jake asked me.

"She always has been," I replied.

Taking our time winding through the heavily treed forest, I felt something like home. Birds were singing in the trees, and everything was green.

The next eight miles were some of the best we had encountered.

The woods, cool and dark, rolled past with our hodgepodge of misfit travel companions all looking forward to a few days' rest.

"Up ahead," I called over the radio. "The bridge is a half-mile up. Stop just before it."

Slowing to a full stop before the 150-foot-long bridge, I walked out to the center with Jake and Lonnie to meet David, Mark and Mel at the halfway point.

"It's been a long time, my brother," I told David, hugging him with two pats on the shoulder.

"You must be Mark," I added, shaking the young man's hand.

"Mel over here," pointed David.

"Jake and Lonnie," I pointed, as we all traded handshakes.

"You look like crap, Lance," said David, sporting a perfectly groomed black beard of a millennial logger look-alike, except David could actually log.

"I feel like crap, buddy. It's been a hell of a trip so far, and I, for one, am looking forward to you serving me breakfast every morning for the next few days."

David laughed with Mark, who was not getting the lighthearted banter.

"Sarcasm, my boy," said David, "and my old buddy Lance is the ringmaster. His picture was included in the Wikipedia file under the word *smart-ass*."

He and I were laughing, with Jake and Lonnie just smiling.

"Can I go back now?" Mark asked his dad.

"Sure, son, but wait at the end of the bridge, in case we need some help with their vehicles."

"We ran into a few of the guys about nine miles back," I told David.

"You ever hear of a guy called 'the Keeper'?" Lonnie asked him.

"Yeah. That guy's an idiot, a real piece of work. I wouldn't be surprised if he's gathered a small army by now, with his preaching of a new and better life with him as the leader," replied David.

"Not anymore," I told him, nodding back towards our caravan. "The position has been passed down..."

"All right, let's get your group across this bridge," said David. "The lightest cars first, with a driver only."

I had forgotten about the drop from this bridge. "About 30 feet?" I asked David.

"Yep. Over 40 when the river is low. Who can swim?" he asked, only half joking.

Jake and I both nodded our heads. "That's where I'm out!" said Lonnie. "I never did learn how to swim."

"I'll take the first one, buddy," I told Jake, "and we can switch off, each having one trailer."

"Like a game of Russian roulette," added Lonnie.

"Slow and steady," said David. "Keep your windows rolled down and don't stop unless I signal."

Squeezing the first SUV past the trailer in front, I edged out on to the bridge. The old wooden structure creaked and vibrated but held its position. Three miles per hour, and I was across in two minutes.

We did the same with the other vehicles, switching off drivers.

"So, I get the first trailer?" asked Jake, a bit sarcastically.

"Don't worry, buddy. I've got the next one, and you know the second one across is always the hardest."

"I'm going driver's-door-wide-open on this one," said Jake. "I don't mind going for a swim, but I'm damn sure not going down inside a truck," he added.

"Ha! That's not a bad idea," I told him. "Think I'll do the same on my trailer run, unless you go for a swim first, of course."

Everyone was out of the vehicles and crossed the bridge on foot.

They watched intently as Jake lined up the truck and trailer, just to the right of center so he could keep his driver's door open.

Easing on to the bridge, it was apparent that the bridge strained under the weight.

"Real slow, Jake," David called out, the bridge now shaking back and forth under the total weight of truck and trailer.

Everyone held their breath, as Jake hung half out of his door, barely reaching the gas pedal with his right foot and with one hand on the steering wheel.

I thought about how to get down to the river if it got bad quickly. Thankfully the guns were on the second trailer, but it would be much heavier.

"Halfway across!" called out David, as the bridge seemed to slump under the heavy weight.

I could see Jake's face looking over his opened driver door. He looked nervous as he glanced back and forth from the end of the bridge up ahead and the rushing river below.

"Don't jump unless you have to!" I called out, hearing the distinct sound of splitting wood.

"What do you think?" I asked David.

"We reinforced it, but it was never meant to carry this much weight."

"Forty feet to the end of the bridge!" called out Lonnie. "Thirty-five...thirty..."

While we could all see from our vantage point how close he was, it seemed comforting to hear Lonnie closing the gap with each call.

"Snap!" came the sound from Jake's passenger side, as one of the three large cables dropped towards the river below.

The bridge was shaking and now leaning 5 degrees to that side.

"Punch it!" called David to Jake.

"Go, go, go!" we all joined in.

Jake, pressing hard on the gas pedal, propelled the truck and trailer off the far end of the bridge, scattering some members of our group in all directions.

Safely off the bridge, I ran to see how Jake was holding up.

"That was not fun," he announced, looking a little pale.

A smile took hold as he said, "Okay. You're up next, buddy," jingling his keys.

"Plan B," said David, before I could answer. "Can't let you break our bridge, guys. There is another way around, but it will take a couple hours… Just you and me, my friend," he said, grabbing my left shoulder.

"Not so fast," called Joy, walking up with Tina.

"You must be the David we've all been hearing about," said Tina, with a flirty smile. "You're even more handsome than Lance described!"

"Now wait just a minute," I interjected. "All I said was he was tall and had dark hair!"

"And you are far prettier than I'm sure Lance would have described you!" replied David. "Lance, why didn't you tell me about Tina?"

"Are we really going to do this for the next two hours?" I blurted out, intentionally rolling my eyes.

"I just thought they should meet," said Joy, giving me a wink. "Maybe Tina and I should go ahead and get our camp ready, while you *strong* boys get the trailer over," she continued, acting out of character.

David and I crossed back over the sturdy bridge, now only carrying our weight. Jim and Steve offered to drive the third trailer around, following David and me in the lead.

"Sorry about your bridge, buddy," I told him.

"No worries," he replied. "It's still good for anything not carrying a trailer, I'm sure."

Backing the trailers 200 feet, David pointed out a side road I completely missed on the way. Overgrown trees and bushes flanked the nearly hidden fire road, plagued by deep ruts down the middle.

"Real slow," said David, riding passenger. "If we get the trailers stuck here, they stay," he added.

Maneuvering down the winding path, we were at the river's edge in 40 minutes.

The conversation went quickly from catching up, to Tina…with no mention of his father so far.

"Why didn't you tell me about Tina?" asked David.

"I don't know… It didn't even cross my mind.

"There are a few things about her you should know," I added.

"Here we go," announced David.

"No, nothing negative," I told him. "Just reality.

"She had a boyfriend before the lights went out, and he was in Los Angeles on business, so no way to connect.

"Veronica and Suzie are two awesome little girls we found orphaned the first day the lights went out, and Tina has taken them under her wing.

"We're also headed to Colorado, so I'm not sure how that plays out."

"Me neither, but it was you that told me my destiny may show up on my doorstep," David pointed out.

"That's true," I replied. "And if I'm being honest, she's kind of just floating along with our group... Not in a bad way... I mean, she picked out all our clothes at an outlet mall, and she's been awesome with Suzie and Veronica. She's a great cook, as well."

"I get it," replied David. "We will see what happens..."

"Not bad on time," I said, looking at Jake's watch he lent me.

"This road leads to the only place to cross this river for nearly 40 miles," pointed out David. "It's not usually attempted at springtime, though, with the river this high."

"I've got to be sure before we try it," I told him. "All the weapons are on this trailer, with the four-wheelers and bikes on the back one."

The crossing was easier than I expected, even with the trailers.

Slowly navigating the road to David's, he told me what happened to his father.

"There's no way you could have known," I consoled.

Pulling into the newly formed camp an hour later, now early evening, I stopped the truck 30 yards out.

"Look at that, buddy," I said, pointing to the kids all playing nerf gun wars with Jake and most of the adults cooking an outdoor dinner.

"This rarely happened in the old world. And despite the hardships, we still get to do this," I added.

Supper was on, and Beatrice, with Joy and Tina's help, whipped up a hodgepodge of venison, fish, and macaroni with cheese for both groups.

Suzie and Veronica were eager to learn from Beatrice, asking question after question.

"Okay, girls," called Tina. "Let's leave Mrs. Beatrice to her cooking."

"Oh, nonsense," said Beatrice, smiling. "I love teaching young girls life skills."

"Smells good," said David, as we walked up.

Veronica and Suzie officially met David, commenting that he had a beard like their daddy.

David asked Tina if she would like to go for a walk after dinner. "I would love that," she replied.

Recapping the story of how they found the girls as they walked the property perimeter, Tina told David she planned to officially adopt them, once everything got back to normal.

"That's nice," he replied. "They seem like great kids."

Returning Tina to her tent, she thanked him for the walk with a kiss on his cheek.

* * * *

Joining his mother for breakfast, David asked, "What do you think, Mom?"

"About Tina, I'm guessing? She's kind and helpful, and she wanted to know everything about you."

"What about the girls, Mom?"

"I like them, too, son. But they're all only here for a few days."

"I know… But a few days is better than no days…

"We will all be eating here tonight," his mother said. "Let everyone know we will eat supper early, as Mel has a surprise for you.

"And son, your father would be proud of you for how you are leading us and helping other good folks along the way."

David and Mel gave me the grand tour after lunch. Mel proudly showed me many of his provisions, promising to send us off with a good supply of coffee beans.

"I hear you have a surprise for me tonight, Mel?" asked David.

"I guess your mom told you," he said, smiling. "You'll like it, I promise. Everyone will, especially the kids."

David spent the afternoon with Tina and the girls.

Beatrice rang the dinner bell at around 4 p.m.

"That's for us," announced Tina. "We are helping your mom in the kitchen for tonight's surprise dinner."

The squealing girls ran towards the house.

This time Tina kissed David on the lips. He watched her leave, with the first smile on his face in quite some time.

Turning, she blew him a kiss.

"That's what I'm talking about!" said Mel, walking up a couple of minutes later. "The lady-killer smiles we've been missing around here, and you didn't even need a wingman!"

"Thanks, buddy, but it's short-lived at best," replied David.

"Who knows?" answered Mel. "I was a lonely paranoid man, alone in a big house. My house burns to the ground, and I gained a new group of friends, old and new, and a girlfriend, both of which I consider family… Just don't overthink it," he added.

"Okay, buddy. I'll see you later," said David.

"Love that smile, David. Love that frickin smile!" Mel shouted, as he walked away.

David shook his head back and forth, laughing.

He spent some time with Mark, who seemed to be getting better.

The dinner bell rang an hour later, and everyone headed to Beatrice's house.

"We made your favorite," said Tina, grabbing David's hand and leading him into the kitchen.

"Linguini with clams!" he said, smiling, as he recognized the unmistakable smell. "I thought we were nearly out of clams, Mom."

"We were," his mother replied, "but Tina here made up the difference so we could all enjoy it."

David raised an eyebrow at Tina.

She smiled. "It seems your old buddy Lance also loves that meal. He grabbed 16 cans of clams the very first night from the grocery store."

The meal was paired with canned spinach, sautéed in garlic salt and dehydrated butter.

David led a prayer for both groups.

The men drank ice-cold beer, thanks to Mel, cooled in the trailer freezers. The women had wine, hand-picked by Tammie from Mel's extensive selection.

David made a toast to friends, new and old.

"Lance and I used to frequent a little Italian place in Boulder, called The Gondolier, when we were in college. They had a dish called Linguine Alle Vingole—also known as Linguini with Clams. We both got hooked, and apparently it's still one of our favorite meals on earth."

"Here! Here!" I called out, holding up my glass.

Mel was grinning after dinner, having a broad audience to show one of his surprises that he had been promising David.

A sizeable green tarp covered the object Mel carried from his house and set onto the edge of the trailer.

Tammy followed, opening a large box and stacking items neatly in front but out of view from the rest of us.

Gathering everyone's attention, Mel asked David to come forward.

"David, my friend, I give you the first of several gifts that will separate our group from the uncivilized rest of the country.

"Please do the honors…but carefully," he added, holding out the corner of the tarp to David.

"On the count of three!" said David, standing in front of the excited children.

"One…two…and three!" he counted, carefully removing the tarp.

The children squealed, looking up at the 70-inch flat-screen television, lit up with the letters *BIG* across the front and an image of a young Tom Hanks.

Mel smiled as questions were fired off from the adults, wanting to know how it was possible.

"One large faraday cage and solar-powered batteries," he responded, holding up four other titles.

"Fifty-seven classic movies in all," he announced. Everyone clapped and hollered.

Beatrice covered her mouth, tears rolling down her cheeks, and quietly slipped away towards home.

Spreading blankets on the ground, Nancy and Lonnie's wife made popcorn for the kids over the Coleman stove.

Tina asked David to sit with her in the back, spending the next two hours talking quietly, as the children were mesmerized by the extended edition of the timeless movie.

"The right girl may just show up on your doorstep one day. Isn't that what you told me, Lance?" said David, helping me return the television to Mel and Tammie's house after the movie.

"You were talking about Tina, right? We'll see, my friend," I responded, with a smile.

"I don't know what will happen over the next few days, but I'm a happy man tonight, brother," David replied.

David and Tina stayed up most of the night, deep in conversation that felt effortless for them both.

Beatrice was up early, clutching the DVD in her shaking hands.

She read the cover, as she had done a hundred times since losing her husband:

April 29, 2016
For David and Mark
Love, Dean

To be continued…

ABOUT THE AUTHOR

Lance K. Ewing lives with his wife, three boys (Hudson, Jax and Hendrix), Ringo, Mini and Bobo (dogs and a cat) in McKinney, Texas. When he is not at work, he can always be found with his family, preferably outdoors.

Lance grew up in the foothills of the Colorado Rocky Mountains, with the Rockies quite literally in his backyard.

Families First is his debut novel. Volume three is being written now.

Lance is a Chiropractor in Dallas, Texas. His new *Chronic Pain* quick-read series of books are now available for pre-sale on Amazon Kindle.

He can be contacted at **familiesfirstnovel@gmail.com**.

Join our e-mail list for news about upcoming volumes and sneak peaks at **familiesfirstnovel@gmail.com**.

Look for the *The Road* Audible version to be available on Amazon soon.

Visit the Facebook page: *Families First*
https://www.facebook.com/groups/447305392509202

Made in United States
North Haven, CT
17 October 2024

59042360R10214